DANSE MACABRE

ALSO BY GERALD ELIAS

Devil's Trill

DANSE MACABRE

A DANIEL JACOBUS MYSTERY

GERALD ELIAS

Minotaur Books

New York

DANSE MACABRE. Copyright © 2010 by Gerald Elias. All rights reserved. Printed in the United States of America. For information, address St. Martin's Press, 175 Fifth Avenue, New York, N.Y. 10010.

www.minotaurbooks.com

The Library of Congress has cataloged the hardcover edition as follows:

Elias, Gerald.
  Danse macabre / Gerald Elias.—1st ed.
     p. cm.
  ISBN 978-0-312-54189-7
  1. Violinists—Fiction. 2. Murder—Investigation—Fiction. I. Title.
  PS3605.L389D36 2010
  813'.6—dc22

                                                            2010021994

ISBN 978-0-312-64179-5 (trade paperback)

First Minotaur Books Paperback Edition: August 2011

10 9 8 7 6 5 4 3 2 1

Dedicated to the memory of my former violin teachers,

Amadeo William Liva and Gerald Gelbloom,

whose joy of music and life was inspiring

DANSE MACABRE

VALSE DIABOLIQUE

Zig, Zig, Zig—hark! Death beats a measure,
Drums on a tomb with heels hard and thin.
Death plays at night a dance for his pleasure—
Zig, Zig, Zig—on his old violin.
What are those moans from the lindens betiding?
Dark is the night, and the wind bloweth keen.
Skeletons pallid come out of their hiding,
To dance in their shrouds over tombstone and green.
Zig, Zig, Zig—how they jostle each other!
List to the rattling of bones as they dance!
But hush! In a twinkling the dancing is over,
Each strives to be foremost—the cock he hath crowed.

—Henry Cazalis (1840–1909), translated by Rosa Newmarch

The young African Prince, whose musical talents have been so much celebrated, had a more crowded and splendid concert on Sunday morning than has ever been known in this place. There were upwards of 550 persons present, and they were gratified by such skills on the violin as created general astonishment, as well as pleasure from the boy wonder. The father was in the gallery, and so affected by the applause bestowed on his son, that tears of pleasure and gratitude flowed in profusion.

—*Bath Morning Post* (1789), review of a performance by George Augustus Polgreen Bridgetower

PRELUDE

ONE

"Can't you get this thing to go at one speed?" Malachi asked. "It's bad enough I have to inspect a corpse at this time of night."

"I'm doin' the best I can, Detective," said Fuente. "Ziggy's the full-time elevator boy. I gave him the night off after he found the body. He was all shook up."

The vintage, manually controlled 1904 Otis elevator needed skill to manipulate, and Fuente didn't possess it. Under his untrained hand, the antique jolted upward in fits and starts, and even at its quaint seventy-five feet per minute, Malachi's stomach lurched downward.

"If you don't smooth it out, I'm going to be all shook up all over the floor."

Mercifully, they arrived at the fourth floor, but before the elevator came to a halt, Fuente cautioned Malachi, "Careful you don't trip over him."

The door swung open on silent, oiled runners. Malachi took a deep breath and entered the crime scene. He wasn't the first cop there. In the eerily funereal hallway, dimly lit by low-watt wall sconces, with its dark green flocked wallpaper, aging and faded, and maroon wall-to-wall runner, Flannery was already in action snapping one photo after another for purposes of analysis and protection for the NYPD in anticipation of the inevitable complaints. Otherwise the hallway was quiet, undisturbed by nervous whispering behind closed doors.

Allard had taken only a step or two from the elevator before he had been cut down. Dressed in his immaculate concert dress of white tie and tails under a black cashmere overcoat, his body was frozen in a strange position on the carpet, like a statue of an obsequious beggar kowtowing to a rich overlord with his shoulders on the ground and his legs pulled underneath him. Malachi couldn't see Allard's head from where he stood directly behind the body, so he slowly began a counterclockwise circumnavigation, continuing to breathe deeply, trying to ward off something distinctly disagreeable he felt creeping uninvited into his gut.

Allard's right arm was under his torso, as was his violin case, which he was still clutching with his right hand. It appeared to have been unmoved since Allard collapsed upon it, which would tend to rule out theft as a motive, unless the killer had been spotted and made his escape before he could wrest the priceless instrument from his victim.

The position of Allard's left arm gave Malachi the impression of a beggar. The arm was partially extended with only the elbow touching the ground; the fingers of the raised open hand were in a clawlike formation like an arthritic awaiting alms. Presumably, rigor mortis had begun to set in.

As Flannery, now kneeling for close-ups, continued to shoot, Malachi resumed his slow inspection. He stepped in front of the body, where Allard's head should have been. Disconcertingly, it seemed to be missing. Malachi knelt down and, as he peered under Allard's chest, saw that it was the head as well as the violin case that had propped up the torso from underneath.

Malachi quickly rose and took three frantic strides to get behind the photographer, and made it to the standing ashtray by the elevator before throwing up. Flannery wheeled around and took a photo of him retching. "The boys at the precinct will have a ball with that one!" Flannery said. Malachi, doubled over, could respond only with an upraised middle finger.

Holding a handkerchief at the ready, Detective Malachi returned to his examination, forcing himself to kneel down and peer once more at the Picasso-reorganized head. The neck had not been cut in the strict sense but was attached to the body by only a frail thread of dreadfully bruised and twisted tissue that had been bent forward so that the head was facing directly upward into the chest and rotated so that the chin was where the forehead should be. Then with the weight of the body on it, the head had been turned another ninety degrees so that it faced the left hand. The neck must have been crushed with great and sudden force, like whacking a salami with a sledgehammer, as a multihued variety of fluids extruded from every orifice in the head—eyes, ears, nose, and mouth—gluing strands of Allard's famous mane of white hair to his face. The eyes and tongue themselves had shot out from the face. There were also superficial—certainly not lethal—lacerations in the area of Allard's temples, but overall the head was such a gooey mess that there was little to read into that.

"So, Detective, what kinda weapon you suppose did that kind of damage?

"Between you and me," Malachi said, "offhand I would say I don't have a clue."

"You and me both," Flannery replied. "You and me both."

Malachi pushed himself unsteadily to his feet, wiping his mouth with the handkerchief. He made sure Flannery got all the shots he needed—of the corpse, not him—and instructed him to wait there until forensics arrived, to protect the crime scene and make sure no one came back to steal the violin.

He buzzed for the elevator and when it finally arrived said to Fuente, "You say Ms. Henrique is in 4B?"

"Well, that's where she lives, but she's not there right now."

"Where is she, then?"

"Mount Sinai. She went into shock. The ambulance took her there before you got here."

"What about the elevator guy?" Malachi consulted the scrawls on his notepad. "Sigmund Gottfried."

"Ziggy? Like I said, I sent him home. He was almost as bad off as Hennie."

"Where's home?"

"Downstairs. Basement Two. Want me to take you there?"

"Can you do it slow and smooth?"

The entire back wall of the elevator was a mirror—a single sheet of beveled, leaded glass, so Malachi had an unobstructed view of himself with the contorted corpse of René Allard behind him as he reentered. At that moment it was a toss-up who was paler and, in his worn gray wool jacket and coffee-stained plaid tie, Malachi was not nearly as well dressed as the body behind him. As the elevator descended, he had time to take more than a perfunctory glance at the rest of the interior. The side walls were oil-finished mahogany, as was the ceiling, which also had an elegantly paneled emergency trapdoor and detailed molding suitable for Versailles. The black rotary phone next to the door, a later addition no doubt, had not a single visible fingerprint, nor did the cherrywood stool have a scratch. The glossily polished parquet floor had an Escher-like border framing an intricately inlaid lyre in alternating colored hardwoods. The latticed safety door and the antique levers used to operate the elevator were gleaming brass.

"They don't make them like this anymore," he said.

"You're not kidding," said Fuente. "Last year one of the gears wore out and we had to shut down for three months to have Otis make a new one from scratch. Forty-seven hundred bucks for one little piece of lead."

"Where are the buttons for the floors?" Malachi asked.

"Prebutton era. Just a buzzer to tell which floor to go to. As you said, they don't make 'em like this no more."

The buzzer went off.

"Main floor," said Fuente. "Mind if we stop?"

"Go ahead."

The buzzer sounded again from the main floor. Then again. Then one constant, irritating nonstop buzz.

"Who the hell's so impatient?" asked Fuente.

"Forensics, maybe," said Malachi, going over his notes one more time. "Get there before the crime scene's disturbed. Or the medics. Maybe a Halloween reveler."

"With a lead finger," said Fuente.

The elevator bounced several times like a Ping-Pong ball before coming to a stop. Fuente swung the door open. Malachi glanced up from his notebook.

"Jacobus!" he said.

TWO

"Malachi!" said Jacobus, instantly recognizing the voice of his nemesis.

The two men had not encountered one another for several years and, at least from Jacobus's perspective, he had hoped that status quo would continue for the remainder of his natural life. Daniel Jacobus, a blind, aging, and increasingly eccentric and reclusive violin teacher, had lived in self-imposed exile on the fringes of the music world for decades, less bitter over the loss of his sight than what he perceived as the corrosion of the aesthetics of his art and the ethics of his profession. What was hailed as progress when the newest wunderkinds hit the scene he termed "regress." Music had become a job rather than an art, pension trumped practice, and new compositions being written for the concert stage were, in his not-so-humble estimation, crap. So Jacobus withdrew from the world. He'd reveled in, yet railed against his isolation until he had been drawn kicking and screaming back into eye of the storm by his friend Nathaniel Williams when the infamous Piccolino Stradivarius was stolen from Carnegie Hall, and the two men had become improbable partners solving crime rooted in the classical music world.

During that investigation, Jacobus had been the primary suspect not only in the theft but also in the subsequent murder of his self-professed rival pedagogue, Victoria Jablonski. Malachi had tracked Jacobus halfway across the world to a small mountain town in Japan, where Jacobus had fled with his student, Yumi Shinagawa, and Williams, and brought them back to the United States to face charges of theft and murder. Ultimately, Jacobus found the missing Strad and the murderer of Victoria Jablonski, and he and his friends were exonerated, but the respect he and Malachi bore each other was grudging and tentative.

The most unexpected result of the escapade, however, was that the notoriety Jacobus had received thrust him back into the limelight of the musical world. He had become the talk of the town, was invited to sit on the boards of cultural institutions and faculties of conservatories, and letters and calls from would-be students pestered him incessantly. When he bothered to respond at all, he turned everything down, teaching only a handful of students recommended to him by the few people in his field he trusted.

Both Nathaniel Williams and Yumi Shinagawa were now with Jacobus, standing before Malachi. Yumi held a bouquet of roses in her hand.

"Well, if it isn't the Mod Squad," said Malachi. "What brings you here on such an auspicious occasion?"

"We're here to pay our respects," said Jacobus.

"How did you know?" asked Malachi. "It's been less than two hours."

"What are you talking about, Malachi? We went to his recital at Carnegie tonight. René invited us to his soirée. So we're a little late. Big deal."

"Sorry to break the news even to you, Jacobus, but the party's on hold. Permanently." He then told them, leaving out almost all the details, of the murder of René Allard.

Jacobus was devastated. Allard was among the last of the artists from the "old school," whose dedication to music and only music was unimpaired by onstage theatrics and offstage politicking. Allard was one of the few violinists whose recordings, along with those of great opera singers, were required listening for his students. His death was a loss to Jacobus not only on a personal level—though his acquaintance with Allard had been sporadic and superficial—but on a profoundly spiritual level, as music was Jacobus's only religion.

Yumi Shinagawa, still holding the roses, asked Malachi if they could take them up to Hennie. Malachi explained that even if she were there he couldn't allow them up to the fourth floor at this time. He did, however, ask, "Do any of you know a Sigmund Gottfried, the elevator operator? I'm on my way to talk to him."

"For about half a century," Jacobus said. "He was in that elevator when I was just a kid going up to Dedubian's shop on the twelfth floor to get my fiddle fixed. Sweet guy. Knows all the violinists who come here."

Yumi recalled how polite he was the first time she came to the Bonderman Building with Jacobus. Nathaniel Williams concurred and suggested it might be a good idea to go with Malachi in order to help make Gottfried more comfortable talking to a stranger.

They arrived at Basement Two with a soft thud. Malachi's stomach arrived shortly thereafter.

"You remember," Malachi asked Jacobus, "when you once told me the expectation of viewing a corpse was no different from the expectation of going onstage to play a concerto? That once you were confronted with the reality of it, the nausea went away?"

"Yeah. So what?"

"You're full of shit."

Fuente slid open the safety grate, which was so well-balanced it almost opened on its own.

"Welcome to Shangri-la," said Fuente. "Let me know if you need anything."

The four of them—Malachi, Jacobus, Williams, and Shinagawa—were immediately struck by the gloom. And by the music.

"You believe in ghosts?" Jacobus asked Malachi.

"Why?"

"That's 'Danse Macabre'!" said Yumi. "That's René Allard playing!"

The spectral waltz, "Danse Macabre" by Camille Saint-Saëns, was eerie enough under any circumstances, but as all the world knew, the piece was the signature encore of Allard, who had performed it with piano accompaniment at Carnegie Hall only a few hours before.

"But unless there's an orchestra down here," said Williams, "that's a recording. An old one too. The one he did with Barbirolli and London, I'd say."

"Shangri-la!" said Malachi. "More like Dante's *Inferno*."

Jacobus could feel the dark, dripping, and dismal gloom seep into his pores. He could hear and feel the rumbling of subways passing somewhere underneath, to the side of, or perhaps even above the basement. It was hard to tell. Dominating the entire floor, like Scylla and Charybdis, an ancient black furnace and incinerator stood side by side, caked with decades of blackened grease and dust. Jacobus heard their banging and hissing, throbbing and knocking as they blasted heat and hot water through numberless ducts.

"I don't like it down here," said Yumi.

"I'll second you on that," said Nathaniel.

Around the perimeter of the furnace and incinerator were some rooms that were obviously later add-ons. A laundry room with industrial-sized but long obsolete machines. A rusting and foul-smelling bathroom with toilet, sink, and curtainless shower stall, paint peeling, faucets dripping. A closet cluttered with mops, buckets, and cleaning supplies. Another one, or maybe a changing room, with a bench and some plastic hooks on the wall.

"Don't worry, there's nothing too ominous," said Malachi. "This place looks like Disneyland compared to some of the lovely back alleys I've been to."

"Thanks for inviting us," said Jacobus. "I'm a big fan of theme parks."

The four followed the music to a closed door. Malachi knocked, and it was opened almost immediately by a short, stocky, bald man with gray hair well trimmed around bigger-than-usual ears. His small eyes were swollen, tear brimmed, and red. He was dressed in heavy, cuffed gray wool pants that came almost all the way up to his armpits and were held up by a black belt and red suspenders stretched over a clean white T-shirt. A key chain attached to his belt led to a pocket, and he held a sodden handkerchief in his hand.

"Detective Malachi, NYPD."

"Welcome, Detective Malachi," said the man, wiping his eyes with the handkerchief. "I was told to expect you." He narrowed his eyes, gazing beyond Malachi into the gloom. "And, can it be? My old friends! Mr. Jacobus! Mr. Williams! And the young lady . . ."

"Yumi Shinagawa," she prompted.

"Of course. Of course. Please come in. Please."

"Long time," said Jacobus. "Sorry . . . the circumstances."

Sigmund Gottfried's one-room apartment was not exactly cheery by Martha Stewart standards, but it was a welcome oasis from the drear of the basement around it. Lit only by a single incandescent bulb in the center of a yellowing plaster ceiling veined with cracks, everything was tidy, well organized, and immaculate. On the wall opposite the door was the source of the music, an old-fashioned console Victrola with its trademark acoustical horn, on which the nasal and raspy 78 recording of "Danse Macabre" was spinning.

"Please have a seat, Detective, friends," said Gottfried, offering them the bed next to the Victrola. Gottfried sat in the only chair, a folding one, at the secondhand wooden desk, which had three drawers. Jacobus felt the link chain of the ceiling light clatter against his dark glasses as Yumi escorted him to his seat.

"So you're a music lover," said Malachi, more as a comment than a question.

Gottfried's lips quivered. He pointed to the Victrola, handkerchief in hand, as if that would explain everything, and began to cry.

"Take your time," said Malachi. He himself had studied the violin when he was a boy. To the dismay of his parents, when he graduated Yeshiva University he chose law enforcement over music or his religious studies. He still went to concerts and to synagogue on the High Holy Days, but Friday nights were too busy with police work for either cultural or spiritual enlightenment.

Jacobus, on the other hand, listened to the old recording with more than passing interest. Murk and gloom meant nothing to him, a blind man. Sound was his umbilical cord to the world, and he sat, transfixed, ears attuned only to the now posthumous performance of René Allard. He ignored the conversation around him, hearing only the music. The perfect elegance, charm, and refinement of the violin playing created a chilling irony to the waltz's ghoulish subject.

That notion turned Jacobus's thoughts to the immediate depressing circumstances. Even for Allard's performance, Jacobus had to be almost bodily dragged out of his home in the Berkshires by Nathaniel and Yumi. The concert had been worth it, though, and with unaccustomed enthusiasm he went backstage to congratulate Allard. All the luminaries were there for the historic event: The violinists, of course—Steinhardt, Zukerman, Mutter, and BTower, that so-called crossover violinist whom he avoided like the plague, were among the many voices that Jacobus recognized. And of course the conductors, the managers, the agents, the wannabes were there too. No critics were there, as they assuredly were sharpening their pencils for the review, but they knew if they dared criticize Allard, who was second to the American flag in the hearts of the public, their jobs would have been in jeopardy.

Jacobus, trying to figure out how to convey his gratitude to Allard for keeping the tradition of great music making alive while at the same time attempting to keep his distance from the throng, suddenly felt a soft cheek against his, and then again on his other cheek. The scent of seductive French perfume was matched by the voice that came with it.

"*Allo,* Jake. I should tell you, I'm not wearing a stitch of clothes."

"If that were true, Hennie, I'd hear every man in this room panting."

Hennie laughed. "Yes, I am teasing you, but I am so happy that you came to René's recital tonight. You must join us for a little soirée later. Don't worry. It will be an intimate gathering, not this three-ring circus. And by all means bring your two friends." Jacobus hadn't refused the invitation even though he was more comfortable here in Gottfried's hovel than he would have been rubbing elbows with the hoity-toity. But now here he was, listening to Allard playing "Danse Macabre" while his corpse was stiffening six floors over his head.

"Please forgive me," said Gottfried. "It has been such a shock. Maestro Allard. He meant so much to me. To the world. I cannot speak."

"Yes," said Yumi, "it—"

"What did he mean to you?" asked Malachi, interrupting.

"He himself gave me this recording that you hear. It was a special present." Gottfried stopped. "I'm sorry. I'm getting ahead of myself. May I start from the beginning, Detective Malachi?"

"Please do."

"Thank you. I'll try not to bore all of you—you must be so

tired—but I must tell you something of how my life started in America. In 1946, my mother, Winifred, put my sister, Seglinde, and me on the boat. It was after the war and there was nothing for us in Germany. It was the last time I saw my dear mother. We arrived in New York and found a cheap room together in Washington Heights. In those days it was possible— eight dollars a week. Then Schatzi met a young man, Orin Oehlschlager, from a wealthy Mormon family."

"Who's Schatzi?" asked Malachi.

"Oh! I'm sorry. That is what Seglinde and I called each other from the time we were children."

"Nickname," offered Nathaniel.

"Ja, nickname. Or pet name, as you sometimes say."

"Go on," said Malachi.

"Young Mr. Oehlschlager, he was just then finishing his—what do the Mormons call it—'mission' in New York, and he was good-looking and spoke German very well, so they became married and moved away. I had no job, of course, when I arrived, but a friend of a friend of a friend—you know how it works—had suggested an interview for the elevator-boy position at this famous building. 'The Bonderman Building, in midtown Manhattan,' the friend of a friend of a friend said, as if it were the center of the world."

Gottfried managed a wistful chuckle, then blew his nose.

"Something funny?"

"Only, Detective Malachi, that when I went for my interview, I had never yet set foot in an elevator in my life! My friends! I am so impolite. I haven't even offered you tea! Please, let me make you some."

"Have any scotch?" asked Jacobus.

"I'm so sorry. No."

"Actually, I wouldn't mind some tea, Mr. Gottfried," said Malachi. "I could use something to settle the stomach." Yumi and Williams also accepted.

"It would be my pleasure," said Gottfried. "It would help me too, to forget some of this terrible thing. And, Detective, please call me Ziggy. Everyone does."

Gottfried's minuscule kitchen consisted of a hot plate, minifridge, and sink, all gleaming from daily cleaning. On the front edges of three simple wooden shelves above the hot plate were tacked handwritten tags for each day of the week. Above the Tuesday tag were carefully stacked cans of Campbell's Beans 'N Franks; over Wednesday was Dinty Moore Beef Stew. Thursday was Chef Boyardee Meatballs and Spaghetti night, and so on. Monday was the only day that didn't have any cans above it. The bed was made with military wrinkle-free precision. Pillows were propped along the length of it to enable day use as a couch. Papers on the small desk in the other corner were stacked and lined up perfectly with the edge of the desktop. Above the desk, carefully aligned rows of black-and-white snapshots were thumbtacked to the wall. Apparently they had been there for many years, as there were some lightened spots below the bottom row of photos that suggested some of them had been removed more recently. Not a speck of dust blemished the concrete floor or old braided rug that covered half of it.

His back to the others, Gottfried continued his story as he filled a cast-iron kettle with water from the sink, put it on the hot plate to boil, and removed tea bags from an ancient Chase & Sanborn coffee can, which he placed in unmatched cups.

"I apparently made an impression on the building manager. Mama had taught me to be polite, tidy, willing to work, make something of my life. So even with my 'Kraut accent,' as they called it, I was given the job for fifty dollars a week plus a free room in the basement. That alone was a huge savings, as until then I was paying the full eight dollars a week for the room in Washington Heights, plus I would save at least another two dollars a week on commuting. In return I would work a twelve-hour shift daily, alternating with a lad named Tom Congden, and would be required to maintain the elevator and the uniform they provided.

"I am very proud of my uniform, Detective, as I'm sure you are of yours. It has no stripes or stars like Papa once had, but I honor it much the same. The way you see me here at this moment is not the way I am proud to be seen. There are not many elevator boys left in the world, Detective Malachi. I am one of the few remaining. They call this 'progress.'

"Now, here is your tea. Am I talking too much?"

"Not if you get to the point before sunrise," said Jacobus, who was trying to concentrate on the recording of "Danse Macabre" that was now spinning to an end.

"Ah! I understand. That was a good joke. Excuse me a moment, please."

Before the old stylus had the opportunity to scratch, Gottfried whisked the arm of the Victrola off the 78.

It was over. Jacobus had the sinking feeling that Allard had just been buried.

"I think Allard made four recordings of that piece," said Nathaniel. "He must have loved it."

"Yes, Mr. Williams! And I have all four! This one is my favorite, with the English conductor Barbirolli, and like all the recordings made in those days, it had to be done in one take! No splicing or dicing! I'd like to see them try to do that today!"

"I knew it was Barbirolli!" said Williams, nudging Yumi in the ribs.

"Ah, so you are a music lover too!" said Gottfried. "Music. It helps one grieve, does it not?"

It might help, thought Jacobus. But it's still grieving.

"What's wrong with Monday?" asked Malachi.

"Monday? I don't understand."

"You have your canned food lined up for every day of the week. Monday's empty."

Gottfried chuckled.

"You are very observant, Detective Malachi. I am a man of simple needs. I know what I like and don't like. I am no epicure, so I have my cans—the same every week. And I have my elevator. That is my castle, and I have people from all over the world visit me in my castle and say, 'Hello, Ziggy, nice to see you again.' That is all I need to be happy. But every Monday, Max the butcher on Sixty-ninth and Amsterdam Avenue has a sale on pork chops. So on Mondays I buy a pork chop from Max and fresh cabbage from the Korean and make myself the dinner I had when Schatzi and I were children, though of course it's not nearly as delicious as Mama's cooking.

"But now I go back to my story," Gottfried said as he caressingly slid the precious record back into its brittle antique jacket. "I was overjoyed with my good fortune and moved into my new apartment the next morning. That my neighbors were the clanging furnace and the mops in the supply room was of no concern to me. There was no difficulty immediately moving my belongings to my new home. Everything fit into Papa's valise that Mama gave me for my voyage across the ocean, except for the wonderful Victrola phonograph that Schatzi, knowing how much I loved music, gave me as a going-away present when she went west. Ach, young people these days with their Walkmans do not appreciate their possessions—of course, young lady, you may be an exception—but you are not here to listen to me carry on about that. With the Victrola I could listen to my beloved recordings—singers like Elisabeth Schwarzkopf, an angel, Fritz Wunderlich, Björling, McCormack. And the violinists—Fritz Kreisler, Mischa Elman the Jew, the young Russian David Oistrakh."

Gottfried sighed. "And they are all gone now."

"Including Allard," said Jacobus, not bothering to correct Gottfried that Schwarzkopf hadn't yet kicked the bucket.

"Ach, yes. And of course, he was the greatest. Do you know the story that one time Kreisler was asked if he resented that Allard was called the French Fritz Kreisler, to which Kreisler responded, 'What! It is I who would be honored to be called the Austrian René Allard!' "

"I can't say I've heard that one," said Malachi.

"Well, Allard's recording of Kreisler's 'Liebesleid' makes me cry to this day. I believe he is . . . pardon me, he *was* . . . the greatest. But I obviously was not alone in that opinion. And a Frenchman! I listen to his recordings every day. It is important you understand this."

Gottfried took a sip of tea. Placing the cup on a fading cardboard Bonderman Hotel coaster, he paused for a moment.

It gradually dawned on Jacobus how much he and Gottfried shared, unlikely though it was on the surface. Jacobus had also come from Germany as a youth, albeit under much different circumstances. It was before the war and it was to study the violin, not to flee a destroyed country. That he had remained in the United States was the result of his parents' death at Auschwitz at the hand of the butchers Gottfried's father worked for. He did not begrudge Ziggy the failings of his countrymen, but it was ironic nevertheless.

The main thing, though, that struck Jacobus was their shared taste in music and their choice to opt for seclusion and isolation in the way they lived, Gottfried here in his underground den, Jacobus in his hovel in the woods of western Massachusetts. Jacobus, not one for introspection, wondered if there was an element of escape in Gottfried's life, and attempt to hide from the present, listening to 78s while tucked away from the world. And he wondered whether that was a mirror into his own soul.

"Because I was the new boy," Gottfried continued, "Tom gave me the graveyard shift from ten P.M. to ten A.M., six days a week. That was hunky-dory with me, because even though I was busy at the beginning of the shift with residents coming home after a night on the town, and at the end with them going to work in the morning, the middle of my shift, from midnight to six, was very peaceful and I had much time to dwell on my good fortune. When I finished my shift I would have a piece of bread or such and then sleep until five o'clock, when I would make myself dinner. As I at first had no refrigerator, dinner was, as you see, usually from a can—and it was wonderful what was available in cans and I have very modest needs, so it was very satisfactory. The seventh day—for me it was Monday—Tom and I switched shifts. We rarely had days off.

"My first day at work was the happiest of my life. Surely, some of the people ignored me. But that's to be expected, as they were very important people and I was just an elevator boy. In those days the number of famous musicians living in the Bonderman Building was probably greater than in some entire countries! Not only Americans, they came from all over Europe after the war. So close to Carnegie Hall, it was like living next to Valhalla. Those were the days before people traveled across the ocean on airplanes in six hours, so when they came here to concertize they stayed a lot longer and kept an apartment here. And with all the violin dealers in this building there were always great musicians coming and going. It was like a beehive, and the honey was music. Was that not so, Mr. Jacobus? You have been here many times over the years."

"Yeah. But more like wasps than bees. For violin dealers it's not so much the music. For them, honey is money and the buzzing is business."

"Maybe that is so. Yes, yes, you are right. But there were some nice people who did say hello and a few even noticed that I was new to the elevator and wished me luck. I have always had a good memory and learned people's names quickly and what floor they lived on, and what time they went to work, so that when the buzzer sounded for the fourth floor at seven fifteen, I knew to say, 'Good morning, Mr. Blackman,' when I opened the door. Or, when Mr.—oh, I won't say his name—had a little too much to drink at one in the morning, I did not have to ask what floor to go to but instead would not only take him to the eighth floor, but would assist him to Apartment 8F, take the right key attached to his key chain, and help him to bed.

"But, Detective Malachi, the best part of my job was the elevator itself. I was in a palace. It is the original elevator from when the Bonderman Building was constructed in the earliest years of the twentieth century. I believe I was told this so that I would be sure to take good care of it, but that wouldn't have been necessary because the elevator was more my home than this room is. In the quiet hours I loved polishing the brass and rubbing the wood with linseed oil. I was occasionally complimented on the way I maintained the elevator by the ladies and gentlemen who lived in the building.

"It did not take long to learn from Tom how to operate the elevator, though since there are no longer many elevator boys, few people realize that there was an art to operating it well. Not, of course, like the art of playing music.

"Once I learned the basics, I began to experiment a little, to move it as fast as possible without the passengers feeling the speed, and then to slow it down and bring it to a stop with no bump. My goal was to be the René Allard of elevators! Isn't that a funny thought, Detective?"

"Go on."

"After a few weeks I was already better, I must say, than Tom at this, but what was I to do? Mama was very proud when I wrote her that Mildred Rivkin, one of the oldest residents at the Bonderman, had said to me, 'What a wonderful ride, Ziggy.'"

Gottfried stopped. It was close to 2 A.M. Yumi had fallen asleep and Nathaniel was close behind her. Jacobus was listening less to Gottfried and more to the underworld surrounding him: the groans of the guts of the building pumping energy upward through the thousands of tons of steel and concrete and pipes and wires above their heads; and the more distant rumblings of the dark underground city, separated from them by only a cement wall. It may have been only a subway, but from its low, moaning vibrations Jacobus felt as if he were embedded in the innards of a great churning organism.

"I am getting off the subject, aren't I?" said Gottfried. "I am so sorry. It isn't often I have visitors here to talk to. But I am almost at the end of my story."

Jacobus grunted. Malachi sipped his cold tea and didn't say anything.

"I had been at my new job about a month, and I knew everyone in the building. At least I thought I did. One night, shortly after I began my shift, I opened the door at the lobby and who entered but René Allard. This man who was my hero.

"Here I must tell you something of my appearance. Not that I was handsome or am showing off. Quite the opposite. Looks mean little to me. But I was short—not as short as I am now—and began to lose my hair at an early age. Other than that, you could say I was not ugly. René Allard, on the other hand, could have been—was—"

"A matinee idol?" Jacobus suggested.

"Just so. A matinee idol, as they used to say. He was tall. He had that wavy hair. And for some reason, Americans always have an attraction for Frenchmen. I maybe had better posture than Allard.

"Of course, we were both relatively young then, in 1946. I was sixteen and Allard was I think thirty-five. So he was already on top of the world, and I was going up and down in an elevator. You can't understand how well known he was then. These days, you think classical musicians like Itzhak Perlman and Yo-Yo Ma are famous. They were nothing compared to Allard. Everyone in the world knew his name—like the singer Frank Sinatra or that Negro baseball player Jack Robinson—and the women were crazy for him.

"He had left France for America shortly after the beginning of the war, and I left, of course, when it was over, but I had no idea where he lived, so, as I say, it was a shock to see him in my elevator, but it was not such a shock to see him with a beautiful woman on his arm. They were both very elegantly dressed and Allard was carrying his violin case.

"Without looking at me he said, 'Fourth floor, please,' in his French accent, and I said, 'Yes, sir, Mr. Allard,' in my German. He turned to me and said, 'You are new here, are you not?' and I said, 'Yes, Mr. Allard.'

"Allard paused for a moment, inspecting me, then said, 'Well I wish you well in your new job,' and I said, 'Thank you, Maestro.' That was all. By the time we arrived at their floor I gathered from their conversation that they had just returned from one of his concert tours. As they left the elevator, Allard turned to me and said, 'By the way, our bags arrive tonight sometime. Would you kindly make sure they are delivered to 4B immediately?' 'Of course, Mr. Allard,' I said. He said, 'Thank you. Good evening, Mr. . . .' You see, he didn't know my name, so I said, 'Gottfried, sir. Sigmund Gottfried.' And Maestro Allard said, 'Then good evening, Ziggy.' And that, Detective Malachi, is how I was named."

Malachi finished his tea.

"You were the last one to see him alive," he said.

"You were?" asked Jacobus, who until that moment had been more interested in finding a way to drink himself out of his grief.

"Ja. That is a terrible honor, gentlemen," Gottfried said in a low, slow voice. "A most terrible, terrible honor."

"That puts you in a rather uncomfortable position, doesn't it?" said Malachi.

"I understand what you are saying, Detective. If that is my fate, so it is one I must bear, and I must learn to live with it."

"Tell me about how you left him."

"Of course, Detective. It was around midnight that he entered my elevator. He was very, very happy. As everyone knows, this was the fiftieth anniversary of his Carnegie Hall debut. He said to me that he thought this one was better than all the others. Would you agree, Mr. Jacobus?"

"Better? Who knows? He's played that same program there every ten years at Carnegie. I haven't heard all of them. But the ones I've heard, they've all been great."

"Did he mention any problems with anyone?" asked Malachi. "Muggers? Critics? Anyone at all?"

"No, no. Only that at the same time he was happy about the concert, he was sad that it was a farewell also. You see, he and Hennie—Miss Henrique—were planning on leaving for Paris tomorrow. When he said good night to me tonight, it was also goodbye. When he said, 'Good-night, Ziggy . . .'"

Gottfried covered his face with his hands and shook. Neither Jacobus nor Malachi said anything.

"This is very unmanly," said Gottfried, recovering.

"Don't give it a second thought," said Malachi.

Gottfried took a deep breath. "So I said, 'Good-bye, Maestro. It has been an honor.' And he stepped out of the elevator. That was all. I went back down to the lobby and waited for the late-night Halloween crowd to return. About fifteen minutes later, Mr. Fuente, the building manager, came running to me. He told me that Hennie, who was worried that Maestro was late for their party, went into the corridor and saw Maestro on the ground. She called 911 and Mr. Fuente. She will take it very bad, I am sure. So Mr. Fuente and I went back up. I'm thinking, Is this some kind of Halloween trick? I do not like this Halloween. It is too wild. When the elevator door opened, I could not believe my eyes. Mr. Fuente was very kind. He told me, 'Ziggy, I'll take care of the elevator. You're in no condition.' And he was right."

"Tell me about the photos on your wall," said Malachi.

"Photos? Oh, just these old snapshots. Thank you for trying to take my mind off my troubles. Papa gave me his Leica before he went off to the war. I still have it. It takes wonderful pictures."

"German technology," said Jacobus.

Gottfried proceeded to describe each photo, starting from the upper left and ending with the bottom right of all six rows. There were a few wintry photos of him with Seglinde and Mama before leaving Germany and some others with his sister after arriving in the United States. With each photo, his spirits seemed to lift.

"Who's older, you or your sister?"

"Neither, Detective Malachi! We are twins. Not identical, of course. You see, Schatzi is much taller than me . . . and much prettier."

"No kidding," said Malachi. "She could be Ingrid Bergman's sister."

"Yes, and I am more of the Uncle Fester type from the TV show. Schatzi got her looks from Mama. I unfortunately got mine from Papa."

There were several snapshots of people standing outside the elevator with him, many of them musicians of varying degrees of renown. Malachi had no difficulty singling out Allard in the photos. His continental flair was a magnetic presence even on a black-and-white snapshot. Some of the musicians held their instrument cases. Others had an arm around Gottfried. Some had signed the photo, meaning there had to have been a second encounter after the film was developed. All of them were smiling next to the obviously proud little man.

"I recognize some of these," Malachi said. "Yehudi Menuhin, Ricci, Francescatti. Hey! Look at this! Could this be the young Daniel Jacobus?" He showed the photo to Gottfried, who confirmed that it was.

"Well, who would've guessed you were such a handsome fella?" asked Malachi.

"Up yours, Malachi."

"And here's one of Isaac Stern before he added the avoirdupois. When I was still a violin student I went to the Ninety-second Street Y to sit in on an Isaac Stern master class."

"Yeah, you and two million others," said Jacobus. "Is that why you quit?"

"Believe it or not, Jacobus, there's some truth behind your

dismal effort at humor. I realized the world would be much better off with me not playing the violin.

"So, Ziggy, what about the missing photos?"

"Missing photos?" asked Gottfried. "Ah! I understand! You are very perceptive, Detective Malachi. You see the blank spots on the wall. Let me get them for you."

Gottfried went to his desk, opened a side drawer, and removed some more snapshots. "They're just copies of the family photos, with dates on the back. I think you've seen them all." He handed them to Malachi.

"May I keep these for a while?" he asked.

"Of course. They're just more of the same. That's why I took them down."

There was a knock at the door, rousing Yumi and Nathaniel from their slumber. Gottfried said, "Excuse me, please," and went to answer it.

"Ah, Mrs. Bidwell!"

"Ooh, it's creepy down here. They told me I should come here for the policeman."

Malachi introduced himself.

"I'm Mabel Bidwell," Mrs. Bidwell said. "4C?"

"Well, Mrs. Bidwell in 4C, can I help you?" he asked.

"Can you help *me*? That's a good one. I'm here to help *you*."

"Okay. How can you help me?"

"Only that I saw the man that killed René Allard."

THREE

The "Two Maestros," as the media had dubbed it, had all the buzz of the Scopes Monkey Trial. A murder in which either the accused or the victim was a celebrity was always enough to get the public's juices flowing, but in the case of the murder of René Allard, with BTower, arguably the world's most famous—as well as physically appealing, controversial, and eligible—living musician as the defendant, the public couldn't get enough. Newspapers, selling as fast as they could be printed, were saturated not only with coverage of the protagonists but also with stories scouring the lives of the lawyers, the judge, the jury, the police, the witnesses—anyone remotely connected to the trial.

Nielsen ratings of the hard-hitting weekly news program *Op-Ed* went through the roof when moderator Ed Fallon interviewed the attractive young prosecutor, Michelle Brown. "Pit Bull" Brown, so dubbed by Fallon for her dogged determination to seek the death penalty for BTower, aka Shelby Freeman Jr., became America's most beloved darling since Shirley Temple. A recent summa cum laude graduate of Fordham University Law School, Brown had aspirations of ascending the political ladder, and she had already mounted the first rungs with swift tenacity. This was her first capital case, and it was as big a plum as she could ever hope for.

"Will the defense play the race card?" asked Fallon, knowing that it was what America wanted to hear and also knowing the answer.

"Race has nothing to do with this case," said Brown. "Only guilt or innocence."

"Is it true, Michelle Brown, that you've been handed this case by your mentor and former professor, District Attorney Adrian Garn, because you're having an intimate relationship with him?"

"Again, that has nothing to do with this case."

Only two people refused interviews. One was BTower, whose attorney, Cy Rosenthal, shielded him from all publicity, which undoubtedly would have been negative. The other was Daniel Jacobus, who took his phone off the hook.

Now, on the first day of the Two Maestros trial, Jacobus was ensconced in the packed courtroom. His turn as a witness for the prosecution was some time off, but he felt compelled to be there. Nathaniel and Yumi hadn't needed to haul him into the city as they did the year before to hear Allard's last performance. He was so eager to see justice done that when Brown interviewed him to determine whether to call him as a character witness, he ended up coaching her on the finer points of the classical music world.

As he leaned forward to listen intently, the eyes of the courtroom and the world were focused on Brown. Conservatively dressed in a gray wool suit with a midlength skirt and white silk blouse, all of which managed to highlight the curves of her figure, she began in practiced understated fashion by summarizing the accomplishments of the great violinist and humanitarian, René Allard, in the unlikely event anyone might not have been aware of them.

"There is no need, ladies and gentlemen of the jury, to go into detail how, even after René Allard's perilous *Casablanca*-like

escape from France to the United States in 1941, he continued
his heroic work for the liberation of his native land. Or how in
1961 he was invited to the White House by John and Jacqueline
Kennedy to perform the Brahms Double Concerto with Pablo
Casals. Or how in 1968 he was named the first Ambassador of
World Peace by UN Secretary General U Thant. The list, ladies
and gentlemen, goes on and on.

"One day, René Allard spotted a young man, alone and virtually
penniless, on the streets of New York. That young man, Shelby
Freeman Jr., now known to the whole world as BTower, was just
one among thousands of poor, listless youths from Harlem,
lacking direction and a future. The one thing Shelby Freeman
Jr. could do differently was play the violin. Shelby Freeman
Jr. had the good fortune to be busking with an open violin case
lying on the sidewalk on a day that was so sunny and pleasant that
René Allard decided to walk from the UN to Carnegie Hall.
Hardly anyone passing by noticed Shelby, and even fewer tossed
a coin or two into his case. But it was Allard who immediately
recognized his raw talent and admitted him to be among a select
number of his students. It was René Allard who gave free lessons
to Shelby and made him a part of his family. It was in fact Allard
who inspired Shelby to change his name to BTower, when one
day at a lesson Allard turned to his pianist, Virgil Lavender, and
said, 'It looks like we have here a young Bridgetower,' referring
to the nineteenth-century black virtuoso George Augustus Polgreen Bridgetower, for whom Beethoven's monumental Opus 47
Violin Sonata was composed."

Brown took the comparison a step further. She likened Bridgetower, who had a permanent falling-out with Beethoven (so that

Beethoven ultimately dedicated the sonata to the French violin pedagogue Rodolphe Kreutzer, who incidentally never performed the piece, thinking it too difficult), to BTower's estrangement from René Allard.

"No one knows exactly what transpired between Bridgetower and Beethoven, but be assured, ladies and gentlemen of the jury, we do know what accounted for BTower and Allard's irreconcilable differences. Allard had demanded hours of hard work every day, hours devoted to the practice of scales and études, and the study of solfège, and music theory, and composing fugues. This was the way Allard had learned when he himself was a student in the Paris Conservatory. He knew in his heart it was the only way to true greatness.

"René Allard taught everything he knew, in the only way he knew, to help ensure the success of Shelby Freeman, but Shelby Freeman Jr. decided he didn't want to put in those hours of drudgery. Shelby Freeman Jr. chafed under the bit of disciplined hard work. Shelby Freeman Jr. rebelled, and ultimately—personally and professionally jealous of René Allard's stature as a musician and humanitarian, which he realized he could never achieve— Shelby Freeman Jr. repaid René Allard's efforts with death.

"Shelby Freeman Jr. needed to do it his own way. He needed to create a new style. But even though relations with his former mentor turned icy, isn't it ironic that when Shelby Freeman Jr. transformed his persona he remembered René Allard's compliment and changed his name to BTower, and often performed the 'Kreutzer' Sonata, which he had learned under the tutelage of René Allard?

"But he did more than just play the violin, as the world knows.

Strikingly handsome, a Muhammad Ali look-alike some have said, Shelby Freeman Jr., now BTower, grew his hair into dreadlocks and dressed unconventionally in tight black jeans and tight black T-shirts for performances. He danced around the stage with a light show going on behind him, even when he performed Bach sonatas. He was the only person in history ever to be on the cover of *Rolling Stone* and *The Strad*. Indeed, BTower was so popular, especially among young and African-American audiences, who had been awakened to the greatness of classical music, that he was the only performer who could command a fee close to Allard's.

"Let me remind you that there is nothing necessarily wrong with what BTower called his concert 'enhancements.' I myself share with millions of people open admiration for what BTower has done on the concert stage. I readily admit that I had never enjoyed classical music until going to a BTower concert. His innovative style refreshed what was perceived by many as a stodgy, white bread art form, so please, jury, do not consider what René Allard, renowned for elegance and good taste, might have thought about BTower's style. But I must also caution you, do not be deceived by BTower's good looks, or by his indisputable flamboyance and personal magnetism. Consider only that a rivalry had been created, a pernicious rivalry not only between two people but also between two worlds, and as time progressed that rivalry intensified into hatred . . . and into murder."

Jacobus, content with Brown's opening statement, leaned back in his seat, but only briefly as at this point Brown suffered her only minor setback. At the defense's request, the judge refused to permit her to show the jury the grisly police photos of Allard's body, declaring them too inflammatory. She was not, however, barred from reading Detective Malachi's report. Undaunted, she feigned poor eyesight, and donning fake glasses to focus the court's attention on the words she was about to read, Brown proceeded to recite the report's goriest details, slowly.

Brown concluded her opening statement by summarizing how the State would prove, with eyewitnesses corroborating every step, that BTower had gone to Carnegie Hall the night of October 31 to hear René Allard perform. Afterward he accosted Allard backstage, and then, unsatisfied with the results of their confrontation, stalked him to his apartment in the Bonderman Building, where he was recognized standing above the body with blood on his hands before fleeing the scene of the murder. Jacobus, reassured by Brown's confident delivery, was able to relax again.

Cy Rosenthal, the unlikely lead attorney on BTower's defense team, was neither a criminal nor a trial lawyer, either by training or inclination. A longtime junior partner of the firm of Palmese, Leibowitz, and O'Neil in Uniondale, Long Island, Rosenthal's strengths were litigation and labor law, where he had garnered a well-earned reputation hammering out collective-bargaining agreements for unions in the beer and toy-making industries. It was only when, on the eve of the Two Maestros trial, a late-night drunk driver on the Belt Parkway put senior partner Carmine Palmese in traction from the neck down for six months, that Rosenthal was thrust into the unaccustomed role he graciously but uncomfortably accepted.

Not many other lawyers would have had Rosenthal's courage to carry the flag under such circumstances, especially in this case. The Two Maestros appeared to be an open-and-shut case, and public sentiment against his client was at least ninety-nine to one. Rosenthal just happened to be that one. Though the hallmark of American justice is the presumption of innocence, he knew in this trial that innocence was exactly what he would have to prove.

Rosenthal concocted the story that BTower had rushed to the Bonderman Building to apologize to Allard after their heated exchange at Carnegie Hall, that he was rebuffed by Allard in the lobby of the building, and that he made one final effort at reconciliation by running up the stairs, knowing that Allard would be leaving permanently for France the next morning. When he arrived at the fourth floor, he found Allard already on the ground. He knelt to assist him (in the process accumulating the blood on his hands and clothes) and promptly ascertained that Allard was dead. The defendant, immediately realizing the portentous ramifications of his presence at the scene, and being unable to assist Allard in any way, panicked and fled. Mistake—yes. Murder—no.

Rosenthal, short, balding, and not nearly as kempt as Michelle Brown, using extravagant language and gestures, attempted to make the case that the absence of a weapon and the astounding fact that the medical examiner was unable to determine a specific cause of death precluded a conviction on a first-degree murder charge. All the medical examiner could conclude was that Allard's neck had been violently crushed by some powerful external force, and that death followed "about thirty seconds later, one minute, tops." Without even a hypothesized weapon, let alone an actual one, he contended, how could a reasonable jury convict? This was Rosenthal's strongest card—actually, his only card—but

throughout the course of the trial he harped upon it so aggres-
sively that he ended up overplaying his hand. After he repeated
this line of reasoning once too often, the judge admonished him,
"Counsel, I think you've made your point. Now if you please,
move on." But there was nowhere to move. By the end of the trial
the New York *Daily News* would tag the flustered Rosenthal "the
counsel for the indefensible."

The next day the chain of witnesses began. Sigmund Gottfried
was the first called. Under questioning from Brown, he reluctantly admitted that BTower had indeed been at Allard's side when
Allard entered the elevator that fatal Halloween night, and that,
yes, BTower had seemed nervous. But Gottfried testified that he
could not believe BTower would do such a terrible thing. He had
seen BTower come and go to the Bonderman Building for many
years and he was always such a nice boy. It was impossible for him
to kill anyone, especially another musician like Maestro Allard.

"Would it have been possible for an athletic young man like
the defendant to run up to the fourth floor in the time it took
the elevator?" Brown asked.

"It would have been very difficult," said Gottfried.

"Is it not true, Mr. Gottfried, that the elevator in the Bonderman Building is one of the last constructed by the Otis Elevator
Company before the advent of the gearless traction elevator?"

"That is true."

"And isn't it also true that the maximum safe speed for such a
museum piece is approximately one hundred feet per minute?"
asked Pit Bull Brown.

"Ja."

"And that modern elevators now effortlessly accelerate to twelve hundred feet per second?"

"I wouldn't know that."

"Would you ever exceed a safe speed for your passengers, Mr. Gottfried, especially one as important as René Allard?"

"Not for nobody! I would never go too fast for safety."

"So, Mr. Gottfried, I repeat my question. Would it have been possible for an athletic young man like the defendant to run up to the fourth floor in the time it took your dinosaur of an elevator?"

Gottfried stammered, "But he couldn't have done it."

"Would it have been possible is the question. Please answer."

"Yes, I suppose," whispered Gottfried.

"I'm glad to hear you say that, Mr. Gottfried, because I myself tested that hypothesis and I didn't even break a sweat. Thank you. No further questions."

Next was Alonzo Fuente, the building manager of the Bonderman Building, who fidgeted.

"Mr. Fuente, tell us what you saw when René Allard entered the elevator the night he was killed."

"Well, I was taking down the Halloween decorations from the lobby—that's why I knew it was around midnight, because that's when I always take down the Halloween decorations—when Maestro Allard came in."

"Was he alone?"

"Yes. He was alone. He pressed the button for the elevator and as he was waiting, Mr. BTower runs into the lobby and up to Maestro as the doors opened. Maestro just kind of ignored him and he went into the elevator."

"Then what did the defendant do?"

"When the doors closed, he ran up the stairs. I thought maybe he forgot to give him something, or something. That's all I know."

"Thank you."

Next called to the stand was Daniel Jacobus, a character witness for Allard. He cut an imposing if not handsome figure: sallow cheeked and unshaven, with springy unkempt gray hair and of course his dark glasses. He was a bit of a gamble for Brown because of his penchant to be a combative loose cannon, and his discomfort being in the public limelight, primped up in clothes other than a flannel shirt and corduroy pants. But the jury tended to sympathize with the wizened Jacobus precisely for his unease, his disdain for protocol, and of course his blindness: And with his credentials as a respected violin teacher, they appeared to believe his blunt candor. Jacobus testified he had taught BTower briefly after his defection from Allard. Though Jacobus idolized Allard's musicianship—as much as crusty Jacobus could idolize anything—he had his own idiosyncratic methods of teaching and so hoped he might be able provide something with the young violinist that Allard might not have tried. However, after a short time they too had locked horns. BTower had to do it his own way.

"Mr. Jacobus, do you think the defendant, in a fit of rage, could have been capable of killing René Allard?"

"Yes," Jacobus muttered.

"Can you repeat that a bit louder so we can all hear, Mr. Jacobus?"

"Yes," Jacobus hollered. His distaste at being the focus of

attention was exceeded only by his desire to see the murderer of René Allard behind bars.

"Ánd why are you so certain of that Mr. Jacobus?"

"Because anyone who would play 'Variations on "I Feel Good"' at a serious concert is capable of anything." The courtroom erupted in laughter, but Jacobus didn't see the humor.

It was Rosenthal's turn to question Jacobus.

"You say you and the defendant didn't get along so well when you taught him. That he had to do things his way. Is that correct?"

"Yeah."

"Yet he went on to become a great star."

"What's your point?"

"Well, Mr. Jacobus, if, as you've admitted, you weren't able to teach the defendant effectively, and yet, after leaving you, he quickly became one of the most famous musicians in history, isn't it possible you bear the defendant a serious grudge?"

"Absolutely."

"Aha!"

"Because I would bear a grudge against anyone who murdered another human, especially if that human was René Allard!"

The gavel came down immediately and forcefully, again and again, until the uproar was extinguished. Jacobus was admonished by the judge from making any further incendiary remarks and was ordered to answer the question, addressing the valid point raised by counsel, which was: Do you, Daniel Jacobus, bear a grudge against the defendant, BTower, for his success after your inability to be an effective teacher?"

Jacobus suddenly felt as if he were on trial, as if he had to justify *his* existence. Why should he have to account for a lifetime of dedication to an art and a profession in which success, however it was defined, was anything but guaranteed? That no matter how hard one worked, how much one understood or felt about music, talent in the vast majority of cases took one only so far—and not far enough—and luck often became the determining wild card? How could he say in a few short sentences what would take a life-time to understand?

"Yes, I do bear a grudge, Counselor," he began quietly. "But not for his success in itself. I bear a grudge because of the shortcuts he took to get there. Disguising music as something else—mere entertainment—and covering up his own shortcom-ings as a serious musician.

"When you hear Bach, Counselor, as it should be heard, there is no greater life-changing experience imaginable. But when Bach is thrust into a dog-and-pony show, and that comes to be defined as great art by an unwitting society, that's when I take exception. When I go to hear Bach I want to hear music. I don't need the Flying Wallendas. So yes, I do bear a grudge against the defendant, but it's not for his stardom. It's for having cheapened something that is far more precious than you, or he, is aware."

The courtroom was silent. Rosenthal had no further ques-tions.

When Virgil Lavender, blue eyed and ruddy cheeked in a stylish but somewhat worn beige and white seersucker suit, was called to the stand to take the oath, he politely corrected the bailiff's pro-nunciation of his last name.

"Accent's on the *end*. Like in pretender," he said with a smile as he took his seat.

"Mr. Lavender, you had been René Allard's exclusive pianist for twenty years?" Pit Bull Brown began.

"Actually, thirty."

"Thirty years. And when we say 'exclusive,' what does that mean?"

"It means that during that time I was the only accompanist he played with."

"That's quite an honor. So did you play with him only at concerts?"

"Of course not! We had endless rehearsals—René was a slave driver for rehearsing. And I was also his studio pianist. That means I accompanied his students—he didn't have that many actually, he was so busy performing—at their lessons."

"And in the thirty years that you spent all this time with René Allard, did you ever see him get angry?"

"Never. He was the most amiable person I've ever met. I remember one time—"

"Did you ever see the defendant get angry, specifically at René Allard?"

"Holy moly, did I? Almost every lesson he would argue. He felt his time was being wasted because he considered René too methodical. I would just sit there and try to be invisible. I never heard anyone talk to René like that, not even—"

"And the night of the murder?"

"Ah, yes. The night of the murder, BTower came backstage at Carnegie Hall after the recital. It was a madhouse. René and I had just finished 'Danse Macabre.' René was putting his violin back in its case and I was on the other side of the room making out a check for Miles . . . he was my page turner. A piano student from the Mannes School. Very talented, but somewhat—"

"Please stick to the subject, Mr. Lavender."

"Yes. Sorry. Out of the corner of my eye I saw BTower go up to René. They chatted. There must have been a misunderstanding. I didn't hear specific words because everybody was talking, but BTower got very heated and then just stormed off. René shrugged but didn't mention anything about it. I just thought it was BTower being BTower, having a hissy fit."

"And why would BTower have a 'hissy fit'?"

"Envy, I suppose."

"Tell us about the concert at Carnegie Hall. It was a special event, was it not?"

"It was the end of an era."

"How do you mean?"

"This was his last concert. His farewell. He was leaving the next day to return to France. Forever. Ms. Brown, there *are* no more musicians like René Allard anymore. Music will never be the same. And to think that after thirty years of collaboration this was the last time for us."

There was silence in the courtroom.

"Thank you, Mr. Lavender."

No one moved.

"Thank you, Mr. Lavender. That will be all."

Next was elderly Mabel Bidwell, René Allard's next-door neighbor. For the occasion she had had her hair blued and permed, and had taken her mink stole out of mothballs.

"Mrs. Mabel Bidwell, what happened moments after twelve o'clock midnight on October thirty-first?"

"I was in my apartment, Apartment 4C, where I've lived for forty-four years."

"Thank you, Mrs. Bidwell. We appreciate your endurance. Please just tell us what happened."

"So I hear a thud from the corridor, which is very unusual for that time of night, though maybe since it's Halloween, who knows? You know what I'm saying? So I crack open the door—I keep the chain on, of course—to see what's all the malarkey."

"And what did you see?"

"I saw that man there"—she pointed dramatically at BTower—"bending over somebody. I didn't know who it was at the time—I mean the body, but it was him all right who was bending over it. Then he gets up. He looks around, all scared—his hands looking all bloody—and runs away down the stairs."

The defense objected to the witness making assumptions.

"Why didn't you call the police right away, Mrs. Bidwell?" asked Brown.

"Because that's when Hennie came out of 4B, and when she saw who the body was, I'm telling you, I had to take care of her first, police or no police."

"Thank you, Mrs. Bidwell."

Finally was Detective Al Malachi.

"Detective Malachi, did you find anything at the defendant's apartment when you went to arrest him that might corroborate prior testimony?"

"Yes."

"What did you find?"

"On the wall of his study, where he kept all his music and CDs and things like that, was a part of a review of one of his recitals, from April 12, 1988. It was written by Martin Lilburn, music critic of the *New York Times*. It had been enlarged and certain passages were underlined in red and it was framed. It was clearly not an artwork."

"Please refrain from editorial comments, Detective. Do you have a copy of that review?"

"Yes."

"Could you please read it to the court?"

Malachi cleared his throat.

" 'When BTower performed the Paganini Twenty-fourth Caprice and the Wieniawski D-Major Polonaise, one forgave him his lack of musical insight, because the sheer power of his mechanical execution combined with his obvious visual stage appeal made for a compelling show. However, when he tried his hand at the profound Bach A-Minor Sonata for Unaccompanied Violin and the ostensibly straightforward Mozart G-Major Sonata, K. 379, his lack of artistic presence became woefully evident, particularly in the insouciant charm of the second movement variations. René Allard, on his worst night, would have brought more reflective intelligence and good taste to the table. And that goes without mentioning the gaping disparity of their sounds—Allard's with his legendary vocal and lustrous warmth, like a vintage Burgundy; and BTower's, strong but cold and colorless as cheap beer.' "

"Thank you, Detective. Was there anything else of relevance you found on the defendant's person?"

"Yes."

"And what was that?"

"Blood was found on the clothing the defendant was wearing at the time of his arrest. It was also found under his fingernails. He apparently tried to wash it off his hands."

"Was it the defendant's own blood found under his fingernails and on his clothing, Detective?"

"No."

"Whose blood was it?"

Malachi leaned forward in his chair as if to emphasize his response. He looked, unflinching, at the jury.

"The blood of René Allard."

"Is there any doubt about the blood, Detective Malachi? If there is any doubt, it is your obligation to tell us. We do not want to convict the wrong man based upon questionable evidence."

"There is no doubt."

When she addressed the jury in her closing statement, attorney Brown rubbed it in. "Now, the defense will try to have you believe that the simple absence of a murder weapon is sufficient to render a verdict of not guilty. They will try to have you believe that between approximately midnight and the time of his arrest, a period of more than two hours, the defendant was unable to dispose of a weapon in a city of eight million inhabitants. They will strain any reasonable level of credulity and have you believe that in the approximately one minute between the time Mr. Allard exited the elevator on the fourth floor of the Bonderman Building and the time that the defendant claims to have discovered the body while on a mission of reconciliation, that during those sixty seconds, the real killer—a phantom who no one saw, who no one can account for—magically appeared, brutally killed René Allard—a heroic and kindly eighty-one-year-old man, the most beloved violinist in the world—and evaporated into thin air. All in sixty seconds. And that the defendant—an athletic, headstrong young man, obsessed with the greater legacy of his elder rival—seeing himself in the predicament of being spotted alongside the body, with the victim's blood literally on his hands, suddenly panicked because he was worried he would be wrongly accused.

"That, ladies and gentlemen of the jury, is what the defense would have you believe. The State's case rests, confident that you will believe what you will believe."

BTower, sitting next to Rosenthal at the defense table, said, "I know what the jury will believe they believe. I just hope they give me death and not life without parole." After just under four hours of deliberation, the jury found BTower guilty of the murder of René Allard. He was also right about the sentence.

VALSE

FOUR

ONE YEAR LATER
DAY 1: THURSDAY

Even for August, the morning was unseasonably hot and humid. The relentless droning of the horsefly and of the NPR pledge drive competed to send Jacobus's irritability over the edge. He lay inert and panting on the musty sofa to which his back was sticking, his head perched awkwardly on the plywood exposed by the couch arm's frayed fabric. He shifted his buttocks, seeking a less uncomfortable position for his increasingly arthritic, aging right hip. The fly landed in his left ear with a pugnacious *tzzzt*. Jacobus instinctively responded, boxing himself painfully as the fly, satisfied with the annoyance it had achieved, calmly sought greener pastures.

"Here's a good one," said Nathaniel, finishing a bag of Cheetos. "Seven letters. 'Leopold, Arturo, or Lenny.' *M* blank blank *S* blank blank blank."

"Don't you have anything better to do?" wheezed Jacobus, blowing cigarette smoke out of his mouth. He crushed the butt in his favorite ashtray, what once might have been a back of a Stradivarius violin, which sat on a folding bridge chair next to the couch on which he was lying. Beside the ashtray was his favorite mug, a toby jug of a blind pirate. The coffee in the mug, abandoned shortly after it was brewed at dawn, was beginning to be reheated by the day's quickly increasing temperature. By now the flavor would be bitter and rancid, reflecting Jacobus's mood.

"Like what? Killin' myself on nicotine?" replied Nathaniel.

"Hey, it's my house. I don't believe there are any No Smoking signs posted here."

After his testimony at the trial of BTower, Jacobus concluded he had had enough and decided he would gradually withdraw from decades of full-time violin teaching. The trial had, unpredictably, left him feeling empty and unfulfilled, unable to commit himself with full energy to his students' needs. He had continued working with his current students until they went on to bigger and better things, or quit, while not taking on any new ones. By this method of attrition he'd winnowed his studio to only a few stalwarts—masochists, he called them—and even those came to see him only intermittently. He hadn't yet concluded, though, which was worse: telling one faceless student after another what his or her problems were, or not having students to tell them what their problems were. In any event, in his semiretirement he was feeling restless and even more ornery than usual.

"Schmuck," Jacobus said.

"Say what?" asked Nathaniel. He was frequently surprised but rarely offended by Jacobus's out-of-the-blue remarks. Williams had been Jacobus's longtime friend from the time they had performed in a trio as Oberlin conservatory students after World War II. They were an improbable pair: Jacobus—blind, eccentric, haggard, an iconoclast; Williams—a large (very large) African American, thoughtful, organized, congenial. Their paths had diverged when Williams became a freelance consultant to insurance companies in the field of musical instrument theft and fraud. Jacobus, whose promising career as a concert violinist was nipped in the bud when he was stricken by foveomacular dystrophy—a complex term for sudden adult blindness—had became a renowned, if unorthodox, teacher.

"You said seven letters," said Jacobus. "Three conductors—Leopold Stokowski, Arturo Toscanini, Leonard Bernstein. The answer is schmuck."

"Ah! Wait a minute; you've got the *M* and *S* backward."

"No I don't. The puzzle's wrong. It's 'schmuck.'"

"I've got it," said Nathaniel. "It's 'maestro.'"

"Whatever." Even lying semicomatose on his back on his frayed and mildewed couch, in the dingy living room of his Berkshire home—what others might call a shack—Jacobus felt hot and prickly. The blades of his 1950s-era double window fan were caked in grease and dust. One of the fans was inoperable; the other was ineffectual except in regard to the volume of noise it made. It had two speeds, loud and loud, so Jacobus, who hated noise, never turned it on. Though his brown flannel shirt was fully unbuttoned, Jacobus could feel the sweat already beginning to pool on his belly.

"So," began Nathaniel, "what's a four-letter word beginning with *O* for 'Business is up and down?'"

"'Otis.' Where's Yumi? She's late for her lesson."

"Tanglewood traffic's probably holding her up," said Nathaniel. "She'll be here. She's never missed a lesson yet. Uh-oh."

"What's 'uh-oh'? You get another word wrong?"

"No, just here in the Arts section. Lilburn has a story about BTower. 'Rarely has a star fallen in as precipitous and calamitous a degree as BTower's. Just a short time ago, at the zenith of stardom in both the classical and pop music galaxies, the onetime darling of the concert stage now finds himself a burned-out supernova, close to his own extinction. BTower's legal team, headed by Cy Rosenthal, confirmed that BTower has adamantly refused to allow death penalty attorney Thomas O'Neil of the Long Island law firm Palmese, Leibowitz, and O'Neil to request any further appeals delaying or preventing his execution. BTower's dyed-in-the-wool fans have nevertheless organized round-the-clock candlelight vigils outside Sing Sing Correctional Facility in Ossining, New York, and in front of Carnegie Hall, demanding clemency from the governor, and vowing to stay there until BTower's scheduled execution, seven days from today. A prevalent claim from his supporters is that the trial and punishment of BTower was racially tinged from the outset; others simply lament the imminent loss of yet a second musical icon as a consequence of the ongoing tragedy of the René Allard murder. Rosenthal says—'"

"Never mind what that shyster says!" Jacobus barked. He was up and pacing. "When he calls, tell him I'm out."

"Why would he call you?"

"To go governor groveling with him. For clemency. The blind man who taught the con, hat in hand. 'Please, Your Excellency! Please spare the life of this poor young man. I know he's done a terrible thing and he should pay, but please let him live. You are his last hope. What a tragedy it would be, blah blah blah.' Forget it."

"Well, if he does call—and I'm not saying he will—why don't you just tell him that?"

"Because," Jacobus said, hearing the knock on the door, "I've got better things to do."

"Like what? Lyin' there swattin' flies?"

Jacobus was saved from a response when the kitchen door with its torn screen creaked opened on rusty springs and then slammed shut, and his prize student, Yumi Shinagawa, entered without ceremony, secretly filling Jacobus with pride. When years earlier she came to him for her first lesson from a small mountain town in Japan, she had bowed in the traditional Japanese manner. He had impressed upon her that as a violinist the only entity she had to bow to was the music, and now, finally, she understood. Yumi had become as much of a daughter to Jacobus— who had no family—as if she were his own, though at this point she was less of a student and more of a young professional whose playing just needed an occasional spit and polish from Jacobus. At first she had all the attributes of a good student: intelligent, hardworking, dedicated, and extremely talented; a rough-hewn teenager with boundless potential. But she had something else too: a perilous family secret. Not only did Jacobus develop her exceptional aptitude on the violin, he had unraveled her secret and ultimately saved her family from ignominious exposure in their role in the theft of the infamous Piccolino Stradivarius, and she in turn had saved his life.

"Sorry I'm late, Jake," said Yumi. As she headed directly into his cluttered study he grunted, buttoned up his shirt with only moderate inaccuracy, and followed her footsteps. Yumi hunted for a flat surface to put her violin case and found one atop a precarious pile of LPs on the floor. "I had to finish packing. This is my first tour with the quartet and I couldn't decide what I need to take."

"That's not my problem, is it?" said Jacobus. "What are you playing today?"

"Beethoven. 'Kreutzer' Sonata."

"Play, then."

Yumi tuned her violin, then, without even warming up, dove right into what may be the most taxing sonata in the violin repertoire, a sonata that Beethoven himself, on the title page of the music, wrote "like a concerto" for violin and piano. Starting with the Adagio sostenuto and throughout the relentless Presto, Yumi played with flawless and dynamic energy.

"Very impressive," Jacobus said after the final tumultuous A-Minor chords of the movement echoed into silence.

"Thank you, Jake," Yumi said, out of breath.

"But not very musical."

Yumi laughed. "I knew there would be a 'but.' What didn't you like?"

"First of all, why the hell are you moving around so much? Trying to put on some kind of show?"

"How can you tell I'm moving around if you can't see me?"

"Just by listening, my dear hyperactive one. When the sound goes in and out like an AM station in the middle of the night, it means you're twisting your body and changing the orientation of the violin to the audience. Your sound is suspiciously inconsistent, which means you're changing the angle of your bow arm in relation to the instrument, causing the bow to slide all over the place, which means you're raising and lowering the violin to the extremes. When you stomp all over the floor—"

"Okay, Jake, I think I'm getting the message."

"But worse than that, I got the feeling that you were using the music as a vehicle for you to try to impress the audience. That's ass backwards. You should be a liaison between the music and the listener, not the center of attention. For example, you shouldn't vibrate like crazy in the second theme. It's a hymn, not a scream. Beethoven wasn't a religious guy, but he knew where his bread was buttered so he's not going to yell when he prays to the almighty, is he? And the way you whacked at the eighth notes. What're you trying to do, kill the violin? In the end it's not *impressive*. It's *oppressive*."

"But what about the idea of musical personality? Isn't that what you always said separated violinists like Allard and Heifetz from 'the rabble'?"

"Personality, yes. Caricature, no. Interpretation, yes. Imitation, no. Isaac Stern, yes. BTower, no. People like Stern and Allard did their homework. Allard studied with Eugene Ysaÿe, the greatest violinist at the beginning of the twentieth century and a damn fine composer too, and went to the Paris Conservatory. You think they would have let him get away without doing his counterpoint homework? Just think for a moment about

Allard's accomplishment. He played exactly the same program at Carnegie Hall once every ten years, from 1942 until the night he died: Leclair, Debussy, and Franck sonatas. Then, for encores, his little improvisations and finally 'Danse Macabre'—people came to expect it, like the Boston Pops playing 'Stars and Stripes.' Most musicians, they play the same program twice, the second time you yawn, but with Allard, it was always a different interpretation, yet somehow always in good taste and always distinctly Allard. You know, there's a commemorative CD of all six concerts that's just come out on Vanguard. I suggest you listen to it. Guys like Allard knew the music inside out, so their personality was just a natural extension of the composer's."

Jacobus heard the phone ring in the living room.

"Sorry, he's out," Jacobus heard Nathaniel say.

A voice at the other end of the line continued to jabber.

"I told you to tell him to forget it!" Jacobus shouted.

Nathaniel put his hand over the receiver and whispered, "I think you've blown your cover, Jake. It's Rosenthal. He said he's relieved to hear you're no longer out."

"Gimme the phone, dammit." Jacobus reached out and Nathaniel shoved it into his hand.

"Forget it, Rosenthal," rasped Jacobus, declining to indulge in pleasantries. "I'm not going to help your client get his sentence reduced."

"Mr. Jacobus," said Rosenthal.

"Don't 'Mr. Jacobus' me," said Jacobus. "I said no way."

"That's not what I'm asking for. Please give me a minute and then you can hang up on me," said Rosenthal.

"Okay, but only for the pleasure of hanging up on you."

Jacobus lifted his index finger to Yumi to signify she had only a minute to wait.

"Thank you," said Rosenthal.

"Fifty-five seconds," said Jacobus.

"It's been almost a year since BTower was convicted of killing Allard. Both great violinists in their own right. The murder weapon was never found. No cause of death."

"Yack yack yack. So what else is new that we haven't known for, what, ten, twelve months?" asked Jacobus. "Forty seconds."

"Just this, Mr. Jacobus," replied Rosenthal, speaking faster. "My team's used up every chance we had for effective appeal. The guy's innocent, and there are just so many parallels to when the cops were after you for killing Victoria Jablonski."

"Wait a minute, Rosenthal. Are you meaning to tell me"—Jacobus was shouting now—"you've got the chutzpah to ask me to try to get BTower totally off the hook? Look, Counselor, the difference between your guy and me was I was innocent." Jacobus understood that people sometimes got killed. He read it in his Braille *New York Times* every day. In certain cases homicide seemed almost justified to him. But when the greatest violinist, and perhaps the greatest humanitarian, of the twentieth century is cut down in so vicious a manner as Allard was, and for such a petty reason as professional jealousy, Jacobus had a difficult time finding any sympathy.

"Your guy was convicted, and if you remember, I was a witness for the side that put him where he is now."

"Look, Mr. Jacobus," said Rosenthal, speaking with the speed of a prescription medication disclaimer, "if you gave me more than a minute I'd explain to you why I think he's innocent, but between you and me, I'm grasping at straws."

"Well, you can make me the last straw," Jacobus said. "And you're the camel. Nineteen seconds."

"If we don't find who did kill René Allard, not only will the true murderer still be on the loose, but an innocent man, and another great violinist—whatever your own personal opinion—will be lost to the world."

"If the cops haven't been able to find this phantom killer for how long—almost two years, what makes you think I can, assuming he or she actually exists?" asked Jacobus. "Five seconds . . . four . . . three . . ."

"How would you have answered that question, Mr. Jacobus, when the cops were after you?" replied Rosenthal.

That stopped him. Jacobus thought for a moment. He'd give Rosenthal another minute. "Why do you think he's innocent?"

"Because there was no evidence! Just supposition. BTower was convicted because the weight of public opinion was totally against him. I've negotiated for the unions enough to know what that means. The only thing that keeps management bargaining and keeps us from getting locked out is when we're able to convince the public that we are the good guys. I wasn't able to do that for BTower. The deck was totally stacked against us. Shit!"

Exhaling cigarette smoke into the phone, Jacobus asked, "What is it you want me to do?"

Rosenthal took a deep breath. "Just meet with my client. Talk to him. See what you think."

"How much do you charge per hour, Rosenthal?" asked Jacobus.

"What?" Rosenthal yelped into the phone.

"Hey, you're the fancy shmancy lawyer. You understand English, don't you? What do you charge?"

"My firm's fee is three hundred fifty dollars per hour. Plus expenses, of course."

"Then here's the deal. If I meet with BTower and I decide he's worth helping, from that point on you get zero per hour. Plus zero expenses, of course."

"Do you really think I'm in this for the money? You think I would risk my reputation on an almost impossible undertaking trying to prove a convicted man innocent, for profit?"

Jacobus relished the incredulity in the lawyer's voice. He almost laughed. Then he did.

"Well, considering that the reputation that's so dear to you went down the toilet at the Two Maestros trial and as a result you might not have such an easy time getting new clients, I would say yes, I do think you would risk it. So now you make a decision. You want me in? Then it's pro bono for you. Rosenthal, I've got a deserving student standing here in front of me waiting expectantly for my pearls of wisdom and you're wasting our time. What'll it be?"

"Very well. You've got a deal, Mr. Jacobus. I'll set it up."

"You do that," said Jacobus, hanging up.

"See what you can accomplish in a minute?" Jacobus said to Yumi. "BTower innocent! They should have also convicted him

for first-degree aestheticide. Usually I think I got a raw deal going blind, but after what I've heard about BTower's stage visuals
I think I'm better off. Moving around so much that the orchestra had to back up ten feet from the conductor!"

"But isn't that what audiences like these days?" said Yumi.
"BTower filled Yankee Stadium! For classical music! Isn't that a
good thing? And he played the 'Kreutzer' Sonata and they went
crazy for it. These days people want to see musicians showing they're
into the music. Emoting."

"These days! Those days! It doesn't matter what days. Do you
know that Bach was considered provincial and out-of-date during
his own lifetime? Who did they like back then? Stamitz! But we've
learned, haven't we, what good taste is. Who listens to Stamitz today? Maybe just some moldy musicologists in the basement of the
archives. No, good taste is what lasts. When the original Bridgetower
premiered the 'Kreutzer' with Beethoven, you can be sure he
didn't have go-go dancers behind him. BTower is just another fly-
by-night, and he'll be remembered for murdering a man who had
taste and not for his dubious contribution to the music world."

"Maybe you have a point."

"How sweet of you to say so. Now play it again, and play it like
the classical composer Beethoven was in 1802—with proportion
and tone quality—and not like a prequel to *Phantom of the Opera*."

"You should be happy I've learned not to take your criticism
personally," Yumi said.

"Who said it wasn't personal?"

Yumi laughed, then played through the movement again, this
time with control and attention to detail. The energy was still
there and the music seemed to flow more naturally.

When she finished, Jacobus said, "That time I heard a little bit of Beethoven. And a little Beethoven will go a long way. Thank you."

That was as much of a compliment as Yumi had ever received from Jacobus.

"Jake," she said, "since this tour with the Magini Quartet coming up is my first, I was wondering if you and Nathaniel might want to come to one of our performances."

"Where are you playing, honey?" asked Nathaniel, who had been listening from the living room. He folded up an old *Times Book Review* and entered the studio.

"It's a festivals tour," Yumi said. "We start in Durango, Colorado. Then the Antelope Island Festival in Utah, Teton Festival in Wyoming, Sunriver in Oregon, and we finish at Ojai in California. Two weeks. And we're doing the Brahms Quintet with Virgil Lavender on some of the programs."

"Out west with the hicks?" asked Jacobus. "It'll be a cold day in hell when I fly out west for a concert."

"Well," said Nathaniel, "with this heat I wouldn't mind a little cold. And, Jake, your house here, it ain't exactly paradise."

FIVE
DAY 2: FRIDAY

Rosenthal followed as Jacobus was ushered into the interview room at the maximum-security Sing Sing Correctional Facility by two burly guards for his 7 A.M. meeting with BTower. Four strong hands guided Jacobus to a cheap uncomfortable plastic chair at a counter that divided the unadorned room in half. Along the entire length of the counter was a Plexiglas shield that separated the visitors from the inmates. Opposite Jacobus sat BTower, flanked by a pair of even burlier guards: Bailey Haskell, a muscular African American with short-cropped graying hair, neatly trimmed mustache, and a palm big enough to hide a football; and Gruber Gundacker, a much younger white man, former offensive tackle on the Syracuse University football team, shorter than Haskell but still well over six feet, with a buzz cut and a baby face.

Jacobus felt for the desk phone in front of him and picked up the receiver. "Yeah," he said.

"I just want you to know, man," said BTower from the other side of the Plexiglas, "that this was all Rosenthal's idea. See?"

"Oh, was it?" said Jacobus. "Well, in that case I wouldn't want to waste your time, which I imagine is becoming increasingly precious," and he slammed down the phone and got up to leave, upending the flimsy chair.

"What?" yelled Rosenthal.

"What am I doing here with this punk?" said Jacobus. "I'm out of here."

"You can't!" said Rosenthal and grabbed Jacobus's sleeve.

"Get off of me." Jacobus made a wild and ineffectual swing for where he thought Rosenthal's face would be. Rosenthal, shorter than Jacobus by almost a head, wrapped his arms around Jacobus and tried to wrestle him to the ground. As the two geriatric combatants struggled, BTower shouted out from his side of the Plexiglas, "Jacobus, you son of a bitch! You can rot in hell!"

"Guards!" yelled Rosenthal. *"Guards!"*

The two muscular guards, laughing, had little trouble separating blind old Jacobus from the diminutive Rosenthal. "Whoa, big fella," one of them said.

"What the hell's your problem, Jacobus?" said Rosenthal, panting. "What did you expect, that he would be waiting for you with open arms? You're the one who helped put him here. Now listen to me. You think this is tough for *you*? I represent labor unions. They call me a lot worse than you've ever heard and I'm on their side! Then, guess what, I have to go out there and get them a good deal or my ass is grass. Now here I've got the one-in-a-million client who just so happens to be innocent and you get offended because he doesn't make nice to you.

"You think BTower's been kind to me? You think he appreciates our efforts to clear him? Well, think again. He'd gotten used to associating with the caviar of society, and here I was, pickled herring. The arrogance never wore off, and the longer the legal process went on, the greater the antagonism grew."

"So why bother, Rosenthal? Why not go on to cases you can win, with clients who deserve it?"

"Because the guy's innocent! Mr. Jacobus, let's start over again, please. Let's you and I sit down a minute and catch our breath. Maybe I should've given you a little better preparation. My apologies.

"When BTower was convicted," Rosenthal told Jacobus after the guards had reset the overturned chairs, "we had assumed that an appeal would be successful, that he'd be walking in a few weeks. Certainly not more than a few months. After all, as I said, where was the evidence? So he became arrogant. Cocky. He alienated the prison guards and, worse, the other inmates. When the appeals, one after another, were rejected, everyone got his payback.

He was subject to the worst abuse from both ends of the legal spectrum. The worst abuse, Jacobus. Need I say more? His will collapsed. Playing the violin, and the fame that accompanied it, became a distant memory. They segregated him from the rest of the prison population. He went from combative to morose, and was placed on a twenty-four-hour suicide watch. If there's a fate worse than the death penalty, that's it, so don't expect him to be all peaches and cream. Now, with that in mind, would you please go back and talk to him?"

Jacobus grunted and let himself be escorted back to the chair, which had been put back into place.

"That was quite a show," BTower said. "Just what are you doing here, man?"

"I have no idea. Your ambassador put me up to it."

"Rosenthal. That incompetent asshole. If lawyers got convicted along with their clients, you can be sure a lot more would get acquitted. So now he's trying to cover his damn ass?"

"Maybe you wouldn't be here if you hadn't killed Allard," said Jacobus.

"Whatever."

"Rosenthal seems to think you didn't."

"Didn't what?"

"Didn't kill Allard."

"Whatever."

"Hey, you schmuck!" yelled Jacobus. "I don't like you and I don't like the way you played the violin, and I don't like the fact that the greatest violinist of the twentieth century was murdered. But if you didn't kill him, someone else did. Someone who's been walking around somewhere for the last two years. So you can rot in hell for all I care, but I want the one that did it locked up. *Capisce*?"

"*Played* the violin?" asked BTower.

"Well, I haven't heard you playing with the Philharmonic lately, pretty boy," said Jacobus.

Jacobus heard a sudden clamor, a hard thud against the Plexiglas, quick footsteps, then the sound of a scuffle. A bunch of grunts, *ughs,* and *nnngs,* as Haskell and Gundacker subdued BTower, shoving him back into his chair, which clattered brittlely against the concrete floor. Jacobus smiled. He had found the soft spot. He was getting somewhere.

"What was that?" Jacobus asked with mock innocence. "Someone fall down and go boom?"

"Just my two pals here," said BTower. "Music lovers."

"So tell me," asked Jacobus, "they don't let you play the violin here? You'd think a little music would spruce up this place."

"That's a laugh," said BTower. "I actually tried that, see, during the first appeal. My agent hadn't canceled my engagements yet."

"And?"

"And they beat the shit out of me. Didn't like the 'faggot' music."

Jacobus kept his mouth shut. He wanted BTower to do the talking.

"Then, when they put me on suicide watch," BTower continued, "the powers that be considered violin strings to be a potential lethal weapon, so the violin got nixed. You should be familiar with that one."

Jacobus considered for a moment the murder a few years earlier

of the violin pedagogue Victoria Jablonski, who had been stran-
gled with a G-string that the cops thought, mistakenly, had come
from his own violin. That he had finally been cleared of the murder did not, in the eyes of the authorities, negate the lethal potential of violin strings.

"But it wasn't any violin string that killed Allard. Tell me what
did happen the night he was murdered, and not the BS Rosenthal
spouted in court. How did you end up standing over his body
with his blood on your hands?"

"First let me tell you that René Allard was not the kind old
grandfather that everyone thought."

"That statement makes you a minority of one," said Jacobus.

"Yeah, well, then don't believe me. But after he finished his
Carnegie recital, I went backstage to congratulate him."

"But then you rubbed him the wrong way. What Lavender testified."

"I wore my jeans and T-shirt to his recital."

"Big deal, that's what you always wear. Am I supposed to congratulate you on your nonconformity with the civilized world?"

"Hey, man, if Allard had said that to me, see, I wouldn't have
minded a bit. What he said was, in his dapper Maurice Chevalier
accent, 'So, you have worn your Halloween costume tonight.' I
said, 'Well, it's what I'm comfortable in.' And he just shrugged
and said, 'Once an *Africain*, always an *Africain*,' and walked away."

"Allard said that?" said Jacobus. "I find that hard to believe."

"Why do you give more credibility to the way someone phrases
music than what he actually says? You know all that crap Brown
was spouting about how Allard made me one of the family? The
truth is he made me his errand boy. His gofer. He was actually

saving money by giving me free lessons so he wouldn't have to hire someone."

"But if all that's true about Allard, why didn't Rosenthal harp on it at the trial?"

"Are you that dumb, man? That would have handed the jury even more motives for me to have killed him! The truth is I did follow Allard back to the Bonderman and tried one more time to settle things with him. I'm telling you, I tried. You know, 'go the extra mile'? When I get to the elevator he won't even look at me, see? Won't say shit. That's what pisses me off. That he won't even acknowledge my existence, man. When I run up the stairs after him, it wasn't to apologize anymore. I wanted to tell him off. But I wasn't going to kill him."

"Prove it."

"I'm not the one supposed to prove what I didn't do! You know, Jacobus, you may think I'm some kind of gangsta rapper, but I don't go around wasting the competition."

"That argument certainly made one helluva defense," said Jacobus. "So, hotshot, what kind of stupidity was it to have that review from the *Times* tacked up on your wall?"

"It's a free country. Right? But hey, if I thought hanging something on my wall was going to get me convicted of murder, I might have had second thoughts."

"I'm not talking about that, and I don't need your sarcasm. I'm talking about music. What the hell does a crummy review have to do with music?"

"Let's say it gave me incentive, okay?"

"Incentive to what?"

BTower looked down at his limply hanging hands. "Jacobus,

if you could see my hands. They feel thick and old as those stink-ing canned Vienna sausages my roommate, Wally Walinsky, used to eat when we were students."

BTower smiled. "Walinsky. What a weirdo, who everyone thought was a big-time talent. 'Isn't Wally wonderful? He's sooo smart.' Ended up doing the orchestra grind—playing with the same hundred dudes three hundred days a year with the same asshole conductors. Sell your soul for a pension and health in-surance. Thank God I'm better than that.

"Because of my hands I was as well known around the world as Muhammad Ali, man. I could go anywhere. 'Hello, BTower. Yes, BTower. We'll send it up right away, Mr. BTower. Can I have your autograph, BTower? Can I take you out for a drink, BTower? Would you like to come to my room after the concert, BTower?'

"And you know damn well it's not easy, Jacobus. I paid my dues, man. I taught myself when I was a kid. One hour of prac-tice every day. Then three hours a day. Five hours. Seven. And hey, it paid off, didn't it? Just ask my former agent, Sheila Rath-man of InHouseArtists, Inc. She got her ten percent from me for six—no, seven—years. From the Chicago Symphony, the Ber-lin Philharmonic, the NHK Symphony, the Sydney Symphony. You name it. Maybe she can get me a gig at the fucking Sing Sing Symphony.

"Then, wouldn't you know it, the minute the trial's over, my best buddy Sheila sends me a letter. 'IHA regrets to inform you . . .' Wouldn't want to tarnish their image now, would we? Tarnished image, all right—I'd give that princess her virginity back if it was a medical possibility."

BTower pressed his fingers into his thighs. Jacobus let the silence linger. BTower's bitterness echoed his. Jacobus had suppressed his all these years, but it was killing him. Had BTower not been able to hold it in? Had he finally lashed out? One way or the other, their rage would probably kill each of them, sooner or later.

"I don't even have life with chance of parole, like Wally has with his orchestra job."

"You could practice without the violin," said Jacobus.

"Sure. And you can see without eyes."

"Can't I?"

"I'm on death row, Jacobus. I'm going to be executed. My career is finished, see? My life is over. For a murder I didn't commit. And what are you telling me? That I should be practicing? Hey, smart ass, if I don't have a violin, how do I practice?"

"We do it all the time," said Jacobus. "Sitting in a cab stuck in traffic when you're late getting to the concert hall, what do you do? Close your eyes, see the music. Right? Rest the case on your lap and put your fingers on top of the case like it's a fingerboard. Sense the feel of the bow in your right hand. Feel its balance, its weight, its responsiveness to your grip. Hear the music in your head. Just think about what you could do with the first chord of the 'Kreutzer' Sonata. You know the notes. You know where your fingers go to play in tune. No one played the notes better than you, faster than you, more brilliantly than you. Yeah, you could play the *notes* with the best of them. You just didn't know how to play the *music*."

"Well, and fuck you too, Jacobus. I think our little chitchat is over."

"Fuck you too, pretty boy," Jacobus said and got up. As he was escorted out of the room, he said over his shoulder to Rosenthal, "I want all the police files, transcribed to Braille or CD, at no cost to anyone but you."

S I X

"Ten bucks," said Gundacker.

"You know I'm not a betting man, Gruber," said Bailey Haskell, giving careful consideration to each chew of his sandwich.

"Five bucks, then," said Gundacker.

"Okay," said Haskell, patiently. "Five bucks. If that's the way you want it."

As had become their routine for the twenty minutes that their shifts overlapped, the two big security guards relaxed with their lunch and enjoyed their daily entertainment watching on the audiovideo surveillance monitor as BTower, the only remaining inmate on death row, paced the perimeter of his cell. After finishing their lunches, it would be Gundacker's turn to do the rounds in the cell blocks, delivering what was euphemistically referred to as lunch to the inmates, and Haskell would remain in the office until they were both replaced by the night shift. It was a timetable that had been going on since Gundacker, still fuzzy cheeked and newly married to his high school sweetheart, Clorinda, had moved up from maintenance on the penal system's ladder. Haskell had been there many years longer, and in his quiet moments calculated his monthly pension and consulted his astrological chart to ascertain the most propitious day he and his wife, April, could retire to their mobile home in Sarasota. He was still strong and could handle most of the prisoners without difficulty even without Gundacker, but he felt his batteries gradually slowing down and was just about ready to pack it all up.

As he did every day, BTower first paced counterclockwise, banging the door and each wall three times with his clenched right fist. He then about-faced and repeated the ritual, now pounding with his left hand. Repetitiveness did not cause any reduction in his virulence; the ritual had remained frenetic and brutal from day one, as the bruises on his hands confirmed. Except for his mattress, his stainless steel cell had the antiseptic sterility and cold hardness of an oven interior, the impersonality of which had goaded BTower toward greater and greater rage.

"How's Clorinda?" asked Haskell.

"She's okay," said Gundacker, keeping his eye on the monitor. "I guess."

"You guess? You don't know?"

"Well," Gundacker said, "she's thinking she wants to have a kid."

"Somethin' not okay with that?" asked Haskell.

"You and April never had kids," said Gundacker.

"Well, Gruber, that doesn't really prove anything."

"I'm just not sure it's the right time. I've only had this job for a couple years. Haven't saved shit yet."

"Same thing with April and me. There was always something we were savin' for or waitin' for so we never did think it was 'the right time,' and now it ain't never gonna be 'the right time.' When I look back on it now, maybe it was our thinkin' that wasn't right. Maybe we should've thought there's never a 'wrong time' to have a child."

Gundacker took a bite of his peanut butter sandwich, which Haskell referred to as the 'choke on white,' that he brought from home every day. It was as predictable to Haskell as his alarm clock going off at 5:45 every morning.

"There! Look, he's stopping!" said Gundacker suddenly. He poked excitedly toward the monitor with his left index finger as if Haskell didn't clearly see it already. "Hand it over, mister," he said to Haskell, holding out a newly freed open palm for his five-dollar prize money.

BTower had paused in his perambulations and was examining his own palms, which even from the distance of the camera showed red with swelling.

"*Not so fast,*" *said Haskell, his careful eyes intent upon the monitor.* "*He ain't sat down yet, now, has he?*"

Motionless, BTower stared fixedly at his bed as the seconds ticked, but rather than sitting down with his head between his knees as had been his custom, he turned a hundred eighty degrees and resumed pacing.

"*Yaah!*" *shouted Haskell.* "*My man, BTower! That'll be one Mr. Lincoln from you, Gruber Gundacker!*"

"*Damn,*" *grumbled Gundacker.* "*How about I owe you? Put it on the account?*"

"*Okay for now,*" *said Haskell.* "*But one of these days, your account be overdrawn.*" *Haskell took a leisurely bite of his pulled pork with horseradish sauce on a kaiser roll. He had another six hours in the booth. He was in no hurry.*

Gundacker, defeated yet again, got up to leave, giving the monitor one final glance.

"*Hey, get a load!*" *he said, his enthusiasm restored, like a child searching for his favorite marble lost in the bushes, who finds a red toy truck waiting to be discovered in its stead.*

BTower had stopped pacing and had moved to the center of his eight-by-eight cell. For a moment he stood stark still, then raised his left arm, elbow bent, so that his hand was at eye level.

"*What the hell?*" *said Gundacker.* "*He gone totally ape shit?*"

Haskell just watched.

BTower then raised his right arm, not as high and palm down.

"*If I'm not mistaken, I'd say we're about to get ourselves a little concert,*" *said Haskell.*

BTower's face was intense, jaw taut. He began to move his right arm like a high-speed horizontal piston. The fingers of his left hand moved like lightning. Haskell and Gruber watched, fascinated. Whatever it was that BTower was silently playing on his invisible violin, they had never seen such a frenzied performance, or anything at all for that matter, move so fast.

The pantomime concert ended as abruptly as it began.

"They all get crazy when they get this close? What's he got, six days?" asked Gundacker.

"Five," said Haskell.

With renewed interest, Haskell and Gundacker observed BTower glare at his throbbing hands, then viciously hurl down the phantom violin. The silent melodrama continued as he stomped on it on the cement floor. He picked it up and swung it against his cell door, bringing no result other than to bruise and scrape his hands even more. Next he attempted to rip the mattress off the bed frame but soon realized that even in the heat of his frenzy it was fastened down.

"Someone like that, angry like that, surely could be capable of killing someone," said Haskell.

"Should we send for the doc?" Gundacker asked Haskell.

"Let's give it a minute. I'm guessing he'll calm down momentarily, but I ain't betting on this one, Gruber Gundacker."

BTower, panting heavily, eyes closed, suddenly collapsed on his back onto the mattress, his hands over his face, his body shaking.

"Show's over," said Gundacker.

"Not quite, Gruber. Look."

BTower lifted himself into a sitting position and peered directly at them into the surveillance camera.

"Fuck you, Jacobus!" he yelled, piercing the silence.

SEVEN

The Columbus Circle subway station was its usual whirlpool of activity. At the confluence of Central Park West, Broadway, and Central Park South, it served the needs of camera-toting tourists decked out in I ♥ NEW YORK T-shirts, Carnegie Hall and Lincoln Center concertgoers, diners heading a few blocks uptown to the boutique restaurants, exercisers jogging to the park, and the usual mass of humanity that just happened to work for a living.

Like horses at the starting gate, the crowd bolted out of the subway, racing toward the finish line of its appointed tasks. Jacobus, hoping to avoid being trampled by the herd, tried to maintain his balance by allowing himself to be carried along in the flow. The rumble of trains, the jackhammers of construction, the relentless roar of humanity filled his ears as he sought the escalator out of the station. He was on his way to see Camille Henrique—Hennie, as most of the musical world knew her—to satisfy his curiosity why she hadn't testified at the trial of the murderer of her longtime companion. Not that it made any difference in the end, but he thought the prosecution would have drooled to have the beautiful woman in mourning take the stand.

Over the years, Jacobus had become adept at maneuvering in crowds, instantly absorbing and analyzing and responding to all sorts of stimuli—sounds, smells, incidental physical contact, even taste, when all else failed. People said that he had a sixth

sense, but in reality it was an exquisitely honed ability to assimi-
late his four functioning ones that enabled him to walk without
a cane, Seeing Eye dog, or human assistance. Here in the suffo-
cating underground station he felt the flow of the crosscurrents
of pedestrian traffic, the sounds of which were somewhat obscured by monumental blowers magnanimously situated by the
Transit Authority to create the most noise and the least relief.
He was on the uptown side of the tracks, so he should get to the
escalator any moment now. He sniffed for the invisible cascade
of sweat, garbage, and car exhaust coming down from the street
level to find it. He wasn't being jostled quite as much now.

"And just how would you suggest I begin my reinvestigation?"
he had asked Rosenthal. "Start with a blank slate," Rosenthal
replied, with BTower as just one potential person of interest. So
Jacobus decided to initiate his search with Hennie, René Allard's longtime confidante. He had encountered Hennie on and
off for many years, usually at a concert or a party, where she was
always Allard's appendage. Jacobus had first met her back in the
early fifties, shortly after she arrived in New York from Paris as a
nubile teenager to study violin with Allard. It had been a scandal
of some notoriety when shortly thereafter she moved in with him;
he was already over forty. But Hennie not only became his lover,
she became his concert agent, office manager, and business partner. They had never married because, as Allard had famously put
it, "That would have interfered terribly with our relationship."
Everyone laughed.

When Jacobus had phoned her after his conversation with
Rosenthal to set up the time of their meeting, he made no bones
about the reason for it. Maybe that had been a mistake on his

part, understanding she wouldn't be very pleased at the prospect of reopening old wounds. On the other hand, he couldn't think of another reason to have called her out of the blue that sounded genuine.

As he mulled over just what he would say to Hennie, Jacobus suddenly realized that the usual sounds and smells of humanity had ebbed into the ether. No voices, no scuffling, no car horns, no sweat, no perfume, no exhaust fumes. All he could hear was an echo of dripping water, some jazzily rhythmic tapping off in the distance, and his own uneven footsteps. His arthritic hip responded like a barometer to cooler, musty, and dank atmospheric conditions. Where the hell am I? he wondered. I shouldn't try to do two things at once, dammit. He stopped to reconnoiter, instincts momentarily befuddled. He decided to turn left.

"Hold, Mortal, lest thou will surely perish!" declaimed a voice, followed by a drum riff on what sounded like a set of paint cans and cement.

Jacobus stopped. "What are you talking about?" he asked.

"A yawning abyss beckons ye, of which thou art presently astride." *Bdop-bah.*

"Who the hell are you?" asked Jacobus.

"Men have called me the Drumstick Man, and honored be I to make your acquaintance. Welcome to my dark domain. 'Tis dark here, yea, but I perceive 'tis darker for you still. Thou canst not see this dormant track bed unused, lo, in the memory of man. One more step and thine earthly coil will surely be kaput." *Bop-bop-bop, bop-bdop-baaaah.*

Jacobus turned to his right.

"Egad! Go not that direction, neither, gentle sir."
Brrrrrrrrrrrrrrrrrrrrrr-op.

"Why the hell not? And knock off that ridiculous tapping."

"But 'tis my very nature to tap, sir! I tap on cans." *B-dang, b-dang, b-dang.* "I tap on walls." *Knk-knk-knk.* "I e'en tap 'pon my head. Ow!!

> *"The man that hath no music in himself,*
> *Nor is not mov'd with concord of sweet sounds,*
> *Is fit for treasons, stratagems, and spoils.*

"If thou goest right, m'lord, thou wilst ne'er return. Right is wrong. A community of Gatherers awaits ye yon." *Bp-bp-bding.*

"And what, may I asketh, gather they?" asked Jacobus.

"Everything, kind sir. Everything . . . But fear not! For I will lead you from these things of darkness and this precipice, just as stout Edgar did lead the orbless Gloucester. Follow me. Perchance my tapping will please you now. Dawdle not! It be not far."

"You live down here?" asked Jacobus, following Drumstick Man's tapping.

"Verily. Long has it been since the light of day has crossed my path. Passageways without number abound within these dank, dark depths. Forsooth 'tis a world unto itself. Aha, here is the end of the line for me.

> *"Walk now thou straight and true,*
> *and the world above 'twill be there for you."*

Within moments Jacobus began to hear the familiar sounds of civilization within easy distance.

"How much do I owe you?" he asked, putting his hand into his pocket.

"Never a beggar nor chooser be! Now get thee to a bunnerie. I am awaaaay!"

Jacobus heard the tapping nimbly recede into the distance. Now again with the type of humanity to which he was accustomed, in short order he was shoved up the escalator toward what was—for everyone else but him—the light at the end of the tunnel.

Walking the few short blocks from the station to the Bonderman Building, jostled by people in too much of a hurry to slow their pace even for a blind man, Jacobus contemplated the nature of insanity. On the one hand was this individual he just encountered who lived underground, talked funny, and liked to bang on things. That person had undoubtedly saved his life out of the goodness of his curiously perverse heart. On the other hand was a society that killed people, occasionally the wrong ones, as punishment for killing other people. BTower and Allard, for example. Jacobus wasn't sure which side of the sanity fence he was on. He had little need for creature comforts, and since the world was black to him anyway—in more ways than one—the prospect of living a peaceful subterranean existence, like Ziggy's, far away from all the things that daily annoyed him, didn't seem all that unreasonable. That's one reason he had never given up his hovel in the Berkshires. No one bothered him except for those he desired to bother him, like Nathaniel and his dwindling cache of students.

Jacobus entered the Bonderman Building for the first time

since the night of Allard's murder, and buzzed the elevator. When the doors opened, he stumbled as he stepped inside and had to grab on to the door's metal grate in order to regain his balance. He said, "Jesus, Lon! Fourth floor. Where's Ziggy?"

"Mr. Jacobus! How the hell did you know Ziggy isn't here? And how did you know it was me? You haven't been here for a couple years at least."

"First of all, the elevator floor was a good inch above the lobby floor. Ziggy would never have permitted that. His elevator perfectionism is known far and wide. Kind of sick that way. He also would never have countenanced General Tso's chicken, whose garlicky aroma is infesting the air, on his sacred premises. And I knew it was you because if they got rid of Ziggy, even temporarily, they'd have you fill in because elevator boys are a thing of the past."

"Well, you got that right too," said Fuente. "Ziggy, he moved out to Salt Lake City, of all places."

"Salt Lake City? They have elevators out there?"

"Was going to live with his sister, he said. The elevator here, it finally gave up the ghost and the owners decided they'd had enough. They let him go about a year ago. He cried real tears, let me tell you, even though they gave him a nice Timex."

"But the elevator's still here, ain't it?"

"Barely. They started the process for a new one, because the whole hydraulic system has been shot to hell ever since Ziggy left. They've sealed off what used to be Basement Two, where Ziggy used to live, to reinforce the floor to support a new elevator. Hold on a second."

The elevator came to a jolting halt at the third floor to let in a passenger. Jacobus's knees buckled and he almost lost his balance. "Going down," the passenger requested. "Sorry, goin' up," said Fuente. "Whatever," said the passenger as the doors closed.

"Then they just jimmy-rigged this old trap until the new one is ready," Fuente continued. "Supposed to be aerodynamic or thermonuclear or something like that. All automated, state of the art, high speed. You wouldn't think it would take a year, though. Unions, probably. But definitely no more elevator boy. That's why they had to get rid of Ziggy. No job, no apartment. Gonzo."

"Who said life's fair?" said Jacobus. "You just move on."

"Here's your floor, Mr. Jacobus." Fuente opened the sliding safety door. Jacobus already had his left hand on it in order to keep his balance, but when the brass lattice contracted, his finger got stuck in it.

"Shit, you nitwit!" hollered Jacobus. "What do you want to do, end my moribund career prematurely?"

"Sorry, sir. Are you okay? I just never've gotten the hang of this thing."

"Just remind me to take the stairs next time."

Fuente told him how far down the hall 4B was. Jacobus found the door, slid his hand along the frame, found the buzzer, and pressed it. It was immediately opened.

"Mr. Jacobus," said a no-nonsense female voice.

"Uch! Two lawyers in one day! You must have a really important meeting. Don't mean to keep you, honey."

"My name is Phoebe Swallow, Mr. Jacobus, and I do represent Ms. Henrique. And how, may I ask, do you know I'm her attorney and I have another appointment?"

"If you were just a friend, Hennie would have answered the

door herself. And then there's the stick-up-the-ass officious tone of voice. Not a housekeeper kind of voice, wouldn't you agree? And you were standing right by the door when I knocked. Why would you be doing that unless you were in a hurry to get somewhere, and with the perfume you're wearing even *my* eyes are watering so it's gotta be you're going somewhere where you need to impress someone."

"Be that as it may, Mr. Jacobus, Ms. Henrique has decided to decline your request for an interview."

"Interview? What am I, a job applicant? I've known Hennie for forty years. It's no interview. It's what my ancestors called a conversation. Who was it made this 'decision,' Hennie or you?"

"Ms. Henrique has no further comment," said Swallow, and closed the door in his face.

"Shit," muttered Jacobus. He started back for the elevator and then decided he really would rather take the stairs, using the corridor's runner to stay in a straight line. Old apartment buildings were a piece of cake.

"*Psst!*" someone hissed. "*Psst!*"

"Yeah?" asked Jacobus, turning his head away from the sound in order to hear better.

"You wanted to see Hennie?" whispered the voice.

"That was the idea."

"I'm Mabel Bidwell. I'm in 4C. Come on in." He felt a small bony hand grab his own and yank him into an apartment.

Mabel Bidwell! thought Jacobus, recalling the eyewitness who discovered BTower looming over the body of René Allard. Maybe this was the way he would skin the cat.

Speaking of cats, Jacobus sniffed and perceived that even

an overabundance of flowery air freshener did not success-
fully disguise the distinct background aroma of cat box. The
dulcet tones of Mantovani added to the unpleasantly saccha-
rine surroundings.

"You sit right here," Mabel said, pushing Jacobus down into a
couch whose bottomless cushions threatened to suffocate him.

"Cocktail?" asked Mabel.

"Maybe I'll wait 'til breakfast, if you don't mind," said Jacobus.

"Well, I'm having one," said Mabel. "Now you stay right there!"

Moments later Jacobus heard a clinking glass approach and
felt the *thwuff* of Mabel's body as she plopped herself into the
cushions next to him.

"Now tell me your name again?" asked Mabel. "I remember
you from the trial. I remember everything."

"Jacobus. And it's not again."

"Well, tell me, Jacobus. What do you want to know? I've been
in 4C for forty-six years! And I've seen it all, if you know what I
mean, and that Phoebe Swallow, she doesn't let anyone see Hennie anymore. We used to be like this—I'm holding up two fingers
in front of your face, Jacobus—but now I can't even call her."

"I'd like to find out if there was anyone who would have
wanted to harm Hennie or René Allard."

"Why, of course I know that!"

"Really! Who would that be, Mrs. Bidwell?"

"Why, that BTower! I'm the one who saw him kill René! I reported him to that Detective Malachi, who between you and me I
didn't think was a very nice person."

"Did you actually see him kill Allard?"

"Well, just as good! He was standing there looking crazy and all, with blood just dripping and oozing on his hands, paralyzed like, and then he looks around, crazy, like I said, and runs away. And I was the one that saw it—I had opened the door just a crack and was looking through the crack and reported it to—"

"Yes, thank you, Mabel. Anyone else?"

"Anyone else what?"

"Anyone else who might have wanted to harm Hennie . . ."

"Oh, no! Oh, no! Everyone loved them. They were such partiers! They were always throwing bashes. Everyone went. I used to go in the old days. They'd go on for hours. All night! Days even! The food and the champagne. And it wasn't just polite conversation, if you know what I mean."

"What do you mean?"

"There was a lot of, you know, *oo-la-la!*"

Jacobus felt a sharply pointed elbow almost break one of his ribs. Then he heard a wail that sounded like a dying baby.

"What the hell?"

"Oh, don't mind Mimi," Mabel purred, "she's just my pussy. She's Siamese. Would you like to pet my pussy?"

"I think I'll pass petting your pussy, if you don't mind. But tell me, with all these parties in the good old days, there might have been someone in love with Hennie and jealous enough to kill Allard. No?"

"Oh, no. I'm telling you. Their relationship. They did wild things, but they liked it that way. They were French."

Jacobus felt a hand on his knee.

"Mrs. Bidwell."

"Mabel."

"Mabel," said Jacobus. He removed the clammy hand, then

opted to hold it in his to make sure it stayed put. "Is there anyone else? Certainly with your encyclopedic memory of this
building's history, you can recall something . . . untoward?"

"Let me think," said Mabel. "Well, there was the girl."

"But Allard and Hennie never had any children."

"Not *a* girl. *The* girl."

Jacobus kept silent.

"You know. The *girl*. The housekeeper. She was Negro."

"Might the housekeeper have had a name, Mrs. Bidwell?"
asked Jacobus.

"Well, there was Bernice, there was Rose, and there was Pearly
Mae. I think it was Rose."

"Rose what?"

"Just Rose."

"And what happened to just Rose?"

"Rose got fired for stealing from René. I don't know why she
did it. She was always such a nice person. She worked here for
years. In those days here in the Bonderman some people had
apartments like me, and other rooms were rented just like hotel
rooms, and then there were the business offices. Now it's just the
apartments and offices. But getting back to my story, one day
when Rose was cleaning 4B she stole some of René's music."

"Why would she want to steal music?"

"Who knows? But they caught her red-handed. Ziggy found
the music in her purse down in the basement where the help kept
their stuff and reported it to the building manager, Mr. Zipolito.
He's been dead many, many years, may he rest in peace. He asked
her to explain it and she didn't have anything to say so she just
packed her bags and that was it."

"Did she steal anything else? Anything valuable?"

"Nope. Just the music."

"Well, thank you, Mabel," said Jacobus, extracting her bony claw of a hand from his. "You've been wonderfully helpful."

"Anytime, I'm sure," said Mabel. "Want to stay for another drink?"

"I'll pass, for now," said Jacobus, and fumbled his way to the door as quickly as possible, almost falling flat on his face over Mimi, who had silently interposed herself between his feet, and whose lugubrious Siamese moan followed him in his wake.

He resumed his trip to the stairway that had been interrupted by his visit with Mabel Bidwell, but then changed his mind, deciding it might be worth risking the elevator once more. Beyond having little desire to aggravate his leg with three flights of stairs, he had a question for Fuente.

"Think you can get me down alive, Lon?" he asked, as the door slid open.

"I'll do my best, Mr. Jacobus. Just fasten your seat belt."

Jacobus asked Fuente if he could spare a minute to look through the employment records to see if anyone named Rose had worked there when Zipolito was the manager. Fuente asked, "What was the first name?" Jacobus said, "That is the first name." Fuente said, "Shit," and some other things in Spanish.

When they got to the ground floor, Fuente put a well-worn PLEASE USE THE STAIRWAY sandwich board in front of the elevator and escorted Jacobus into his cluttered, windowless office. He ransacked the area behind the mops, Drano, Lysol, and Raid in the closet, hauled out a stack of heavy notebooks, and dropped them on the desk. The flying dust made Jacobus sneeze.

"What years?" asked Fuente.

"Between the time René Allard moved here and when they stopped renting rooms like a hotel."

"Well, that narrows it down to about a century," muttered Fuente as he rummaged through the files. After twenty minutes, during which hiatus Jacobus smoked three or four Camels, Fuente had found two Roses, but only one in the correct time slot. Rose Grimes had worked at the Bonderman Building from 1950 until her firing on July 22, 1965. The handwritten address listed her as living at 74 West 132nd Street but provided no additional information. Fuente checked the current phone directory, but there was no Rose Grimes listed.

"Almost thirty years," said Fuente, copying down the address for Jacobus to take. "Lotsa luck."

EIGHT

As Jacobus and Nathaniel maneuvered through an intractable, inhospitable assemblage lounging with brown bags on the disintegrating front stoop of the shabby brownstone at 74 West 132nd Street, they continued to debate Nathaniel's insistence that he accompany Jacobus to Harlem. "It's not exactly a place where an old, blind, Jewish white man would be met with open arms," Nathaniel had said. Jacobus responded, "So what'll you do when the gangstas jump me? Eat them?"

But other than a few errant sneakered feet placed with dubious

intent in Jacobus's path as he mounted the stoop, they had not
been hassled, though Nathaniel pointedly informed Jacobus that
as they made their way through the neighborhood, they had received glances both curious and threatening on this combustibly
hot late summer day.

The front door of the tenement had a hole the knob once oc-
cupied, its single glass pane had been replaced by plywood in its
final stages of decomposition, and it had been so warped by time
and misuse that Nathaniel had to lean into it with all his abun-
dant might to push it open.

"Where are we? The urinal?" asked Jacobus, stepping over
the threshold. "It stinks."

"This is the entrance," said Williams. "There's a directory on
the wall, but all the names have been spray-painted over. Van-
dalism."

"This is my lucky day, isn't it?" said Jacobus. "Shall we ask one
of the young lads out front if Grimes still lives here?"

Nathaniel told Jacobus to stay where he was and went outside,
shutting the door behind him. Jacobus heard lots of muffled
"muthafuckas," "yo' mommas," and suspicious mirth when Rose
Grimes's name was mentioned, but he couldn't make out anything specific. He heard the door screech open.

"May be your lucky day after all," said Williams. "She still
lives here. Fifth floor."

"Elevator?"

"Nope."

"Don't speak too soon."

They started up the unmaintained stairs with Nathaniel

leading, Jacobus's right hand reaching out for his friend's shoulder for guidance. By the third floor, the pain had set in and Nathaniel had Jacobus by the hand, pulling him up step by step.

"Why don't you get a walking stick for that hip like I told you?" Nathaniel asked.

"You mean a cane? In case you haven't noticed the last thirty years, I don't do canes," Jacobus said, panting.

"Pretty soon you won't be doin' walking neither," replied Nathaniel.

They arrived at the fifth and top floor, sweating and panting, doubled over, hands on their knees, having navigated around splitting bags of garbage, puddles of urine, and a chillingly silent pit bull. There was no fan, let alone air-conditioning, to remedy the stifling heat. The only relief was a rendition of "Take My Hand, Precious Lord" being sung by Mahalia Jackson coming from a transistor radio somewhere. When Nathaniel finally got his breath back, he told Jacobus to just let him do the talking at first. "Be my guest," he wheezed.

Nathaniel knocked. After a moment the chained door opened just a crack, but enough for the gospel music to flow out.

"Who's there?" asked a resonant alto voice.

"My name is Nathaniel Williams, Miss Grimes. I'm here with my friend, Daniel Jacobus. We were wondering if we might visit with you."

"Visit? About what?"

"About a young African-American man who might have been wrongfully convicted of a serious crime."

"Well, there's lots of them, and most of them deserve it. What's it to me?"

"This particular young man has set a positive example for the African-American community." Williams was still trying to catch his breath. "He had been a real role model. Maybe you've heard of him. He's a violinist. His name is BTower. We promise not to take too much of your time."

"Yes. Yes, I've heard of him. Who hasn't? One moment."

The door closed. The chain was slipped off and the door re-opened.

"Please come in."

"Thank you, Miss Grimes," said Williams. "And you can put down the gun."

Grimes gave them a once-over and said, "I guess. You two ain't fit enough to attack an ant. Come on in and sit down. You want some iced tea? I was just making some."

Nathaniel and Jacobus entered a small one-bedroom apartment, spare but clean. It was cooler than the hallway and Jacobus smelled the pleasant scent of fresh-cut flowers. The upholstered chair creaked under his weight when he sat but was otherwise comfortable.

"Now tell me what it is you're needing to say to me," said Rose Grimes, handing them each a glass of tea with fresh mint leaves.

"Just for starters, are we correct you once worked at the Bonderman Building?" asked Williams.

"That was a long time ago. What's that got to do with anything?"

"Did you know René Allard?"

"Why are you asking?"

At that moment Jacobus was startled by a heavy sigh that came neither from Nathaniel nor from Rose Grimes, but from a fourth person in the room.

"What the hell? Who else is here?" Jacobus asked.

"That's my husband, Mr. Jacobus."

"Does he ordinarily siesta when company comes?"

"Jake," whispered Williams, "the man is in a wheelchair."

"That's all right, Mr. Williams," said Rose Grimes. "My husband has been in this condition for a long time. He's not really sleeping and he's not really awake. Maybe he can hear us, maybe he can't."

"And who takes care of him?"

"Why, I do, of course. 'Wives, submit yourselves unto your own husbands, as unto the Lord.' Ephesians, five, twenty-two."

"Well, that's quite devoted of you," said Jacobus, who had a sardonic view of religion. Any religion. "But have you tried medical care?"

"All we can afford, Mr. Jacobus. I took him to the VA hospital when he came back from Vietnam. That was 1965. But I put my trust in the Lord, Mr. Jacobus."

" 'God helps them that help themselves.' Benjamin Franklin, *Poor Richard's Almanac*, 1757," said Jacobus.

"Jake, please," said Williams.

"Don't *you* believe in anything, Mr. Jacobus?" asked Grimes.

"I believe in doing good, not waiting for voodoo spirits to make good things happen."

"And what good have you done lately?"

Jacobus scratched his head. "I gave a pretty good violin lesson. Just yesterday. That's my calling in life, as it were."

Grimes *tsk*ed. "Have you no faith in a higher power?"

"Yes. Bach."

"Is that all?"

"Sometimes Mozart. Have you ever heard his Symphony Thirty-eight in D? It's as miraculous as the creation of the world, Mrs. Grimes, and Mozart did it faster than God did. He did have to make a few corrections, though. That's something God would have been well advised to do."

"That's blasphemy!"

"No, it's true. Mozart did make corrections."

Williams interrupted. "Jake, I think you've made your point."

"Is there anything else you wanted to ask me before you leave?" asked Grimes.

"Can you tell us of the circumstances surrounding your departure from employment at the Bonderman Building?" Williams asked, placing his iced tea on a doily-covered table next to him.

"I was accused of taking some of Mr. Allard's music. After I left I found work cleaning homes in Westchester, two a day, sixteen hours a day including the commute, in order to be able to pay the rent."

"And why did you take the music, Mrs. Grimes?" Nathaniel asked.

"I didn't say I took it. I said I was accused of taking it. 'For the Son of man is going to come in His Father's glory with His angels, and then He—' "

" 'And then He will reward each person according to what he has done.' Matthew, sixteen, twenty-seven. Yeah, yeah, yeah. Did you take it or not?" asked Jacobus.

"I don't have to answer to you, Mr. Jacobus. Jesus Christ

knows the truth, and He's the only one that matters. And frankly I don't see what this has to do with this young man being wrongly convicted."

"BTower is in jail for killing René Allard," said Williams. "The only way BTower's life can be saved is if we find the person who really killed him. That's it in a nutshell, and I'm sorry if it opens up some of your old wounds."

"If BTower is innocent, the Lord will protect him."

"Now that's a comforting thought," said Jacobus.

"'Let the wicked forsake his way, and the unrighteous man his thoughts: and let him return unto the Lord, and he will have mercy upon him; and to our God, for he will—' "

"Mrs. Grimes," said Williams, "I can't help but notice the violin case by your flowers. Do you play the violin?"

"Let's just say it's been in the family a long time."

"How long have you had it?" asked Jacobus, his interest piqued. The religion lesson had been putting him to sleep.

"As I said, it's been in the family. It's all busted up, anyway."

"May I see it? Both Mr. Jacobus and I are musicians, and we're always interested in seeing instruments."

"I have nothing to hide."

Jacobus heard Rose slowly rise with a soft but labored *mhh* as she pushed herself up from her chair and shuffled past him and her catatonic husband. Jacobus considered the toll that years of back-breaking housework must have taken on her health, including her mental health, just to pay rent and take care of a chronic invalid. No paid vacation for Rose Grimes. A heavy price for salvation.

"Here. Look at it," she said. "And if you don't mind, I have to get ready for church choir."

"You leave your husband here alone?" asked Jacobus.

Rose Grimes's husband remained motionless, slumped in his wheelchair.

"He's not going anywhere," she said.

Jacobus heard Nathaniel snap open the clasps of the case.

After a moment, Williams said, "Thank you very much for your time, Mrs. Grimes. Jake, I think we're ready to go."

"Thanks for the tea," said Jacobus. "But just one more question. If you have such faith in the Lord, why is it there's a chain on your door and you kept the gun in your lap the whole time we were here? I heard you put it on the table when you got up."

"Protection. This neighborhood isn't the safest in the world, as I'm sure you have already ascertained."

"No doubt, Mrs. Grimes. No doubt. Just remind me, though. Where in the Bible does it say, 'Praise the Lord but pass the ammunition'?"

NINE

In the cab, Jacobus and Nathaniel bickered all the way to the Bonderman Building. Nathaniel had seen instantly that Grimes's violin was broken and scratched all over. It was useless. He had lifted it up, cradling it in both hands so it wouldn't fall apart entirely, and had given it no more than a cursory glance. He placed it back in the case and handed it to Rose. The only thing they agreed upon was that at one time Rose Grimes's violin, surprisingly, had been a good one, made by Ferdinando Garimberti in

1958 according to the label inside it; and if it didn't look like it had been run over by a fourteen-wheeler would be worth thousands of dollars. Jacobus was apprehensive that the poverty-stricken Grimes could ever have had the financial resources to own a violin of such quality. Nathaniel was offended that Jacobus would be suspicious simply because it was an African American who owned a good instrument.

"It has nothing to do with color," Jacobus had retorted. "Have I ever had any doubts about you owning a Matteo Goffriller cello? That's worth more than Brooklyn! What I'm suspicious of is a *poor* person who owns a good violin, who just happened to have been fired for stealing music from a famous violinist who was later murdered, and just happened to have lived in a building with other famous violinists and violin dealers."

"I know you're no racist, Jake," Nathaniel said. When they played chamber music together as members of the Dumky Trio back in the '50s, Jacobus had stood up to a concert presenter in southern Ohio who would not permit Nathaniel onto the stage for a performance. Jacobus proceeded to play an impromptu program of what he called "traditional concert favorites," music made famous by Paul Robeson, George Gershwin, Tchaikovsky, and others. Jacobus, providing off-the-cuff program notes, did not beat around the bush describing the elite group as a conglomeration of African Americans, Communists, Jews, and homosexuals. The offended audience almost tarred and feathered the trio, but that incident cemented their friendship for life.

To resolve their current dispute, Jacobus and Nathaniel agreed to take what meager information they had about the violin and shuttle from one violin dealer to another in the Bonderman Building, hoping they might find someone to whom Rose had at one time brought the violin for repair or maintenance, and from there, to figure out how she got it. Not much to go on, but it seemed reasonable that if she had shown it to anyone it would have been to someone with whom she had been familiar at her place of employment.

So they started at the Martelli shop on the second floor, then up to Bamberger on six and Lifschitz on seven. No one recognized the name or description of Rose Grimes, or had any recollection of that particular violin. Going up to Dedubian's on the top floor, Alonzo Fuente, who had been their chauffeur in the elevator, joked that they had just become eligible for frequent flyer miles. "Very funny, Lon," said Jacobus. "Maybe you should consider comedy since you still don't know how to operate this contraption."

It was nearing the end of the business day as they entered the elegantly plush nineteenth-century-styled penthouse showroom. Boris Dedubian, the third generation of Dedubian et Fils Violins, Inc., was on his way out the door. A few years earlier, as a result of the Piccolino Stradivarius violin scandal, Jacobus had almost put Dedubian out of business and into the hoosegow, but ultimately he offered Dedubian a way to save face, which earned Dedubian's undying gratitude. Though retirement to his beloved condominium in Montreux had been postponed, he at least retained his prestige in the violin community as one of the world's most authoritative dealers. The millions of dollars' worth of violins, violas, cellos, string basses, and their bows, instruments on display behind climate-controlled glass cases, as well as the fastidiously tailored herringbone suit he was wearing, bore testament to his continued success.

"My dear Jake and Nathaniel!" Dedubian said in his cultivated generic European accent. "What a pleasure it is to see you both again. It has been too long!"

"Probably not long enough, you mean," said Jacobus. "You seem to be back in the swing, though."

"Well, you know the old axiom, 'Where there are violinists, there are violin dealers.'"

"And money."

"Well, yes. That too. What can I do for you today? I was just about to close the shop, but for you the lights are back on. It just so happens an amazing G. B. Guadagnini, Turin, 1781, arrived today. Mint condition! Perhaps you'd care to try it?"

"Maybe another time, Bo. We're actually just shopping for a little information."

"Oh?"

Nathaniel asked Dedubian if he had any recollection of an African-American woman named Rose Grimes ever buying a Garimberti made in 1958. He tried to imagine what Grimes looked like back in the day in order to describe her to Dedubian, but it was difficult to imagine the wrinkled, hunched-over, almost toothless elderly woman as anything but. Instead, he described the Garimberti: the golden orange color of the varnish, the distinctive corners, and the back, which, before it was broken, was a beautifully grained single piece of bird's-eye maple. The problem was, if Dedubian had seen it, it could have been more than thirty years ago.

"Gentleman," Dedubian reminded them, "with the number of customers I have every day, let alone over a quarter century, it is impossible to remember every single instrument. Impossible. Even if the merchandise had been of superstar quality, who can recall them all? Garimberti, an excellent luthier, yes, but he was no Stradivari, and there were so many contemporaries—dozens I could name you—building instruments with solid craftsmanship and beautiful sound quality."

"Maybe," said Nathaniel, "since this particular violin was all busted up you might have repair records even if you didn't sell it."

Dedubian asked his secretary, Mrs. King, who was still in the office, to check their back data. While they waited, he brought out the Guadagnini violin that he had just obtained on consignment. Made in Milan in 1754, it was considered one of Guadagnini's greatest instruments. It was nicknamed the "ex Ysaÿe," meaning it had been owned at one time by Eugène Ysaÿe, the great Belgian violinist at the turn of the twentieth century, and who had been, incidentally, the teacher of the young René Allard. The current owner wanted $800,000 for it, so Dedubian was putting it on the market for $925,000 with a willingness to haggle with both the potential buyer and seller. He handed it to Jacobus along with an equally superior French bow and asked him to play a few notes.

Jacobus put the instrument under his chin. He had a fine ear for tone—he could almost unerringly name the maker of any good violin from the sound and feel of it—but the basic intrinsic tone of the instrument, and even less its market value, was of minor importance to him. It was what the musician could do with the sound that counted. "Anyone can get good paint," he would say to his students, "but only Leonardo could make the *Mona Lisa.*"

Jacobus played the beginning of the Allemande from the Bach Partita in D Minor. With a melodic line that crosses all the strings he could obtain a sense of the violin's capabilities within a few measures. The sound was resonant, full-bodied, and evenly blended from one string to the next, and at the same time, as he varied the bow speed and pressure on the string, responsive to subtle color changes.

"No wonder they call Guadagnini the poor man's Stradivarius— if you call under a million 'poor.' Definitely a Guad," he said as he felt the dimensions of the instrument, tracing his finger around the purfling. "It's got his typical sound and the broad pattern in the middle. Bo, you'll have a sucker paying that type of dough within a week."

"No doubt, but of course we prefer to call them clients," said Dedubian. He reclaimed the violin as Jacobus handed it back to him. "Ah! And here comes Mrs. King."

Mrs. King reported bad news and good news. The bad news was that Rose Grimes had neither bought a violin there nor brought the Garimberti in for repair. The much better news, however, was that Dedubian had in fact written an insurance evaluation for it in 1965. As was typical for such evaluations, he had given a brief description of the instrument and of the inscription on the maker's label inside it, and went on to state that in his opinion the violin indeed was what it purported to be. At the time of the evaluation, Dedubian had appraised it for $1,000. Had it still been in good condition it would have been worth anywhere from $20,000 to $30,000, such was the appreciation of good modern Italian violins. With the damage it had suffered, though, its real market value was nil.

"Are you sure she was the real owner, Bo?" Jacobus asked.

"Hey, Jake!" interrupted Williams. "There you go again. Just because a black woman—"

"Black, shmack," said Jacobus. "If she was guilty of stealing Allard's music, and I say 'if' surrounded by brackets, then it's possible—"

"Gentlemen! Gentlemen!" interrupted Dedubian. "Excuse me, but it doesn't help to argue because in any event I don't know the answer to the question. When clients with violins come into my shop, I don't ask who, where, what, or how. It's not my job to be a policeman. If they say it's theirs, unless it's an instrument I know for a fact to be illicit, I take my clients at their word."

"Then any idea who she insured with?" asked Jacobus. "Seems that if she went to the trouble and expense to get the valuation, she would have insured it."

"I have no idea about that either, Jake," said Dedubian. "That's totally up to the client, though an instrument like that really should have been insured."

"I know what you're thinking, Jake" said Nathaniel. "If Rose Grimes had insured the violin and then broke it intentionally, she could have made a claim for the insurance and collected the cash, never intending to repair it. Seeing how she's struggled all her life, that is something to consider, isn't it?"

"And if she needed that cash fast, like to take care of an ailing husband, she might have been desperate enough to have stolen for it," said Jacobus.

"Well, I think you're getting ahead of yourself," said Nathaniel, "but I'll grant you it's a possibility. In the meantime I can check on some of the main companies that sell instrument insurance—Intercontinental, Counselors, Vermont Mutual—and see if I can track down her policy."

"While you're at it," said Jacobus, "try to find out more about poor old Mr. Grimes, will you? She was hiding information about a broken fiddle; maybe she's hiding information about a broken man. All we've got is his address and when he came back from Vietnam."

"I'll buzz my contacts with the insurance companies and the VA hospitals," said Nathaniel, "and see if I can get some kind of dossier going. They won't give me his medical records, for sure, but at this point anything we can get couldn't hurt."

"In the meantime we just sit on our thumbs and study the police reports?" asked Jacobus. "We've gotta get a move on. There are only, what, four days left."

"Well, actually I was just thinking of something more adventurous," said Williams.

What he had in mind, he explained to Jacobus, was to fly out to Salt Lake City. Jacobus once again balked at this prospect. "I'm not Yumi's nanny," he complained. It was annoying enough for him to have to be drawn from his seclusion in the Berkshires to come to New York. But Salt Lake City? Nathaniel reasoned it was not just to hear Yumi perform. It would also be to meet with Virgil Lavender, who was such a close colleague and confidant of René Allard, and with Sigmund Gottfried, who had moved there to be with his sister and who had been the one to notify the authorities that Rose Grimes had stolen music from

Allard. Maybe he knew something about the violin, Williams postulated.

"Ziggy in Salt Lake City?" interrupted Dedubian. "I miss the little man so! I think he actually brought me business over the years—he was like a tourist attraction. Every violinist in the world must have chatted with Ziggy! Jake, go to Salt Lake City! And please make sure you give Ziggy my best."

TEN

"You what?" yelled Malachi.

"Careful, Malachi, or you'll choke on your kishke," said Jacobus. Because Nathaniel had booked their flight to Utah first thing the next morning, Jacobus had invited the detective to bustling Carnegie Deli for a late snack. The pair wanted to break the news gently that they had taken up the reinvestigation of René Allard's death and that, if they were successful, they would be undoing all of Malachi's investigative work that had led to the conviction of BTower.

"Look, Jacobus, just because you were right once before—" Malachi said.

"And you were wrong and almost got me a life sentence."

"There was nothing wrong with the police work," said Malachi. "Everything pointed to you stealing the Piccolino Strad and killing Jablonski."

"Everything except that you pegged the wrong guy. Me." Jacobus had about as much regard for police work as he did for pastrami on whole wheat.

"Keep your voice down, Jake." Nathaniel placed one of his big hands on Jacobus's forearm. "You're yelling even louder than the waiters."

"Just like you may have with BTower," continued Jacobus, a half decibel softer. "I'm not saying he didn't do it, but the least you can do is give me what I need to find out for sure. Pass the pickled tomatoes, please."

"Jacobus, you're being a pain in the ass. But why should this night be different from any other? Let me say it one more time so you'll understand. You were exonerated. You never had to go to trial. You found the thief and the murderer. But BTower is different. This guy was tried. He was convicted, and he was sentenced to death. This time, there is no doubt. No question. Case closed."

"No question? Nathaniel and I have already discovered that one of the maids who'd worked at the Bonderman Building stole music from Allard, and might have stolen a violin and committed insurance fraud."

Malachi applauded.

"Well, mazel tov to you, Sherlock!" he said. "Who figured you'd ever be Boy Scout of the Year? Please, though, be kind enough to inform me, what does this have to do with BTower murdering René Allard? How's your corned beef? Even if she had stolen the *Mona Lisa* it still wouldn't have anything to do with my case."

"Needs more mustard," said Jacobus. "So why should it bother you if we keep looking? Rosenthal says D-day's next Wednesday. What would it hurt to give us what we need?"

"You've got the report, Jacobus. Why don't you try reading it? Everything we copied to Rosenthal for the trial is there."

"Not quite. Rosenthal doesn't have the photos of Allard's body."

"Believe me, Jacobus, he was dead," said Malachi. "Or do you need us to dig him up to check his pulse?"

"You certainly bolster my faith in the criminal justice system, Detective. But what about that strange pose you wrote about in your report? Your ordinary stiff doesn't do a Rodin when he croaks, now does he? I'm sure your corpses come in all sorts of artistic configurations, Al, but lacking any other hard evidence, I'd think something as surrealistic as Allard's contorted disposition would jump right out at you. And what about those 'superficial lacerations' and the missing bits of scalp and hair—"

"They were obviously left on the murder weapon—"

"Which you never found. What kind of hack detective work is that?"

"Back off, Jacobus."

"And," Jacobus pushed, "in the report you mention Gottfried's photos."

"Jacobus, you're wasting my time, and I've had enough of your meddling. When I write a report I include *everything*. That's my job. Those photos were just family snapshots of happy Germans in lederhosen. Duplicates of what were on his wall. You were there! He didn't even ask for them back after the trial. What the hell good are photos going to do for you, anyway? You're blind as a bat."

"Just be a good boy, Malachi," said Jacobus, "and pretend I'm your Yiddishe mama asking—"

Jacobus felt his collar suddenly tighten around his throat. He was yanked out of his seat, his dark glasses flying off his face. Jacobus heard the conversation in the restaurant come to an abrupt halt.

"You're a crusty old fart," Malachi said, choking Jacobus. "That doesn't bother me. You insult my work. That doesn't bother me, either." Jacobus grabbed at Malachi's hand around his throat, gasping as he futilely tried to pull it away.

"But after a while, when you get personal your act gets old, and you just crossed the line."

Jacobus felt another hand on top of his. A big one. Strong but not aggressive. Nathaniel's.

"Please, Detective," Nathaniel said with quiet insistence.

Malachi threw Jacobus back in his seat, the cue for the chatter in the restaurant to resume.

Williams said, "Jake, why is it you always have to go antagonizing everyone we need help from?"

"Hey, friend," Jacobus said to Nathaniel as he massaged his neck and fumbled for his glasses, "you don't like the n-word. I don't like the b-word. Chances are Mr. Sensitive here missed the boat somewhere. There's more to a photo than smiling faces, and I think it's worth finding out if there's anything there."

Williams, the mediator, asked, "Detective Malachi, what harm would it do to provide us with these materials?"

"Harm? It wouldn't do *you* any harm," said Malachi, "but it would be the end of my job as a cop. Pit Bull Brown is gunning for DA. If she were to just smell that I was trying to futz with her Two Maestros triumph in any way, shape, or form, she'd have my balls on a silver platter."

"Y'know, Malachi," said Jacobus, "there comes a point when career has to take a backseat to justice."

"That's awfully high and mighty of you," said Malachi, "but that's not the way I see it. What I see is that in our society we've got plenty of rights. They're written out chapter and verse by the founding fathers. BTower has a *right* to get you to traipse all over to help him dodge the hereafter. But we also have responsibilities, Jacobus, even if they're not spelled out so tidily. BTower had a responsibility to stick a sock in his ego before he went out and murdered. I'm glad BTower got what was coming to him. I'm glad he is where he is.

"So I don't need a lecture on integrity from you, Jacobus," said Malachi, "but thanks for the kishke. I'll see what I can do." He threw down his napkin and got up. "Bon voyage."

ELEVEN
DAY 3: SATURDAY

With BTower's execution date at the forefront of their thoughts, Jacobus fought off his mounting fatigue. By taking the early morning nonstop Delta flight from JFK, he and Nathaniel arrived at Salt Lake International Airport before noon. Sigmund Gottfried, who had learned to drive since moving to Utah, and his sister, Seglinde Oehlschlager, were waiting to greet them.

"Thanks for coming," Jacobus said, as he and Nathaniel were escorted to the car. Jacobus hobbled, his arthritis acting up after the long flight. "And for being on time."

"My father always told me," said Gottfried, "'Better an hour early than a minute late.'"

Jacobus eased himself into the plush, comfortable backseat, which soothed his aching hip. "Nice car," he said, inhaling the satisfying "new car smell" mixed with somewhat nauseating pine-scented air freshener.

Gottfried confessed to some embarrassment being behind the wheel of the luxury Avalon in which he would now chauffeur his old friends to their hotel. Jacobus joked that it was the first time he had ever encountered Ziggy moving horizontally. With the windows up and the air conditioner on full blast, Jacobus could neither see nor feel the effects of blinding sunshine and searing August heat that he had fleetingly encountered walking from the terminal to the car. On the twenty-minute drive along North Temple to the Waltz Rite Inn where Jacobus and Nathaniel were staying, Gottfried filled them in on his life since leaving New York.

"When my elevator broke down," Gottfried said, "and I lost my job and my home, I felt as if my life was over, and then Seglinde invited me to stay with her and Mr. Oehlschlager until I got back on my feet. So what else could I do but pack my valise and come here? What is it they say? 'Go west, young man!' Except I'm not so young anymore." Gottfried chuckled.

"You packed all your belongings in one suitcase?" asked Jacobus.

"Not quite so, Mr. Jacobus," said Gottfried. "Most of it I left behind in the apartment. You see, I thought of this change the same way as when Seglinde and I left Germany. It would be a new life, a time to leave the old life behind. They were covering up my basement apartment for good. Sealing it away forever. In a way it was like a burial. It was symbolic.

"But now I'm sounding so dark on such a sunny day! I can assure you it was not so sad. You may not believe this, but until then I had never before been outside New York City since coming to America. Other than our journey from Germany, the five-day Greyhound bus ride to Utah was the greatest adventure of my life. Really, it was like an awakening from a deep sleep. And what a beautiful bus it was! So clean! I laughed to myself, the bus was like my elevator but sideways and with windows.

"But I'm going on and on with meaningless detail when I should be the thoughtful host and giving you the tour of the city. We are now going past Abravanel Hall, the home of the Utah Symphony, a very fine orchestra, and across the street—there, to the left—is Temple Square, home of the Mormon Tabernacle Choir."

"Where is Mr. Oehlschlager?" asked Jacobus.

"You are so kind to ask, Mr. Jacobus," said Seglinde. "My dear husband had been ill in the hospital for almost a whole year, and then he passed away last year."

"I'm so sorry," said Nathaniel. "That must have been a very difficult time for you."

"Thank you, Mr. Williams. He had suffered for so long, in a way his death was probably for the better. I know this is easy for we who are still living to say, but I believe it is true. And then Ziggy came, so I have been okay."

"He seems to have left you well provided for," said Jacobus. "Your husband, that is."

"Oh, you mean this car!" said Seglinde. "Yes, Ziggy and I are quite comfortable now. We are very fortunate. But here we now are at your accommodations."

Jacobus and Nathaniel agreed to be treated by Ziggy and Seglinde at JC's, the hotel's restaurant, after checking in and taking a little rest. They would all have lunch together and in the evening go to Yumi's concert at the Antelope Island Music Festival.

Jacobus, finding the accommodations comfortable and quietly air-conditioned, decided to get a few minutes of shut-eye. They had been on the road since 5 A.M., New York time.

Jacobus lay back in the bed, but he couldn't rest. By taking this trip he was certain he was losing the race against time. This all could have been done over the phone, and Yumi would have many more concerts in her blossoming career they could go to. Half a day had gone by and he had learned nothing. He was annoyed that he had allowed Nathaniel to talk him into coming.

For a year, Jacobus had been obsessed by the haunting image of Allard's body as described in Malachi's report. Now it was back in his head and he couldn't get it out, tired or not. There's nothing natural about being murdered, he thought, but the contortions of Allard's body in his death throes exceeded even that aberration.

Cursing, Jacobus got out of the bed.

"Nathaniel, read me the report again."

Williams retrieved Malachi's report from his attaché case. He knew exactly what passage Jacobus wanted, so often had he requested it in the last few days, and turned to the dog-eared pages. This time, however, Jacobus actually got down onto the lime green shag carpet, creaking himself into Allard's contorted position, head twisting excluded, that Malachi had described in so detailed a fashion.

Nathaniel couldn't help laughing.

"What's your problem?" asked Jacobus.

"Only that you look like an inchworm in the grass. Sorry."

Jacobus was not amused. "I think he was holding his violin."

Nathaniel laughed even harder.

"What a time to practice!" he said.

After they were seated at JC's, the four of them—Jacobus, Nathaniel, Gottfried, and his fraternal twin, Seglinde—attempted to engage in polite conversation.

"Ziggy, you seem uncomfortable," said Jacobus. "You're fussing even more than you used to. Spit it out."

"Mr. Jacobus, you see right through me. That is just a figure of speech, I don't mean this personally. But you are right. I just want to say—this is so hard to say—we both told the truth as we understood it."

"Truth?" Jacobus pondered for a moment. "You're talking about the trial?"

"Yes. Exactly so. I couldn't believe the young man *could* do such a thing, and you couldn't believe he *couldn't*. It is still difficult for me, that such a fine young man is in jail, but I want you to know, I always have respected your opinion, even since the time you yourself were a student."

Jacobus recalled the early days, when he could still see, going

to the Bonderman Building to visit Dedubian for new strings or
to have the sound post on his violin adjusted. Gottfried was there
even then, the stalwart sentinel, greeting all who entered his tiny
domain with polite dignity. Jacobus, along with everyone else, he
supposed, had come to take Gottfried for granted, never appre-
ciating the man's acute sensitivity. Gottfried's emotional out-
pouring at the Two Maestros trial had certainly shed new light,
and Jacobus was about to comment on the unpredictability of
events in life and response to those events when the waitress arrived.

"Hi, there!" Jacobus heard the fake smile in her voice. "I'm
L'Norma, and I'll be your server today! Are we all ready to order?"

When it was Jacobus's turn, he said, "Liverwurst and onions
on seeded rye, with butter."

"I'm afraid we don't have liver or rye bread on our menu, sir,
but we do have a special today! We're serving our signature
house-crafted patty melt on freshly toasted artisan ciabatta
bread!"

"L'Norma, hon, excuse me for just one sec, okay?" Jacobus
turned to Nathaniel, who was sitting next to him. "What the hell
is she talking about?" Jacobus whispered in his ear.

"It's a swiss cheese burger on toast."

Jacobus turned back to the waitress. "Okay, L'Norma. I'll
have a plain hamburger. On a bun."

"I can't tell you how much we are looking forward to hearing
your young student perform tonight," said Seglinde after L'Norma
had made her escape.

"*Former* student," said Jacobus. "Yumi seems to have a mind of her own these days. But that's good. Shows I did my job."

"And the chance to hear Mr. Lavender perform with her quartet!" said Gottfried. "I always thought of him only as an appendage of Maestro Allard."

"It doesn't seem to matter who he plays with, though," said Nathaniel. "Lavender fits everyone like a glove. I'll bet they'll do fine together."

"But he must so miss Maestro Allard, like all of us," said Gottfried. "There were many times when Mr. Allard was in terrible poor health, when he could hardly stand up, when you almost thought he might die. But then he would have a recital with Mr. Lavender and it was like a miracle—it seemed to bring him back to life. It happened too often like that, I mean Maestro's resilience. As long as his music was alive, so was his health, because his music was always from the heart."

"Music can do that, I suppose," said Jacobus, who didn't listen to much music anymore. In his view, the way people performed these days was neither intellectually informed nor heartfelt, and a truly great musician needed to be both. Today's concert stage was all smoke and mirrors, all visual, which did Jacobus no good, and even if he could see he considered performances like BTower's, who had taken things to the nth degree, to be blatant foppery. So he contented himself with listening to his old recordings of Heifetz, Kreisler, Milstein, and a few others, and when the vinyl got too scratchy, he'd rip the disc off the turntable and throw it against the wall.

"You know," said Gottfried, "most people didn't know how

close Maestro Allard came to death, even when he was still young. It frightened me. Yes, they looked the other way from his little escapades and his high living because he was so charming. What is the word? The bon vivant. But all the drinking, and the smoking, and the women, who were always on his arm, those things almost killed him."

"Almost," said Jacobus.

"I think here is our food," said Seglinde.

"Yes," said Gottfried. "And I have a good appetite. I have always taken care of my health, and would you believe, Mr. Williams and Mr. Jacobus, to this day I have never been to a doctor!"

"He is like his father," said Seglinde.

"*Mmm*, yeah, good health is so important," said Nathaniel, diving into his nachos and buffalo wings.

"Tomorrow night, Mr. Jacobus, will you go to hear the Mozart G-Minor Quintet?" asked Seglinde. "The Markner Quartet is playing with Simon Baker."

"Sorry, but we're just here overnight. Have to get back home tomorrow," said Jacobus.

"Such a shame. It is the most sublime music ever written," said Gottfried. "I remember hearing this music the first time on WNCN in New York. It was 1956 and I remember that date because it was the two hundredth anniversary of Mozart's birth. I'm sure you know he was born in Salzburg, Austria, but what you may not know is that Schatzi and I were born only just over the border. Maybe that is why Mozart has always been my favorite composer, since we were almost neighbors. When they played his quintet at midnight it was during my shift, but Mr. Zipolito let me switch with Tom Congden just so I could hear it. I tell you, it was a miracle for me. Such music!"

"You've got a great memory," said Nathaniel, inhaling an overflowing corn chip.

"Ziggy takes great pride in his memory," said Seglinde.

"Do you by any chance remember a Rose Grimes who worked in the Bonderman Building?" asked Jacobus.

"Rose Grimes?" said Gottfried. He thought for a moment. "No, I'm afraid that's one name that does not ring the bell, Mr. Jacobus. My great memory fails me for that name. Could you give me a hint please?"

"One of the housekeepers. According to the records she was there for a good fifteen years."

"There were so many housekeepers, always coming and going, over the years. In its heyday they employed twenty-four housekeepers, two for each floor! Is she a friend of yours, Mr. Jacobus?"

"It's just that she has this nice Garimberti violin, which I thought was a little strange. And with all those violin dealers in the Bonderman. Anyway, just curious."

"I agree. It is very curious," said Gottfried. "A bit of a mystery, certainly, for a Negro woman to have a nice violin. No offense, Mr. Williams. But I am sure you will clear it up, Mr. Jacobus."

"Now," asked Seglinde, "shall we have some dessert?"

TWELVE

Less than an hour north of Salt Lake City a seven-mile causeway connects the mainland to mountainous Antelope Island, rising majestically from the vastness of the Great Salt Lake. Relishing his role as the tour guide, Gottfried explained the island's main zoological attraction, an American bison herd managed there for over a century. More recently the Antelope Island Music Festival, sponsored jointly by the Utah Arts Council, Utah State Parks, and the Sierra Club, had been attracting more and more summer concertgoers who loved the feeling of open wilderness combined with the intimacy of classical chamber music in a location accessible to a metropolitan area. Ziggy couldn't decide which delighted him more—the beautiful music or those behemoth bison that roam freely over the island.

Arriving at the southern tip of the island, the car pulled up to the concert venue, the former Garr Ranch, originally built in 1848 by Fielding Garr and now refurbished as a museum. Gottfried insisted on paying for the tickets, after which they were ushered to their seats in the rustically appointed great room. Behind the performers, through a huge picture window, the audience could witness a splendid view of the Great Salt Lake with the sunset-lit Wasatch Mountains in the background.

The concert began with Felix Mendelssohn's heartwarming Quartet, Opus 12, masterfully composed while he was still a teenager. It was followed by the Hugo Wolf "Italian Serenade," a charming but deceptively difficult work. During intermission Jacobus went outside to think, to inhale the intoxicating sage-salt air, and to avoid both the small talk and the fruit-flavored punch that were flowing indoors. The second half of the concert was devoted exclusively to the dramatic and fiery Quintet for Piano and Strings, Opus 34, by Johannes Brahms. The unity of purpose between the members of the quartet and Virgil Lavender made it seem as if they had played together for years, when in fact they had rehearsed the piece only once. Such was Lavender's legendary ability to fit with any musicians with whom he worked. As the last rays of the setting sun vanished from the shimmering lake, the defiantly impetuous final cadence of the quintet brought the crowd to its feet en masse. Even without the awe-inspiring splendor of the natural surroundings, Jacobus, normally a severe critic, considered the performance an artistic success, especially as the ensemble was newly formed and hadn't spent years together developing a distinct, unified voice. Rarely one to express enthusiasm, on this occasion he invited Nathaniel, Yumi, Virgil Lavender, and Ziggy and his sister for a post-concert celebration in Salt Lake City. His ulterior motive was to question Lavender and Ziggy regarding what they knew about Allard's death and when they knew it. The clock was ticking.

"I am honored," said Gottfried, "but Seglinde and I are not the drinking type anymore, and for me the best thing after such a performance is to go home and just remember it in quiet. But many thanks, and please give my heartfelt congratulations to the musicians. They played so beautifully."

Lavender suggested a bistro called Un Peu de Paris he had heard about from the Guarneri Quartet, which had recently performed in Salt Lake, as one of the few late-night places to drink in the still alcohol-shy state. As Jacobus and his entourage entered, a scratchy recording of Edit Piaf singing "La Vie en Rose" crooned in the background. The place was darkly lit, titillating the patrons into feeling that they were doing something mildly illicit, which in Utah was not a difficult effect to achieve. Above the bar, a nineteenth-century-style mural of a bare-breasted Winged Liberty adorned the wall, under which was printed the motto VIVE LA RÉSISTANCE. Posters by Toulouse-Lautrec and Degas adorned exposed brick walls. Waiters and waitresses swirled among the tables, trying to look French, decked out in black berets, black and white horizontally striped short-sleeve T-shirts, and red aprons tied around tight black pants.

Jacobus heard a polite young man say, "Good evening. Are any of you members?"

"Members of what?" asked Jacobus.

"This a private club for members, sir."

"So what do we need to do? Take a loyalty oath?"

"You just need to sign here, sir, and pay a one-time five dollars for temporary membership that's good for three weeks, or a twenty-dollar annual fee, which includes parking validations."

"No secret handshake?" asked Jacobus.

When they were finally seated, Jacobus, Nathaniel, Yumi, and Virgil Lavender discussed the evening's performance. Though it was the same program as the one in Durango two days earlier, everything seemed to go more smoothly. Perhaps it was because they had a performance under their belt and all the butterflies were gone. Perhaps it was the setting, or maybe they just played better. In any event, a special chemistry with the audience tonight had illuminated the performance. Yumi, exhilarated by the concert and the late-night partying, was ebullient. Lavender was more reflective.

"Not too many Kansas farm boys like me have made it in this business," he said. "I think I must've played that Brahms quintet a hundred times since I was a student in Wichita, and tonight was a doozy."

Yumi expressed unabashed admiration at Lavender's uncanny ability to fit in with her group.

"I kind of have a feel for what the other musicians are feeling," he said. "Kind of a sixth sense. And of course there are some traditions in interpretation that everyone does."

"Toscanini said that tradition is the way the last moron did it," said Jacobus.

Lavender laughed. "He may have had a point, you know. But when René and I played together, we knew each other inside out. Sometimes we could get away with the most outlandish things at a performance without even rehearsing it. Partners in crime, it felt like."

Lavender mentioned his upcoming concert at Carnegie Recital Hall.

"I'm nervous as a jitterbug for that one. I haven't done a solo performance in decades," he said. "It's nothing like ensemble playing. Just me and the piano alone onstage. Yeesh! Please, someone put a warm body onstage with me!"

Lavender reflected upon the different styles of American and European chamber music playing. He confessed to a preference for the latter, as their objective was more to fit together as an integrated ensemble and less for each musician to project his or her own artistic vision. He didn't believe one style was necessarily better than the other, "but just, personalitywise, it's more my cup of tea." Yumi said she would certainly pay close attention to the Markner Quartet from that perspective at their concert tomorrow night. It was the Magini Quartet's one night off while on tour, and Yumi had underlined the Markner's concert in her calendar.

Piaf was replaced by Jacques Brel on the tape loop, singing "Ne Me Quitte Pas," and the waiter arrived.

"What'll it be, gents?"

"What do you got?" Jacobus asked.

"You name it, we've got it."

"Scotch and soda. Johnny Walker Black."

"I can serve you the soda with a one-ounce shooter on the side. You have to mix it yourself."

"Okay, then make it a double."

"I'm not allowed to serve you a double, but I can serve you a second after you've ordered your first."

"Fine. Just bring it today, okay?"

"No problem, sir," said the waiter, laughing. "And to eat?"

"Nothing."

"Sorry, but I'm not allowed to serve you liquor without food."

"But I'm not hungry. I'm thirsty."

"Sorry, state law."

"Okay, bring me a damn patty melt! Nothing like a patty melt and scotch. I assume you have a patty melt."

"One patty melt coming right up, sir! And one scotch and soda!"

Yumi ordered a Stella Artois, Nathaniel a Maker's Mark on the rocks, and Lavender the specialty of the house, the Joan of

Arc, which was a margarita with a twist of jalapeño "for the fire," the menu said. And, of course, food to go with their drinks.

The conversation got back to music. Lavender confessed that one of the few people he had a hard time playing with had been BTower.

"He was still Shelby Freeman Jr. when he was studying with René. Unbelievable talent, but I'm telling you . . . technique and pizzazz is one thing, but that kid was over the top! You know, when René put the kibosh on him as a student because BTower wouldn't learn the 'old-fashioned way,' I actually think he was a little jealous of BTower, talentwise. And BTower didn't like it one bit."

Jacobus agreed with the overall assessment. When it came to sheer bravura, BTower could play rings around the elderly Allard. Gradually BTower got the groupies and the PR, the non-stop career and recording contracts, but somehow age seemed to have bestowed upon Allard's playing a degree of poetry and sublime simplicity such that he became an even greater musical legend the older he got.

"So no matter how hard BTower tried, it seemed he was destined never to be numero uno," he said.

Maurice Chevalier was now singing "Thank Heaven for Little Girls." Jacobus called the waiter over and asked if they could play some Marcel Marceau. The waiter said he would ask.

"It's just a shame the two factions couldn't recognize each other's greatness," said Nathaniel. "Things really got bitter."

"You're not kidding," said Lavender. "One time, when BTower had finished a concert, Allard publicly commented, 'The boy gives nuance a bad name.' It looked like BTower could've killed him then . . . I guess he did, after all. Oh, Jesus! This is giving me the creeps."

Lavender's last comment had been spurred by the new background music, a Muzaked rendition of "Danse Macabre," not Allard's recording certainly, but disconcerting nevertheless. Fortunately, their order arrived and they all quickly toasted one another and took a deep gulp of comforting alcohol.

"You know," Lavender continued after raising a questioning eyebrow at his Joan of Arc, "when René first performed that piece in Carnegie Hall back in '42, he had a special reason for playing it. I wasn't with him then—I only did his last four Carnegie concerts, since '62—but he told me about it after. That first Carnegie recital was right after he got off the boat—literally—having just escaped from Vichy France. That's why it was an all-French program. He wanted to show solidarity with his confreres in the Resistance. Then, after the formal part of the program, he did those little improvisations he was famous for, and finished with the 'Danse.'

"You know the piece. It's really a grotesque perversion of the waltz, which of course originated in Austria. Amazingly enough, Saint-Saëns heard Allard play it shortly before he died in 1921—René was just ten but was a real wunderkind—and autographed René's music. '*Les mains d'un petit ange—le grand diable.*' Imagine what that's worth! Anyway, the piece starts out with the chiming of midnight—the witching hour—and then those diminished fifths on the *scordatura* violin. Nowadays the piece doesn't feel scary, but I gather from the history books that for the first audiences in 1874 it was very unsettling."

"*Scordatura?*" asked Yumi. "That's a term I haven't learned."

"Now you will," Jacobus said through a dripping mouthful of patty melt prepared with the bistro's special flair, melted Roquefort and a sickeningly sweet French dressing. He wiped his mouth with his sleeve.

"*Scordatura*'s when a violin is tuned abnormally. Ninety-nine point nine percent of the time the strings are tuned in perfect fifths—G–D–A–E—but in 'Danse Macabre,' instead of E, it's tuned a half step lower to E-flat. The resulting interval, the diminished fifth, was called the devil's interval in the Middle Ages because it has the aural connotation of evil. It's in all the B horror movies when the guy's throat is about to be slashed. 'Danse Macabre' begins with the chiming of midnight in the accompaniment, and then the first thing you hear from the soloist, before the actual waltz starts, is the devil tuning his fiddle. Hocus-pocus kind of stuff."

"And that's why René played the piece," said Lavender. "It was his secret statement against the Nazis. His friends back home knew this, and even though the audience didn't get the message, it always brought the house down. Of course, the rest of the recital was incredible too, and that's why, when he played the same program every ten years at Carnegie, there wasn't a dry seat in the house."

"What was the deal with the improvisations?" asked Nathaniel. "He's the only one I know who did that kind of thing."

"Well, maybe these days," said Lavender. "But don't forget, René studied with Ysaÿe, and like a lot of the virtuosos in Ysaÿe's day—Joachim, Sarasate, Kreisler, Huberman, Ole Bull—improvising was a centuries-old tradition. It was something they learned to do, like jazz musicians today. It was René's little gimmick, though I must say it was very engaging. He would ask for someone's name or initials from out in the audience and make up a piece based on that name right there on the spot. Oh, it was only two or three minutes, but it was always charming and the audience ate it up. At first he did it unaccompanied, but after a while I could pretty well predict what he would do, and I could make up a simple little accompaniment to go with it. To the un-initiated it seemed like magic, the cynics thought we were cheat-ing, but it was neither, I can assure you."

"Give us an example," asked Yumi. "Please."

"Well, one night there was a particularly buxom young lady in the front row—they always seemed to buy the front-row seats for René. Of course, René chose her from all the volunteers. She said her name was Deborah. A slam dunk! René took the first three letters of her name and made a syrupy Brahmsian love song out of it. What else would you expect? That was enchanting enough as it was, but when he got to the climax he started playing the retrograde—"

"Retrograde?" asked Yumi.

"Retrograde means backwards," said Jacobus. "Didn't I teach you anything?"

"Which of course is B–E–D. Anyone at Carnegie who knew anything about music—and that was just about everyone—knew immediately what was up. The young lady turned a bright red, but I'll give you one guess where Deborah spent the night! What a scalawag, that René!

"So it was kind of a trick. A lot of composers did the same kind of thing with their own names—Bach, Schoenberg, Shostakovich—"

"How could they have done that," asked Yumi, "with all those *H*'s and *S*'s?"

"You haven't learned anything from me, have you?" asked Jacobus.

"But you never mentioned that, Jake," Yumi protested.

"That's neither here nor there. Just don't tell anyone I've been your teacher, okay? In Europe, our note B-flat they call B. Our B-natural they call H, and our E-flat they call S. So Bach is B-flat–A–C–B-natural. You can figure out the others on your own time. That'll be fifty dollars for the lesson, please."

Their waiter arrived and asked if everything was excellent.

"I want another scotch and soda," said Jacobus.

"I'm sorry, but you'll have to finish your first one before I can bring you another. I'll come back later."

"Like hell you will," Jacobus said and drained his glass. "Do I have to finish my patty melt too?"

"That's optional," said the waiter, who then left.

"You certainly had a long and rich history with Allard," Nathaniel said to Lavender.

"Yeah, but it was almost a very short one. Very few people know how close to death he came a couple years after that '62 recital. His lifestyle. Moderation was anathema to him. He was only a little over fifty at the time, but physically he was more like eighty. He had a weak heart, emphysema, cirrhosis of the liver, high blood pressure. You name it, he had it."

"Isn't that about when he disposed of the ex Hawkins del Gesù?" asked Nathaniel. One of reasons Williams was the darling consultant of insurance companies was that he did his homework. He maintained up-to-date files on the transaction of every major violin, including the names of seller and buyer, the auction house or dealer, the price, the provenance of the instrument—basically everything that would have to be known in the event of a claim.

Like the ex Ysaÿe Guadagnini that Jacobus and Williams had recently encountered at Dedubian's shop, the ex Hawkins del Gesù was a violin named after a famous owner. The name ex Hawkins was the sobriquet given to a violin made by Giuseppe Guarneri, the only luthier whose instruments rival his contemporary Antonio Stradivari, and who remarkably lived in the same town of Cremona, Italy. The ex Hawkins had been owned by an Englishman—Clarence, Earl of Hawkins—a competent amateur violinist, in the late eighteenth century. Guarneri himself had the nickname del Gesù because he always inscribed the labels inside his instruments with the Greek abbreviation for Jesus, I.H.S. (iota-eta-sigma), and a Roman cross.

The interesting thing to Jacobus, however, was that Allard had disposed of the ex Hawkins del Gesù in an unorthodox fashion, selling it to a private party whose name he never divulged shortly after that first heart attack. Even for someone as revered as Allard, the transaction raised eyebrows. He had defended himself by saying that it was important for him, a Frenchman, to play on a French violin, and indeed from that time on he performed on a very serviceable J. B. Vuillaume, whose violins were the pinnacle of the French school. It was admitted Allard did play as beautifully as ever, but the questions persisted and no one ever found out to whom he had sold the del Gesù.

"Yeah, it was shortly after the heart attack," Lavender continued. "Can you imagine what his medical bills were? I think that's why he sold it. When he had that attack, I thought it was the end. He was in such bad shape we thought it might even be better for him to die, then and there. Hennie and I went to see him in the hospital whenever we could, because we never knew which time would be the last. He had more tubes connected to him than my high school chem lab. But that little guy you were with at the concert . . . what's his name?"

"Ziggy," said Jacobus.

"Yeah, Ziggy, that fellow. He was there every time I went to visit René, sitting by his side."

"A devoted man. He must have lost wages taking time off," said Nathaniel.

"A little creepy if you ask me, but what do I know?"

Another waiter arrived with a tray of four cognacs during a pounding *Les Mis* medley.

"On the house," he said. "And congratulations on your special concert tonight."

"Hey, you're a different waiter," Jacobus said, noting the lower voice.

The waiter laughed. "I try to be," he said. "Maybe you scared off the first one."

"Do we have to leave you a tip too?" asked Jacobus.

"Thanks, I'd appreciate it," he said, laughed again, and retreated into the swirl.

"Let's make this a quick one," Jacobus said to his friends. "I can't take much more of this music."

Yumi excused herself to go to *Les Dames* before the group left the bistro. While she was gone, Jacobus said to Lavender, "What else?"

"What do you mean?"

"There's nothing creepy about a guy going to visit someone he worships who's in the hospital."

"Well, you're right," said Lavender. "There's a little story that goes with it, but I didn't want to tell you in polite society. It's a tad lurid. Some years before René's heart attack, he and Hennie were having one of their soirées, and let me tell you, if there was one thing René was *not*, it was a skinflint when he threw a bash. There was more caviar than at the Romanovs' coronation, and the Bordeaux flowed like the Seine. Hennie was still only about twenty at the time and was as wild as she was beautiful. René and I hadn't played together yet, but I was one of the privileged invitees because we were on the panel of a competition together. I tell you, I was still pretty Midwest milquetoast then, and it was the wildest shindig I'd ever been to. At one point René told me that he and Hennie were 'going for a ride.' She grabbed a bottle of Dom Perignon on the way out. I thought they were going to go and take a taxi somewhere. When they got back about twenty minutes later, the bottle was empty and they both had coy little smirks, were half unbuttoned, and their clothes smelled like champagne and her hair was a mop. I said, 'Well, you've certainly been through the ringer,' and Hennie whispered in my ear, 'We've just had sex in the elevator.' I expressed my astonishment somehow—I'm sure I was speechless, so I don't know how—and René said, 'It was the big mirror, you see. We just couldn't resist. We told Krinkelmeier, take the elevator up and down as fast as you can, for the excitement.'"

"Krinkelmeier?" asked Jacobus.

"That's what René and Hennie used to call Ziggy. It was all in fun."

"Yeah. So anyway . . ."

"So anyway, Hennie gave this silly conspiratorial titter. 'Yes,' she said, 'and we made Krinkelmeier watch. He didn't want to, but with the mirror, he couldn't help it, could he? That made it even better.' Uh-oh, here comes Yumi. But that's the upchuck."

As Yumi sat, Lavender raised his snifter. "To the endearing René Allard, greatest virtuoso of his time, who didn't understand all the fuss. He would but shrug and say, 'I am just me.'"

"And here's to Yumi and Virgil, for an amazing concert," said Nathaniel.

They all downed their drinks and paid the bill. On the way out, Jacobus bumped into a chair, something he had always prided himself on not doing. The others, mildly tipsy like Jacobus, laughed. Perhaps they had all celebrated a little too much. Jacobus tried to steady himself, latching on to a coatrack for support. The background music became blurred, now unbearably loud, now inaudible, giving him a suddenly intense headache. For a moment he had a delusional image of himself as Beethoven in the throes of impending deafness. "What the hell?" he said, and they laughed some more. By the time they got to the curb his head was spinning and he was having trouble breathing. He grabbed on to a parking meter, threw up, then, having lost his sense of direction, plunged headlong into State Street and oncoming Saturday night traffic. His friends were now shouting something at him, but they seemed so far away. What was that? Running footsteps? Before he passed out, he felt himself being dragged and manhandled, but that was all.

THIRTEEN
DAY 4: SUNDAY

BTower sat slumped on the edge of his bed, forearms on his thighs, head on his chest, a position in which he could be found most of the time now. There was nothing to look at or to hear, anyway, that he hadn't seen or heard for his months in solitary.

Through the adjustable-volume mikes on the surveillance cameras, Haskell and Gundacker could hear the sounds in each cell. But the sounds infiltrating from outside the cells were distant and amorphous, as if underwater. Unintelligible, disembodied voices, metal doors sliding open and closed.

"Hmm," observed Haskell. He nibbled around the core of his tart Granny Smith apple. He pointed at BTower's image in the monitor, the apple easily corralled in his massive hand, and said to Gundacker, "Sound was this boy's life. His meal ticket. Got him out of the slum and made him famous. And now, what's he got . . . white noise. White noise. Well, only a few more days."

"That's deep," said Gundacker. He polished off his peanut butter sandwich, getting ready to do his rounds.

"Go to hell," said Haskell, but not meaning it.

"Hey, looky there." Gundacker pointed to the monitor. BTower had just arisen from the mattress. "Ten bucks he starts pacing again."

But BTower didn't start pacing. Instead he walked back to the center of his cell stage and resumed his violin-holding position. Unlike yesterday's manic episode, this time he was controlled, if not calm.

"Damn," said Gundacker. "Gotta go feed the swine. I'll miss the show."

"Hey, Gruber," said Haskell, "don't you worry. I'll keep an eye on him. If he paces, we'll take the ten off your account. Promise."

Gundacker departed and Haskell returned to watch BTower. The wife had her soaps, he had his monitors. He had the better deal, he concluded. No commercials.

Relaxed but attentive, he took the first bite of his turkey and cranberry relish on homemade white. He watched, intrigued, as BTower held his imaginary violin steady, moving only his right arm—the bow arm. That much was obvious even to the musical illiterate that Haskell readily acknowledged himself to be.

Haskell, though, was a good observer. Days before the penal experts, he could tell when inmates needed to be placed on suicide watch by noticing little things: how a guy rubbed his face, or how often he washed his hands or stared at the ceiling. He also knew when trouble was brewing; when an inmate's neck muscles hardened or his breathing got shallow, indicating that violence was imminent. More than his great strength, Haskell believed, it was his awareness of the inconsequential that had enabled him to keep the upper hand on this island of damaged souls.

BTower seemed to be experimenting with different aspects of his right hand. First, he moved his hand from right to left in a line parallel to the ground. Then, deliberate little vertical counterclockwise circular movements with a momentary stop as BTower felt for the balance of the weight of his arm. This went on for minutes—first the motion from right to left, then the circles. Over and over again. Haskell tipped back on his chair, devouring his sandwich at the same patient rate as BTower's practice. Haskell surmised BTower was deciding where to put the bow on the string. Haskell had never been to a concert, but he had seen the violinists on the old TV shows, like Lawrence Welk.

BTower's next effort seemed to be to determine how fast to move his bow once he got it on the string. Haskell lost count of how many times BTower repeated this, but one thing was for sure: Yesterday's furious abandon had been replaced with conscious focus. At first he thought it was just pure repetition, as if BTower was simply trying to memorize a movement. It was getting boring until Haskell realized that BTower was actually doing something minutely different with each and every repetition in a systematic way. It became apparent that BTower had music in his head and was trying to get precisely the right sound. Haskell leaned forward in his seat.

He observed that BTower was not only altering the speed of his arm, he was also altering its level, both at the beginning and the end of the motion The process was so systematic that after a while Haskell, confident that he could predict what BTower was going to do next, put down his almost finished sandwich, stood up in front of the monitor, and started to imitate in advance what BTower was doing. At first his arm felt stiff as a board, but the more he watched and imitated, the more comfortable he felt.

"Loose as a goose," Haskell said out loud.

But he couldn't figure out exactly how BTower was making those adjustments. It all seemed so fluid. Somehow his arm motion was almost circular. At the beginning of a stroke it seemed to go down, but at the end it seemed to go up again, even though his hand itself was moving in a straight line. The camera did not have a zoom lens— Haskell had argued with the warden for an upgrade but was told it wasn't in the budget—so he put on his reading glasses and put his face right up to the monitor, his sandwich forgotten, and stared.

Haskell heard a knock at BTower's door. It was Gundacker, delivering lunch. BTower cursed under his breath and so did Haskell, whose first violin lesson was being interrupted. The tray appeared under the door. They knew that BTower would leave the tray untouched, but those were the regulations.

BTower, his concentration broken, suddenly called out in a challenging voice, as if Gundacker had thrown down the gauntlet and not the Salisbury steak, "It's more than sound, Jacobus! See, I changed it all! I got the public! The public has ears AND EYES! Allard couldn't touch me! Those assholes! Purists! You don't know a damn thing! You hear me?"

But if Gundacker heard, his only response was the sound of his receding footsteps.

Murderers, thought Haskell. They're all different, but they're all the same. What made them different from the rest of us, he wasn't sure.

FOURTEEN

When Jacobus regained consciousness, he had no idea where he was. He knew only that he felt as if he had been wrung through the heavy-duty cycle of a commercial dryer by someone with a year's supply of quarters. Gradually, though, he became aware of the sounds surrounding him, recognizing hospital sounds reminiscent of his bedridden stint after having his skull crunched by a former student, Rachel Lewison, a few years before. Jacobus had unearthed the truth that Rachel had murdered his rival, the renowned if infuriating violin teacher Victoria Jablonski, and if not for Yumi and Nathaniel's last-second intervention, Rachel would have killed him too. As it was, the knock on his noggin had rendered him semicomatose in the ICU for weeks. That he had testified on Rachel's behalf and that she ultimately was declared not guilty by reason of insanity brought Jacobus little succor.

Now, as then, his ears were functioning acutely, and he could hear the intravenous drips, the soft hum of medical technology, and the intermittent murmuring of hospital staff outside his door, but his body ached and his throat was dry as a bone. His parched first words were choked and burned his throat.

"No wonder they don't serve doubles in Utah," he croaked.

"Mr. Jacobus! We were so worried about you. You're alive!"

"Ziggy, that you?"

"When I heard you were in the hospital—your dear friend

Nathaniel called me—I came over right away. You're at LDS Hospital. It was the closest one, but it's also the best. I was praying you would recover."

"Where are the others?" Jacobus whispered.

"They will be right back. They're talking to Dr. Allred. I was just relieving them. They have been here with you. In fact, I'll go get them. They'll be so overjoyed to see you're still among the living."

Jacobus heard Gottfried's footsteps running along the linoleum floor. A few minutes later he returned with Nathaniel, Yumi, Lavender, and the doctor.

"You're a heck of a lucky man, Mr. Jacobus," said Dr. Allred.

"If this is lucky," said Jacobus, "I feel sorry for the sick ones."

"What he means, Jake," said Nathaniel, "is that you were poisoned."

"Like hell I was!"

"Yes, Mr. Jacobus. It's true. To put it in lay terms, someone slipped you the proverbial Mickey. But instead of just trying to knock you out, someone definitely wanted to put you six feet under, if you catch my drift. Your friends described your sudden convulsive symptoms so we immediately forced some amyl nitrite into your lungs, followed by an IV of sodium nitrite, and then sodium thiosulfate."

"For what? I had chicken pox when I was a kid."

"For cyanide poisoning, Mr. Jacobus. You could have been dead from cardiac arrest within minutes."

"Cyanide! So why am I still with the living, pray tell?" Jacobus said, though with his whole insides still burning, he wasn't so sure he wanted to be.

"You really would've been a goner," said Dr. Allred, "except for your vomitus that was apparently triggered by food that disagreed with you, and enough of the poison evacuated along with it to bollix up the whole ball of wax. Mr. Williams here also managed to save you from having your head run over by a Land Rover, and once we pumped your stomach, well, I'd say now you're over the hump."

"Saved by a patty melt," said Williams.

"What a hideous notion," said Jacobus. He thought for a moment. "Doc, if my head had been run over, how long would I have lived?"

"It depends on the speed and weight of the car, the point of the cranium it contacted, for example."

"Well, let's say it squished me real good."

"Death would have been pretty much instantaneous under that scenario. As I say, you're a lucky man. You've dodged two bullets."

"But what about chickens? Don't chickens run around even after their heads're cut off? It takes them a few minutes before they plotz."

"Well, it all depends on how you define life, I guess," said Dr. Allred. "It's a difficult ethical question for us these days. Motor functions working but no longer thinking. Just survival instinct ingrained into their muscles. Those chickens are not really alive, in my opinion, though if you asked the chickens' families . . ."

"Thank you, that's very comforting. When can I get the hell out of here?"

"We've all given our statements to the police," said Williams.

"You'll have to do that too, but Doc here says as soon as you feel ready to go there are people with much more urgent concerns ready to take this bed from you."

"You must be kidding. I feel like shit." His throat felt like a porcupine had just crawled through it, not to mention his head and stomach.

"If you wish to stay longer," said Dr. Allred, "I'd like to read you this pamphlet on the adverse effects of smoking and drinking alcohol, two of your vices, I'm told. Following a few simple guidelines could add five to ten years to your life."

"Nathaniel, where are my clothes?" said Jacobus.

At the Salt Lake airport, Jacobus and Nathaniel said their farewells to Yumi and Lavender, Gottfried and Seglinde, assuring them all—especially Yumi—that Jacobus would be fine, and boarded a Continental flight back to Albany, changing in Cincinnati. Jacobus had had his interview with Detective Lamar Christiansen of the SLPD about the incident the night before. Yumi, Lavender, and Nathaniel had provided a visual description of that last waiter who served them the free cognacs, one of which, Christiansen postulated, had contained cyanide. Other than the outfit the waiter wore, which was the same as all the others, their descriptions of his physical features were all different. This did not surprise Christiansen, especially as the light in the bistro was dim, there was a lot of late-night activity going on, and they all had been drinking. Jacobus gave a description of the way the waiter had talked.

"He said 'spay-shle' instead of 'special,' " said Jacobus. "And instead of 'appreciate,' it sounded like 'a-prishy-it.' It was unique."

"That's great," said Christiansen. "You've really narrowed it down."

Jacobus felt proud of his discerning aural acumen. "So who is it?" he asked.

"Well," said Christiansen, "you've eliminated forty-nine states and most foreign countries that I know of. That leaves only the two million people who live in Utah. If you consider that only about half of them are male, that gets rid of a million, plus or minus, right off the bat. But I'll get started right away."

Jacobus and Nathaniel took their seats on the plane, looking forward to a tranquil, recuperative eight hours during which they could reflect upon their progress, or lack thereof, in determining the true murderer of René Allard and now the attempted murder of Daniel Jacobus. No sooner had they clicked on their seat belts when the surrounding rows were mobbed by a swarm of blond children ages three to sixteen carrying violin cases.

"Are you all part of an orchestra?" Nathaniel asked, addressing the general horde.

A smiling, attractive middle-aged woman responded. "No, we're a family. These are my children. We're going to Institute for the week."

"Institute?" asked Jacobus.

"Why, the American Suzuki Institute in Purchase, New York. Haven't you ever heard of it?"

"Yes, I've heard of it," said Williams. "That sounds wonderful."

Jacobus said, "Hold on. It's probably costing you five thousand dollars for plane tickets and another five thousand for room and

board. You can learn more about violin playing from a CD of
Pinky Zukerman and it would only cost you twenty bucks."

"Pinky who? Does he teach Book Six?"

"Book Six of what?" Jacobus asked. He whispered to Nathaniel,
"Are we talking Utahese again?"

"Book Six of Suzuki, of course," the proud mom said. "Do
you take?"

"Do I take?" asked Jacobus. "Take what? What the hell are
you talking about?"

"You don't need to get upset, sir!" said the mother. "Do you
take lessons?"

"*Take* lessons?" he said. "No, I don't *take* lessons. I give."

The flight attendant asked everyone to take their seats.

"I don't know," said the mother. "How can you give lessons if
you don't know Book Six?"

Jacobus felt Nathaniel's calming hand on his arm, so he chose
to accept the question as rhetorical and did not respond. After
that, the flight was otherwise uneventful. Jacobus and Nathaniel
discussed every angle of the poisoning attempt they could think
of until they were blue in the face. They were baffled by the
whole incident. What had Jacobus said or done to anyone to war-
rant potentially lethal retaliation? Who could have been responsible? Was it all a big mistake? The café had been so crowded.
Could they have given the drink to the wrong sucker?

When they arrived in Cincinnati, Jacobus and Nathaniel headed
to the airport Caffeinds Coffee Corner. While they waited for
their coffee, Jacobus hobbled around to loosen his stiff joints and
Nathaniel got out his cell phone. None of the insurance companies

he called had yet found an instrument coverage policy for Rose Grimes.

"Could you keep looking, please?" he asked Vermont Mutual, as he had asked all the others. "We're in a bind, timewise. It's urgent, you see." They all assured him they would get back to him if they came up with anything.

Second, he called the VA information hotline in Washington, D.C., to find out what he could about Mr. Grimes.

"No, I'm sorry I don't have a first name," he told the records administrator, Yavonne Reid, "but I do have an address." Yavonne said they would get back.

He then called Detective Al Malachi in New York City, cajoling him until he grudgingly relented, to a degree, to their request for additional materials.

"So you'll send us both sets of photos, of Allard's body and Gottfried's family?"

Malachi said, "Not quite, I'm not going to send them to you. I'll send them to Miller."

Roy Miller comprised the entire police force of Jacobus's town in the Berkshires. Only a part-time cop but full-time plumber, Miller had managed to keep the peace in the small village for almost twenty years on a pittance of a salary, so the locals were not complaining.

"You and Jacobus can inspect the photos in Miller's presence. Then they'll be returned to New York by courier. That's the deal. Take it or leave it."

"I really appreciate that," Nathaniel said. "And Jake does too."

"I'll bet," Malachi said. He hung up.

Before Nathaniel made his call to Boris Dedubian, Jacobus

expressed a thought that had entered his head as they were waiting for their plane but had become temporarily dislodged when they were confronted by the Suzuki horde.

"You suppose Lavender might've held something against Allard?"

"Like what?" Nathaniel asked.

"Well, here's a guy who pretty much forfeited fame as a soloist to be in someone else's shadow. When Allard played that last concert at Carnegie, Lavender's career essentially ended with it. He's been pigeonholed as an accompanist, and it's not easy to rebuild a reputation as a soloist, especially someone getting along in years."

"What about this tour with the Magini Quartet?" Nathaniel countered. "Looks like he's doing okay."

"*Maybe* okay. The quartet's good and no doubt'll get better, but they're still a new group with a couple young players like Yumi. When Lavender was with Allard, he was playing with the big boys—the Juilliard Quartet and Emerson. Now he's got to start all over again. Maybe there was some resentment. What the hell, I don't know."

They agreed to put that hypothesis in their back pocket and move on in more substantive directions.

Nathaniel called Dedubian.

"Boris," he asked, "do you recall if your insurance evaluation of the Garimberti mentioned whether there were papers?"

An insurance evaluation is a simple document containing basic information about the instrument, including its value, as determined by the expert writing the evaluation, intended to aid insurance companies determining payouts in the event the instrument is stolen or damaged. An evaluation can usually be obtained from a dealer for a set fee of tens of dollars.

On the other hand, a certificate—what in the business is called the "papers"—is a more official document that verifies the authenticity of the instrument to the greatest extent possible. It lists in detail every one of the dozen or so pertinent measurements of the instrument, plus a very specific description of the varnish and all other distinguishing characteristics. It states what is written on the label glued to the inside of the instrument and often comes with a set of professional photographs of the front, back, and scroll. Most important, the expert who writes the papers states in his opinion who made the violin. The final step is to stamp the document with his personal seal to prevent any possible finagling with it. No value for the instrument is stated in the papers, as the document is theoretically intended to accompany the instrument throughout eternity, and values can change greatly from one year to the next, usually up. Sometimes the papers state the name of the owner of the instrument, sometimes not. There are very few experts in any generation whose opinions are universally respected, so to have an impeccable certificate can make a million-dollar difference in the value of the instrument, regardless of how beautiful it looks or sounds. So important is certification that the document alone might cost up to ten percent of the value of the violin itself.

"Let me have Mrs. King check on that," Dedubian said.

"You think you could get back to us by tomorrow?" Nathaniel asked.

"For you and Jake," he said, "I would do anything."

Nathaniel thanked him and hung up, fully aware that Dedubian said that to all his customers.

The second leg of their flight droned on and on, but by the end of the trip Jacobus and Nathaniel were no closer to understanding the murder attempt in Salt Lake than they were at the beginning. Arriving at Jacobus's home after the one-hour drive from the Albany airport, they were both exhausted and unwilling to give the issue any additional consideration.

FIFTEEN
DAY 5: MONDAY

The phone woke them early the next morning. There was only one extension in the house and that was downstairs. "You get it," Jacobus shouted hoarsely to Nathaniel, who slept in the guest room, which was the size of a large closet and as well appointed. "I'm still an invalid."

The call was from Miles Bardon at Intercontinental Insurance Associates, the same company that had insured the infamous Piccolino Stradivarius.

"I've got some news for you," said Bardon. "A Rose Grimes indeed obtained coverage for the Garimberti soon after she secured the evaluation from Boris in New York."

"Hold on one second, Miles," Nathaniel said. He shouted the news up to Jacobus.

He returned to the phone. "Did she ever make a claim?"

"No."

"No? Are you sure?"

Bardon chuckled. "Listen, Mr. Williams, when we pay out more than a dime, we don't forget."

By the time Nathaniel finished his call, Jacobus was in the kitchen smoking a Camel as he brewed a pot of instant Folgers in his ancient aluminum percolator, wondering where the paucity of their accumulated information left them. The knowledge that Grimes had never collected insurance money on the broken violin stopped them in their tracks. And maybe that's where they should be, he reasoned. The weight of the evidence, if not all the suspicions, still pointed to BTower. As he was about to drink his coffee, the phone rang again. Jacobus answered it himself this time. It was Dedubian.

"I have some information for you," Dedubian told Jacobus. "It seems that the Garimberti has papers, good papers, from Laszlo. He was one of the best."

"Laszlo!" said Jacobus. "Crusty old fart! He wrote papers for my violin. You know my fiddle. It's a terrific eighteenth-century Neapolitan instrument, but Laszlo used to give me hell because I never bought a Strad."

"Yes, he was like that. How did you get him off your back?"

"I told him I did have a great instrument. My ears. What's he up to? He still live in Passaic?"

"No, not for a long time," said Dedubian. "Lazlo's been retired for a few years. His eyesight was going and he was no longer absolutely certain what he was looking at. He didn't want all his earlier work to be invalidated by making a bad call, so he called it a day. I do believe he is now in your neck of the woods, Putnam County, New York. I hear he has become fond of vegetable gardening, of all things."

This was good news for Jacobus, because Novak was now only a half hour away, whereas going to New Jersey would have taken another valuable day off their efforts to preserve the life of BTower.

"What do you think about Grimes not filing an insurance claim for the Garimberti?" Jacobus asked. Dedubian rattled off a few possibilities: ignorance, shame, excessive paperwork. There was no way to know. This led to the subject of the previously stolen Piccolino Strad, which had been recovered by Jacobus, but which had also been seriously damaged in the process.

"There aren't too many pristine Strads or Guarneris anymore, are there?" said Jacobus.

"Very few, Jake," said Dedubian. "Very few. I had a Strad for sale a few months ago but because it had been repaired under the bass bar and sound post it really didn't have much tone. It did have some nice historical value so there was not much trouble selling it. Then last year I had the ex Hawkins, which was in beautiful shape—"

"You had what?" said Jacobus.

"Yes, indeed," said Dedubian. "The ex Hawkins. I was asked to sell it, and I can tell you when word got out—among private circles, of course—that it was for sale, my phone rang off the hook. I did not have it in my shop for twenty-four hours."

"May I ask who the seller and buyer were?" asked Jacobus.

"You may ask, but I am sorry to say I am not at liberty to tell you. Both parties requested anonymity, and if I am to maintain my ability to buy and sell at this level I must respect their wishes.

I can, however, assure you that its provenance and authenticity were indisputable. All the papers were there, and anyone in the world who had ever seen the violin before René sold it and it went underground would attest to it being the original."

"May I ask when you sold it most recently?"

"You may ask."

"Are you at liberty to tell me?"

"Yes, I am."

"Then, godammit, tell me!"

"It was sold the day after BTower's conviction, about a year ago."

That floored Jacobus. Allard's del Gesù, hidden for years, sold the day after his murderer's conviction!

"What do you read into that, Bo? Surely there's some connection."

"Yes, there's a connection," said Dedubian, "but, from the sound of your voice, not nearly as nefarious as you may think. It is nothing new for an owner of a valuable instrument to capitalize on the notoriety of a previous owner in order to maximize profit. When Jascha Heifetz died a few years ago, some guy who had one of Jascha's old junker Mittenwald fiddles put it on the market and got ten times what it should have gone for. With the ex Hawkins, the markup wasn't as proportional; I can't tell you the price, but it was millions more than it otherwise would have been."

"Then why didn't the seller get rid of it the day after Allard died? Why did he wait a whole year until the day after the conviction?"

"Backlash, I suppose, Jake. With someone as beloved as Allard, buyers might have been disgusted that someone would want to profit from his death so fast. Wouldn't you be? So they waited. Really, it's nothing sinister, just capitalism at work."

"Yes, and I'm sure you raked in a proportionally greater commission as well," said Jacobus.

"Well, it's all standard. I'm not complaining, however."

Jacobus hung up, no longer as hopeful as he had been a moment ago. Another thread, perhaps, but a frayed one at best. At least he had Novak. Where that would lead, he had no idea. He chugged his tepid Folgers. "Ah!" he said, smacking his lips. "At least there's something good in the world."

Jacobus called Roy Miller, the town's police force. Miller had received the photos from Malachi. Jacobus invited him to the house, just a few miles down Route 41. He said, "I've got a Jack Daniel's with your name on it."

Miller said, "But it's only nine thirty in the morning."

Jacobus said, "That's never stopped you before."

"I'll be there," said Miller.

First, they looked at the police photos of Allard's body. They had read the report, but now here they were in all their graphic gore. Jacobus ordered Nathaniel to describe in detail what they looked like, but it turned Nathaniel's stomach just to look at them. Nevertheless, Jacobus was relentless.

"Why?" asked Nathaniel. "What is it you need to know?"

"If I could answer that question, I'd only need that one thing. But since we don't know what that one thing is, I need to know everything."

So Jacobus demanded more and more detail. How prone was the body? What did the clothes look like? How far from the elevator was he? Where exactly was the violin underneath him? How was he holding the case? What was the angle of the curious disposition of the left arm? How rotated was it? How straight were the fingers? How far apart from each other were they? Worst of all, describe the head. How was it twisted? What was the color, or colors, of the face? Tell me more about the missing bits of scalp and hair. Jacobus didn't know what he was looking for. He just knew it was too bizarre to be immaterial. He prodded Nathaniel mercilessly, corroborating every detail with Miller, so that he could have a picture in his mind's eye of the gruesome scene.

They took a break. Miller had his JD in a Big Gulp mug loaded with ice, Jacobus his cigarette, and Nathaniel a cup of Earl Grey tea with honey to soothe his throat from all the talking he had done.

Next they pulled out Gottfried's collection. Each one was in a clear, numbered plastic sheath. They appeared to be what Malachi had purported them to be, a bunch of family photos from the old days in Germany. Many of them were copies of each other and of the photos that had been on the wall. Yet Jacobus had Nathaniel describe each one. Ultimately, when his voice gave out entirely, Nathaniel had Miller take over the monologue.

"Take one out," said Jacobus.

"What do you mean?" whispered Nathaniel.

"Out of the plastic envelope."

"Whoa, hold on one minute!" said Miller. "What do you need to do that for?"

"Who the hell knows?" asked Jacobus. "I want to hold one."

"I'm not sure if I'm supposed to . . . but what the hell,"

Miller said, taking another swig of his drink and removing one of the multicopied photos of a teenage Sigmund Gottfried with his twin sister and their mother, Winifred. Seglinde, towering over her brother, had long flowing golden (or so it seemed in the black-and-white photo) locks of hair. The siblings had whimsical smiles on their faces; the mother was more stern.

Miller placed the picture in Jacobus's hands. Jacobus first felt around the edges and corners, which were still impressively sharp—tidy fellow, that Ziggy—then he felt along the back of the photo, which was predictably smooth and unblemished. He was about to turn it over and do the same on the picture itself, but felt a large hand stop him.

"Jake," said Miller, "I don't know if you should do that. It might ruin it. I've had enough run-ins with Malachi." When Jacobus had been a suspect in the murder of Victoria Jablonski a few years before, it had been the trusting Miller who had naively enabled him to flee to Japan. Malachi had been irate, and Miller had almost lost his badge and the modest income that went with it.

"All right," said Jacobus. "For now." He picked up the photo and put it just in front of his nose. He inhaled deeply.

Miller chuckled.

"What's so funny?" asked Jacobus.

"Well, if you could only see it as well as smell it."

"Why?"

"You're sniffing that young lady. She looks good enough to eat." Miller laughed at his joke and poured himself another sour mash.

A moment later Jacobus threw down the photo.

"Nothing!" he growled. "Nothing!" He sat back in his chair, totally dispirited.

The phone rang but he made no move to answer it. Finally Nathaniel picked up the receiver and, his voice gone, whispered, "Hello."

It was the VA. They had some interesting news for him.

"Are you sure?" rasped Nathaniel. A moment later he put down the receiver.

"What is it?" asked Jacobus.

"There is no Mr. Grimes at 74 West 132nd Street," said Williams.

"Hey, he was there. You saw him. I heard him. He wasn't big on chitchat, but he was still kickin'."

"Except he wasn't a Grimes. He was a Freeman. A Shelby Freeman. Senior."

SIXTEEN

Though the pacing continued, it was slower than yesterday, and the hand banging had stopped. BTower, eyes closed, centered himself in the room. He lifted his imaginary violin and bow and began to practice, still only the right hand on imaginary open strings, and all somewhat stiffly.

"Look at that. He's really losing it," Gundacker said to both Haskell and Rosenthal. He removed a sandwich from his lunch bag and unwrapped it. "Cripes, peanut butter again," he complained.

"Is he?" said Haskell, who had brought a container of leftover chili. A few days ago I would've said yeah, he's gone, but y'know they almost always get either more

violent as the big day approaches, or sometimes they get kinda numb. Seems to me that Mr. BTower here is finding something in between."

"By playing charades?"

"I mean he's got three days to go and he's pulling it together, man. I mean he's hearing music. Not crazy music, real music. And he's practicing it. I've been watching. I can almost hear it, the way he's doing it."

"Then you're a fruitcake too," said Gundacker.

Haskell chuckled quietly. "Maybe, man. Maybe. But look at him now. That boy's got a plan."

The two guards and Cy Rosenthal watched the surveillance camera as BTower gently placed his imaginary violin on the mattress. Now that his legal team had suspended its appeals, all that Rosenthal had left was the opportunity to observe his client. He expressed a hope that somehow he and his team might contrive a way to extend BTower's life—a plea for mental health treatment, perhaps, or . . . or what?

"Five bucks he paces," said Gundacker.

"Quit while you're behind, Gruber," said Haskell.

BTower lay on his back on the floor and put his hands behind his head.

"Napping. He's gonna take a nap on the floor," said Gundacker.

"Why don't you let your lips take a nap, Gruber?" said Haskell.

BTower didn't nap. On the contrary, he began to do sit-ups, toe touches, knee bends, and push-ups—basic stuff kids learn in gym class—followed by a variety of sophisticated stretching exercises from shoulders down to knees.

"Well, boys, time for me to go," said Rosenthal, rising from his folding chair. The two security men rose with him. "Gotta head back to the city. Can't say I'm too hopeful, but thanks for your time."

"I'll let you out," Gundacker said. "Time to begin my rounds anyhow. Don't know why he thinks he needs the exercise, though. What's he got, three more days, but he must have had one helluva personal trainer," he said.

"You could use one, Gruber," said Haskell. "Those choke sandwiches, they all going right to your stomach."

"Fine, give me a thousand bucks a week and I'll call Paunchless Pilates today."

As soon as Rosenthal and Gundacker had gone, Haskell put the bowl of chili on the desk and stood up, ready for Lesson Number Two. He had an inkling that BTower's exercises had something to do with playing the violin. He now mimicked BTower, again in center stage painstakingly seeking a relaxed and balanced posture. Stand straight up, feet shoulder distance apart, knees slightly bent like a linebacker before the snap. BTower bounced on the balls of his feet a bit, making sure he was relaxed from the neck on down.

BTower rotated his head from side to side. Haskell did likewise. Ah, the neck! The more he turned his neck in either direction, the more tension he felt going down his spine. He was relieved that BTower finally settled on a position looking almost straight ahead as he held the violin, though he wasn't sure he'd be able to see the fingers on his left hand (when it was finally time to use them). But then Haskell asked himself, why should he need to see where his fingers were going, anyway? He had ears to hear, didn't he? What did he need eyes for? After all, that guy Jacobus who BTower hated, they said he could play the violin and he was blind.

Now BTower began to raise and lower his outstretched left arm, finally settling on a level with his left hand raised to a height that would keep the violin more or less parallel to the ground. Haskell followed suit. It felt comfortable and practical. Though Haskell couldn't know for sure, he ascertained it would also be best for keeping the bow on the string and making the best sound.

Now BTower began to play, still without moving any fingers on his left hand. Haskell tried to imitate, but BTower was doing things with his right arm and hand that were beyond him to follow. He executed bow strokes that started totally connected but gradually became spikier until, by the end, he was doing these short choppy motions with only his fingers. Haskell soon gave up and just watched, finishing his chili, which was now almost cold, but he had an idea for the next lesson, if there would be one.

SEVENTEEN

The more dirt they unearthed, the more Jacobus felt buried by questions. BTower, the progeny of Shelby Freeman and Rose Grimes? What about the Garimberti? What about this possible new triangle of Grimes, BTower, and Allard? Why hadn't Grimes revealed any of this to them? How did all the pieces fit together? If nothing else, all these new questions upped the ante on Jacobus's visit with Laszlo Novak.

An hour after the call from Dedubian, they arrived at Novak's tidy white-clapboard, green-shuttered cottage at the end of a tree-shrouded gravel lane. Before they even knocked on the screen door, a voice as gravelly as the lane barked, "Hey, I'm on the can. Just come in. Food's on the counter."

Nathaniel and Jacobus found their way to the kitchen, the former by sight, the latter by smell. Jacobus bumped into the refrigerator, knocking off a calendar and some newspaper clippings stuck to it with a magnet.

"Klutz," said Nathaniel, picking the items up off the floor and replacing them on the fridge. "Can't you see where you're going?"

"Sure I can," said Jacobus. "I just like walking into things."

They helped themselves to a plate of spicy homemade Hungarian salami with fresh cut-up tomatoes drizzled with olive oil that was sitting next to a few beat-up old violins and a can of varnish. Novak joined them as they were polishing off the salami.

"Never know when nature'll call at my age," said Novak. "So you guys starving or something? You just finished my lunch."

"Sorry," said Nathaniel. "Couldn't help it."

"Well, what the hell," said Novak. "There's plenty more. You can take some home with you. Take my zucchini . . . Please! So what are you overstuffed gents here for? Dinner?"

Jacobus licked his fingers. "We're trying to find out the owner of a violin that you wrote a certificate for."

"Yeah? When? You want a beer? I got some Rolling Rock in the fridge."

"Sure," said Jacobus, and Nathaniel added, "Make that two."

"About thirty years ago," said Jacobus.

"You guys must be off your rocker," said Novak, handing out the bottles. "I can't even remember what I did before I went to the bathroom. What is it? A Strad? Del Gesù?"

"Garimberti. 1958."

"What? That's not a big fiddle. How d'you expect me to remember who brought in a Garimberti?"

"Don't you have records? Copies, at least?"

"Jesus, they're in a bunch of cardboard boxes in the attic covered with mouse shit. I haven't looked at them since I retired. You want me to go through all that for a Garimberti? What else can you tell me?"

"The present owner is an African-American woman," said Nathaniel. "Rose Grimes."

"Nope," said Novak. "Don't ring a bell."

"I'm guessing," said Jacobus, "that's she's had the fiddle since about 1965, because that's when she left the Bonderman. Maybe she took it when she left." Nathaniel winced.

"Strike two," said Novak. "Modern Italian violins. They're a dime a dozen."

"Garimbertis?" asked Jacobus.

"Garimberti, Antoniazzi, Bisiach, Pedrazzini, Ornati, Sgarabotto, Sderci. You want me to go on? There was one little guy who used to bring them in by the truckload, but that was before '65."

"Who was that?"

"You expect me to remember his name? Jake, there are some days I wake up in the morning and I ask myself, 'Who am I?' Then I look in the mirror, and say, 'Oh, yeah, it's Laszlo.' Not that it's such a pretty face. Plus I can't see a thing. Not as bad as you, though, Jacobus—yet! Getting old ain't all it's cracked up to be. All I remember, he was a little bald guy and talked with a German accent. I remember that because I don't like German accents."

"Was he a polite little guy?"

"They're all polite because they all want me to write good papers. But yeah, he was polite. Too polite if you ask me. A little bit off his noggin, but who am I to talk? And he dressed like he talked. Not a thread out of place, but nothing fancy. I used to write up certificates for him a couple times a year. Always pretty good stuff. Not great. Good. And in good condition."

Ziggy! thought Jacobus. Was it possible? But how could Ziggy have the money to own all those violins? And why? Why be an elevator boy all your life if you have all those assets?

Jacobus asked, "Lazlo, was this guy's name by any chance Ziggy? Sigmund Gottfried?"

Novak laughed. "Nope. Don't ring a bell. You shoulda brought the Avon lady with you, Jake, because you're not ringing any bells today. I don't remember what it was, but I know what it wasn't, and it wasn't no Ziggy." He laughed again.

"Is it possible," asked Nathaniel, "that this person with the German accent wasn't the real owner?"

"Nathaniel," said Novak, "you know better than to ask me a dumb-ass question like that. Are you saying I should've asked for a photo ID from everyone who ever brought me a violin? Maybe their rap sheet? Should I ask my customers, 'Excuse me, madame, but is your violin by any chance hot?' They bring in a violin, I tell them what I think it is, they pay me. Boom-boom, bye-bye."

"Laszlo," said Jacobus, finishing his beer and wiping his mouth with his sleeve. "Do me a favor. See if you can find the certificates for this guy. After all, you said there were a bunch of them. It might be important. It might not. But all we've got are loose ends and it's starting to piss me off. You find the name, and Nathaniel will buy you dinner at Csardas."

"Give me a week," said Novak.

"How about a day?" said Jacobus.

"Then it's going to be dinner and girls."

EIGHTEEN

Nathaniel's 1974 red VW Rabbit swerved onto the Taconic Parkway on their way to New York City. Though Jacobus would have preferred to endure sitting through a Bruckner symphony than to climb those four flights of stairs again, he knew that a return visit to Rose Grimes was unavoidable. Jacobus asked Nathaniel to make a few calls on his cell phone.

"You're not supposed to make calls while you're driving in New York," said Nathaniel, his foot getting heavier on the pedal. Time was getting short for BTower and they were treading water.

"They can make an exception for you," said Jacobus. "No way your driving could get any worse. Never mind. I'll call."

His first call was to Detective Malachi. He told Malachi he wanted measurements of all the angles and distances in the positioning of Allard's left hand and arm. Malachi asked him why, and Jacobus told him that it just seemed very unnatural.

Malachi said, "You think getting your neck twisted in a vise is natural?" but agreed to do it if it would get Jacobus out of his hair.

Jacobus also gave him an update on his findings and asked if it was sufficient information to get Brown to agree to reopen the case.

"Are you kidding, Jacobus? All you've got is a lot of *gornisht*. Zilch. *Bobkes*. Nada. Nothing. You need me to make that any clearer? And none of your nothing has anything to do with Allard."

"What about BTower's paternity? His mother works in the Bonderman Building. She's got a shady violin. A guy who fits Gottfried's description is buying and selling violins, and don't forget Gottfried's the one who ratted on Grimes and got her fired."

"Is there a law against buying and selling violins, Jacobus?"

"Well . . ."

"Does any of this have an iota of anything to do with Allard? I repeat, Jacobus, all you've got is *gornisht.*"

"I'm almost right about this, Malachi. I know it."

"Like Mark Twain said, Jacobus, the difference between almost right and right is like the difference between a lightning bug and lightning. I'll get you the measurements, and that's it."

"Smart-ass," mumbled Jacobus, as he dialed the next number.

"Rosenthal here."

"Why the hell didn't you tell me about BTower's parents?" Jacobus shouted without preamble.

"What are you talking about?" said Rosenthal. Jacobus explained BTower's ancestry. Rosenthal said BTower had told him only that he and his family had become estranged when he was a kid, so he moved in with an aunt for a while, and then with friends. He had refused to disclose more than that, saying it had no relevance to the case. Besides, Rosenthal asked Jacobus, "Why didn't *you* know anything about his parents? You taught him, didn't you?"

"Ah, never mind," said Jacobus. Rosenthal was right. Jacobus had a very broad definition of what were a good teacher's obligations. It was more than teaching the mechanics of the violin, more even than conveying the mystery of musical aesthetics from one generation to another. It was taking on the role of mentor, career guidance counselor, instrument consultant, psychologist, philosopher, parent. That's why teaching had exhausted him and was the main reason he couldn't keep going as he had. He was unwilling to lower his standards, and for Rosenthal to now remind him that he already had done so in BTower's case was a painful recognition. "We're going to talk to the mother now, anyway. The father is non compos mentis. How's the son doing?"

"Believe it or not, Jacobus, he seems better. Not happy, maybe. But calmer. Something you told him, he admitted. But he's changed. I watched him on his cell monitor, and sometimes he just stands there like he's holding up his violin. I don't know. It's a little odd, but at least he's not banging his head against the walls anymore."

"Well, I don't know what I told him that he wouldn't knock me over the head for," said Jacobus, "but maybe you could ask him if there's anything about his family background that might give me some direction."

"Will do," said Rosenthal. "And Mr. Jacobus?"

"Yeah?"

"Thank you."

"You say that now, but wait'll you get the bill."

NINETEEN

Jacobus banged on the door. "It's Jacobus. Put your gun down, Grimes, and open up!"

"And why should I?"

"You lied about the name of that zombie in there!"

"Jake," said Nathaniel, "that's no way to talk."

"No one lies to me," he said.

The door was suddenly flung open. Jacobus heard it bang against the wall.

"I lied to no one!" said Rose. "You never asked me his name. You just assumed his name was Grimes. I never said it was."

"And what about BTower? You forget he was your son?"

"Your sarcasm is offensive, Mr. Jacobus."

"Sarcasm doesn't stink as bad as dishonesty, Mrs. Grimes. Or is it Mrs. Freeman?"

Nathaniel intervened. He pleaded with the two to go inside and sit down. Yelling at each other in the echoing hallway was not doing them any good.

Once they were seated, Nathaniel continued. "Mrs. Grimes, is that your name?"

"Yes. I kept my maiden name, Mr. Williams."

"Mrs. Grimes, you do have some explaining to do. You might not have outright lied to us, but what you said, and didn't say, was certainly misleading. Can you please start with how you got the violin, other than that it had been in the family for a long time?"

"All right, Mr. Williams. I'll tell you everything, and then I
hope you and this other person will leave me in peace.

"In 1965 my husband, Mr. Freeman, returned from the war.
When he went to Vietnam he and I had just married. He was not
a highly educated man but he was a good man who worked hard.
We promised each other that when he got back we were going to
have a family, but then they told me he had been wounded in the
head, so when he came back he was as you see him. But I never left
his side, and I did . . . what was necessary to have a child because
I intended to keep our promise. Shelby Junior was born later that
year.

"As you can see, Mr. Williams, this is not a proper neighborhood to raise a child, but financially we had no choice. So you
would think it would be very difficult to keep a young boy out of
trouble. But Shelby Junior was different. From the time he was
born he would sit on my lap and the two of us would listen to
music on the radio, and I would take him to choir rehearsals and
I would hold him in my arms. He was never difficult.

"When he was old enough, I gave him the violin. He could
barely hold it—he was such a small child—but I couldn't afford a
smaller one, what with caring for my husband and all. But somehow he managed to teach himself—couldn't afford lessons
either—by playing along with the gospel. I tell you, Mr. Williams, it was the happiest time of my life."

Rose Grimes sighed.

"But then, you know, Shelby Junior got older, as children do.
As his talent became clearer to him—he could play anything that
he heard by ear—he started to become full of himself. He began
to go to clubs to play jazz and he would sneak into concerts with-

out paying. Gradually he stopped listening to gospel. Then one day . . ."

"Go on, Mrs. Grimes," said Nathaniel.

"Then one day he ordered me to turn off my music. Ordered me, his own mother. I told him he was arrogant and that he should get down on his knees to thank the Lord for being blessed with God-given talent. 'The Lord lifteth up the meek: he casteth the wicked down to the ground.' "

"And what did he do, Mrs. Grimes?"

"He laughed at me. A nasty laugh. Told me God had given him nothing. That here he was, living in a slum, and he learned to play the violin all by himself without any help from anybody, and that if God wanted to give him something, he'd get him out of this place."

"And what did you do, Mrs. Grimes, when Shelby Junior said those things?"

"God help me, Mr. Williams. I picked up the violin and smashed it. Not even one's child can blaspheme the Lord and not pay a price."

"So Shelby Junior left?"

"Yes. Without another word. He moved in with my sister for a while. Then, I don't know. We haven't spoken since that day, so I didn't know where he went or what he did, except that he was so ashamed of his name that he changed it."

"Where did you get the violin?" asked Jacobus.

"It was a gift."

"From?"

"I don't know."

"You know, Mrs. Grimes," said Jacobus, "it's kind of hard to take your holier-than-thou crap when you keep lying. We're trying to save the life of your son, the son you denied was yours, and all you do is obfuscate. Have you ever considered the possibility that your Bible-toting proselytizing might have been one reason your son ditched it out of here and became a rebellious son of a bitch?"

"If we're talking about obfuscating, Mr. Jacobus, don't forget that you were his teacher at one time."

"Just for a while."

"'Just for a while'! Oh, I am so sorry. Of course, no one of your character could possibly have any influence over an impressionable young man in such a short time. And where, may I ask, did you get *your* violin?"

"Mrs. Grimes," said Nathaniel, "if I might just get a word in edgewise here. I'm not going to editorialize on your faith or your relationship with your son, but you have to admit that after all we've heard, it's a stretch to believe you don't know where the violin came from."

"As I said, you may believe what you want. The truth—and may the Lord strike me down here and now if it isn't—is that one day I opened my door and the violin was there. There was no letter, no explanation, no address where I could return it or say thank you. It was a gift from God."

"Or the devil," said Jacobus.

TWENTY

In recent years, Jacobus felt his age. Now, aching and exhausted both physically and mentally, he felt even older than his age. The traveling, the questions, the arguing, the misgivings, not to mention the attempt on his life had worn down his will. And for what? After having turned over all the stones and seeing the roaches scatter, there was still nothing convincing, nothing substantial or demonstrative to prove that BTower did not kill Allard. Some strange things, no doubt. Coincidences, maybe. Maybe not. But where would it all lead? The only certainty was that unless something happened, in a few days BTower would pay the price.

Nathaniel suggested that Jacobus spend the night in Manhattan rather than driving the two and a half hours back to the Berkshires. Jacobus, for once, agreed, so they drove the short distance to his apartment on Ninety-sixth Street.

"Want to go get some coffee?" asked Nathaniel. "Perko-Late's still open down the block." Jacobus declined. It was atypical for him to need more than five or six hours of sleep, but this time he said he just needed to go to bed.

They sat at the counter of Nathaniel's cluttered but spacious kitchen and reviewed what remained to be done. Nathaniel offered to make tea. Jacobus said, "Tea? You must be kidding. Scotch." He still didn't believe a word of what Rose Grimes had told them. Nathaniel disagreed.

"Look at it from her point of view, Jake. She's got two total strangers walking into her quiet life and turning it inside out, bringing up old painful wounds she'd spent a lifetime trying to forget. All she wants is for us to go away, so she tells us what she needs to and no more. There's no crime in that. You can understand that, can't you?"

"I wouldn't think a mother could . . . Ah, what the hell," said Jacobus. "Maybe you're right. Just check out what you can of the facts. Birth certificates, dates, whatever. You know the routine. Call Laszlo tomorrow. Make sure he didn't forget we were there. Did you call Malachi? We'll need those measurements. I'm gonna hit the sack."

"Hold on a minute, Jake," said Nathaniel. "I'll need to write this all down." Nathaniel rummaged for a pad in the drawer next to the stove and sat back down. Dossier, Novak, Malachi. He tore the page off the pad and went to put it on the cork bulletin board glued to the side of the refrigerator.

"Darn," he said. "Outta thumbtacks. I should get those magnets like Laszlo." Jacobus heard Nathaniel again rummaging through the drawer.

Jacobus swallowed some scotch and put his glass down. "What'd you say?"

"Nothing," said Nathaniel. "I'm just looking for thumbtacks to put the note on the board. Here they are."

"Thumbtacks," said Jacobus.

"Yeah, thumbtacks. You've heard of thumbtacks, haven't you?"

"Ziggy's photos. Malachi's report. He said the photos were thumbtacked to the wall. The photos we saw with Miller. They had no thumbtack holes."

It took them a moment for the significance to sink in.

"The photos we saw," said Nathaniel. "Are you implying those weren't the ones that Ziggy took down?"

"What I'm saying is that lonely Mr. Gottfried, who enjoyed surrounding himself with pictures of famous violinists, might also have enjoyed the company of pictures of Italian violins. Violins for which he acquired certificates. What time is it in Salt Lake City?" he asked Nathaniel.

"Two, three hours earlier. Something like that."

Jacobus dialed the number for Seglinde Oehlschlager. He spoke to her for five minutes and hung up, shaken.

"What is it, Jake?" asked Nathaniel.

"Ziggy. He's dead. Suicide."

TWENTY-ONE

Seglinde—calm but clearly distraught—had explained to Jacobus that Ziggy had driven up to the Antelope Island Music Festival.

"He went to hear the Markner Quartet with Simon Baker perform the Mozart G-Minor Quintet, just as he had told everyone," Seglinde said. "After the concert he drove to the edge of the Great Salt Lake and threw himself into the water, Mr. Jacobus. He wrote a long note. It rambled and rambled—it was so much like Ziggy. He left it on the dashboard. The police have it now, but I can tell you Ziggy wrote about both his joy and his sadness—after such sublimely glorious music in that setting. He so loved Antelope Island—he felt he was already almost in heaven. But there was the sadness at leaving his friends behind, and I think this is something he would want to you to know, Mr. Jacobus, a sense of responsibility for the attempt on your life, since you had gone to Utah to see him."

Ziggy responsible? Jacobus thought. His stomach tightened. It was Jacobus who now felt like an accomplice in Ziggy's death.

"Mr. Jacobus, are you still there?" said Seglinde.

"Yes. Yes," he said. In his most sympathetic voice, Jacobus said he recalled that it was in fact Seglinde's idea to go to the concert. Hadn't she gone?

Her response was tearful.

"If only I had," she said. "If only I had, then none of this could have happened. I have no excuse. I feel I let him down so."

Jacobus did not know how to end the conversation. Eventually Seglinde composed herself and continued.

"The police are still searching for the body in the lake," Seglinde explained, "but one way or the other there will soon be a small memorial service to which you and Mr. Williams are of course invited." If they couldn't make it, she would understand perfectly. It was so far away. "And I'm bearing up reasonably well, thank you, considering," she said. "We were very close, the two of us."

"What about possessions?" Jacobus asked as politely as possible.

"Possessions? There was a will in the safety-deposit box. But don't worry, Mr. Jacobus, I'm comfortable enough."

"Were there belongings from New York? Memorabilia? Photos, perhaps? Things to remember him by?"

"No. I'm quite sure nothing like that. Everything Ziggy brought from New York was in his father's valise. Just bare essentials. No photos. The Leica, of course. That had been his father's also."

Jacobus thanked Seglinde, muttered a few more condolences, and hung up. After relating the conversation to Nathaniel, he rubbed his face, now rough with whiskers, with both hands. The crow's-feet that had years ago sprouted from the outer corners of his eyes now traversed the entire sides of his face.

Why? he asked himself. And why *then*? What had been going on inside Ziggy to drive him to kill himself? For Jacobus, who had known despair, whose life had taken dizzying downward spirals, the very contemplation of suicide had been sufficient to prod him away from the abyss. Even when he lost his eyesight literally overnight in his sleep, his response had not been despair. It had been anger and defiance, and the next day he won the audition for concertmaster of the Boston Symphony, playing the audition, unbeknownst to the audition committee, entirely from memory. Only then did he grudgingly accede to his friend's insistence that he go to the hospital.

He had been at the precipice only once, when he no longer cared what the outcome would be—when the love of another human being was offered to him and he realized his capacity to reciprocate had been irretrievably taken from him in his childhood in a manner he would never divulge. At that moment, there on the edge, he had been almost happy to let go, and would have but for Nathaniel's strength. Nathaniel, who had literally pulled him from a watery suicide. Was that the way Ziggy had felt at the last moment? It seemed so from his note. But for what reason? Jacobus had never told anyone his story. Had Ziggy kept his own secret? Or was there some reason he simply could not handle his newfound freedom after his cloistered life? He had seemed so content, with his fancy new car and his easy generosity.

Yes, there had been something going on with violins. Of that, Jacobus had little doubt, but in the violin business there was a fine line between unscrupulous transactions and outright illegal dealing. Jacobus did not know whether Ziggy had crossed it, but even if he had, would that have been sufficient reason to take his own life? Was there more? Guilt? Despair? A harmless little man caught up in something too big? If so, Ziggy had concealed it well.

"That's all she wrote," Jacobus said to Nathaniel. He had never felt so tired. "I think it's time to pack it up."

"Jake, I know how you're feeling, but let's not give up yet," Nathaniel urged him. "I've still got those other calls to make, and maybe if Ziggy's photos weren't in Salt Lake City, he might have left them in New York. Let me call Alonzo Fuente to see if we can get into the old basement."

"Whatever," said Jacobus. He jiggled the almost melted ice cubes in his diluted scotch. "I know what you're doing. Trying to buoy my spirits. I suppose I should thank you."

"No need."

Nathaniel called Fuente and told him that Ziggy had died. He and Jacobus wanted to see if there were any effects he might have left behind they could send to his family out west. Fuente, after expressing his sorrow at the passing of "the little guy," explained that in order to build the new elevator, the weight of the new shaft had to be supported by an entirely new bracing system.

"They installed those braces in Basement Two and reinforced the floor of Basement One, where they installed a new furnace and incinerator, the new kinds that work real good, but they still weigh a ton. That means all the access to Basement Two had to be cut off, totally. No stairs, no emergency access, no elevator. The only way to get down there would be to jackhammer through the new floor, and I don't think my boss would be too thrilled to do that. We're already about eight months behind. Sorry about that."

"As I said," said Jacobus after Nathaniel hung up, "case closed." He asked Nathaniel to dial first Rosenthal, then Malachi, and admit defeat. Their responses were somber but respectful. They knew what it meant.

Jacobus rose slowly and stumbled toward his bedroom, groping along the way, tired and forlorn. He felt that somehow he had caused Ziggy's death, something he said or did. Somehow he was responsible. And for what? Trying to exonerate someone who probably committed the murder of a great man? It was now time to let the chips fall where they may. He just needed to lie down.

TWENTY-TWO
DAY 6: TUESDAY

The next morning Jacobus dragged himself bleary and morose into Nathaniel's kitchen, having for once overslept. Nathaniel had gone out early and returned with coffee from Mud in Your Eye and cheese Danish from the Lower Crust, Jacobus's favorite bakery.

"Thought these might cheer you up," said Nathaniel.

"Thank you," said Jacobus. "That was very kind of you."

They ate without talking. The only sound intruding upon

Jacobus's despondence was the Bach cantata "Ach Gott, wie man-
ches Herzeleid," broadcast on WNCN. "O God, how much heart-
ache," the chorus began. The music and text, like so many of Bach's
cantatas, had the uncanny ability to expose his innermost feelings.

"Just forebear, forebear, my spirit, Confronteth me within
these times." The words alone did not cut through his devout
atheism, but Bach's genius to perceive their musical and spiritual potential combined with his supreme ability to mold them
into profoundly articulated counterpoint moved Jacobus to his
core.

"I am content in this my sorrow, for God is my true confidence." Jacobus sighed and was about to say something, but then
decided against it and picked at the crumbs of his pastry. His
resignation and his catharsis were complete.

"Well, I guess we should be going," said Jacobus, though he
had eaten only a few bites.

"Whatever you want, Jake."

The phone rang. Nathaniel answered it.

"Just one second, Yumi. I'll put him on. Jake, it's Yumi. She's
got a problem."

Jake took the receiver. "Hello, dear."

"What's wrong, Jake?" Yumi said. "You never call me 'dear.'"

"No, no! Everything's fine." Jacobus decided he would not
burden Yumi with the news of Ziggy's death. It was, after all, her
first tour and she didn't need any distractions. Besides, she hardly
knew Ziggy, anyway. "What can I do for you? Is there a problem
with the tour?"

Yumi explained that the concerts were going extremely well.
The tour had so far been a big success and they were being treated

like royalty wherever they went. The problem, she explained, was that Aaron Kortovsky, the first violinist, "was getting personal."

"Well, you can't say I haven't warned you; playing string quartets is a very personal thing, Yumi," said Jacobus. "That's one reason why it's so difficult for quartets to succeed. Each member feels very deeply about the music, and after a while any suggestion to change things even the slightest from the way you want it starts to feel like an affront. But don't worry about it, Yumi. Aaron is a pro. He's been around the block, so feel free to stick up for what you think."

That's not what she meant, Yumi explained. Kortovsky had come to her hotel room after the Markner Quartet concert and had put his hands where he shouldn't have.

"You mean he tried to put the munch on you?" asked Jacobus, appalled.

"I'm not sure what you mean by that, but I think that's what he did. I told him no, but now I'm worried he might try to kick me out of the quartet if I don't say yes. What should I do, Jake?"

Jacobus was rarely in the mood to play the role of the counselor, and at this moment it was the last thing he needed. Why couldn't teaching the violin just stop with teaching the violin? But with Yumi it was different. Yumi was like a daughter to Jacobus. Their relationship had endured the gamut of emotions. Not that it had all been peaches and cream. There had been a time when there was mistrust, and even a moment when Yumi thought Jacobus intended to bring harm to her and her family. But that was before; now their bond was unbreakable. For Yumi to have been taken advantage of and put in a position of personal and professional vulnerability incensed Jacobus, adding yet another layer to his misery. It wasn't fiction for women to be given the take-it-or-leave-it threat. He had seen it happen between orchestra conductors and female musicians, and even between conservatory teachers and their students. All too often he heard credible stories of that type of behavior among testosterone-overloaded male musicians, and Yumi was not one to exaggerate.

"These guys," said Jacobus, his voice rising, "when they go on the road, think that just because they leave their wives at home, the world becomes their personal harem."

"But Jake, Aaron's wife is Annika!"

Annika Haagen was the violist in the Magini Quartet and was on tour with them.

"Jesus! Either that guy has too much chutzpah or too little brains," said Jacobus. "Yumi, if Kortovsky is dumb enough to make another advance, what you've got to do is make it abundantly clear that although you greatly value playing music with him, his actions are both immoral and illegal. You got that? You don't need to have him reported to the police, but you got to give him the impression it's a possibility. I know it's a tough balancing act, but if you want to keep your position in the quartet, you need both to be respected and to have a good relationship with the guys."

"Okay, Jake, I'll do my best," said Yumi. "Maybe that's why the Markner Quartet has lasted so long. All four of them are male." Jacobus was relieved to hear Yumi laugh.

She began to talk about the Markner's compelling performance of the affecting Shostakovich Eighth String Quartet in which, to her delight, Shostakovich included extended use of his "signature" motive that they had talked about at the café.

"But Jake," she said, "I'm still not sure how he got D–E-flat–C–B out of the name Shostakovich."

Jacobus, considering Yumi's unsettled state, explained with uncharacteristic patience. "D is for his first name, Dmitri. That's easy enough, isn't it? E-flat represents the *S* at the beginning of his last name, C replaces *K*—it's Russian spelling, after all—and the B is for the *H* at the end of the name. Shostakovich, conveniently for us, skipped over the other letters.

"And now that I've given you yet one more free lesson, tell me, how was the Mozart?"

Yumi related how wonderfully they played, their uncanny sense of what each musician in the ensemble was doing, their beautifully blended sound, and, of course, Mozart's incredible ability as a composer. She said it had been a spiritual experience for her.

Jacobus replied that he hoped that it had been educational as well, and that to a certain extent it might have balanced the negativity of her encounter with Kortovsky.

"Look, Yumi," he said, "call me whenever you need to," though he hoped she wouldn't have to anymore.

Jacobus hung up and sighed again. Everyone has their tsores, he thought. Allard, BTower, Ziggy, now Yumi. But why was it he always seemed to be in the middle of it? He sat there in Nathaniel's kitchen for what seemed only a moment, when he felt a hand on his shoulder.

"Car's all packed, Jake," said Nathaniel. "Whenever you're ready."

There was very little conversation on the two-and-a-half-hour drive to Jacobus's house. Even if he had his sight, neither the brilliant azure of the August sky nor the friendly flitting of wood thrushes, chickadees, and robins in the forest surrounding his home would have lifted him from his deep resignation.

"There's a salami on your doorstep," said Nathaniel.

"Is that a punch line to a joke, Nathaniel? If it is, don't bother."

"There's a note attached to it." Standing on the stoop to Jacobus's house, Nathaniel picked up the salami and read, " 'Hey, Jacobus, you putz! Where you been? Call me. Novak. P.S. Why don't you get yourself a damn answering machine?' "

Jacobus didn't respond.

"Well, don't you think we should call him, Jake?"

"Would it make a difference?"

Nevertheless, once they were inside Nathaniel dialed Novak's number and handed the phone to Jacobus.

"Aha!" said Novak. "I found them. I found copies of all those certificates."

"And?" asked Jacobus.

"I told you it wasn't a Sigmund Gottfried. It wasn't anything like a Gottfried. I was right."

Jacobus was perplexed but only slightly interested. He thought it would have been Ziggy, but it was too late to close the barn door. Who was it, then? he asked.

"You won't believe this. A guy with six consecutive consonants in his name. Never trust a guy with six consonants."

"Dammit, are we going to play Will Shortz, or are you going to tell me?"

"Hey, Jake. Don't get hot under the collar. The name is Orin Oehlschlager. Got that? Double O. Oehlschlager."

TWENTY-THREE

When Haskell arrived at the surveillance room after his morning rounds, Gundacker reported that BTower had already been "practicing" for hours. No more pacing. No banging or shouting. Just calm and collected in the middle of his cell.

"Damn," said Haskell. He had brought a magnifying glass with him so he could see what BTower had been doing with the fingers of his right hand. He also figured that with only one day left, BTower would be starting to play some notes with his left hand. The glass would undoubtedly have come in handy for that. Now it appeared he had missed the boat for his third lesson. He slumped in his chair, resigned himself to an uneventful day, and rummaged through his lunch bag to extract his sandwich.

"Whatcha got today, Bailey?" asked Gundacker. "Looks good." He stared at his limp peanut butter sandwich.

"Eggplant parmigian on baguette," said Haskell.

"Jeez!" exploded Gundacker. "Every day you got something great for lunch and all I get is this damn peanut butter sandwich. I'm sick of it!" He hurled it at the monitor, where it stuck momentarily, causing no damage that a spray bottle and a paper towel couldn't remedy.

"Look, Gruber," said Haskell, patiently. "All I bring for lunch is just leftovers. Whatever we don't eat the night before, April just puts together for the next day. Now, why don't you just go and ask Clorinda to fix you something other than peanut butter?"

"Clorinda?" asked Gundacker, bewildered. "Clorinda doesn't make my lunch!"

"Then who does?" asked Haskell.

"I do!" said Gundacker.

Haskell leaned back and examined the man he had been working with for the past two years.

"What're you lookin' at," asked Gundacker. "What'd I say?"

"I thought I knew you, Gruber, but sometimes people can fool you, what they really are. But you just taught me one real important lesson."

"I did? What's that?" Gundacker said.

"Only that in life, Gruber, you make your own peanut butter sandwich. And now because of what you have just taught me, I need to go see that young Mr. BTower personally. It's against regulations, I know, but I got to do it. You don't mind if we switch shifts just for today, Gruber? Here, you can have my lunch."

"Be my guest," said Gundacker, already reaching for Haskell's bag.

Haskell made his way to BTower's cell. He could have used his key to enter. He could have hollered, "Hey, BTower," but instead he knocked. For several moments there was no response. Then finally, "Slide the tray under the door if you have to."

"It's not lunch," said Haskell. "Can we talk?"

"You've got the key," said BTower.

Haskell entered the cell. BTower was still standing in the middle. Haskell eyed him in two new perspectives. Physically, BTower was no longer a two-dimensional object on a monitor, a character on the soaps. More important, Haskell bore with him the new insight provided, unknowingly, by Gundacker.

"You got something to say?" asked BTower. "Go ahead. Or are you going to just stand there."

Haskell, older by at least a generation, towered over BTower, but he was momentarily at a loss for words. He hadn't actually planned what he was going to say to the young celebrity, whose fame and notoriety unaccountably made him even more tongue-tied.

"I been watching you practice," he said. "On the monitor."

"So?" BTower asked.

"*I was just wondering, when are you going to do something with your left hand?*"

"*You mean,*" asked BTower, who was now smiling, "*because I only got twenty hours left?*"

"*That's partly what I mean,*" said Haskell.

"*You play the violin?*" asked BTower.

"*Nohow,*" said Haskell, "*but I've been followin' right along. This would've been my third lesson, but Gundacker say you've been workin' all morning.*"

"*Well,*" said BTower, "*you haven't missed anything. I needed to get the sound right before practicing the left hand, but I think it's time to start practicing the note.*"

"*One note?*" asked Haskell, who for someone rarely surprised was clearly caught off balance. "*These last few days I guessed you been practicing everything that's ever been written. Y'know, for old time's sake. Now you talkin' one note?*"

BTower laughed. "*Jacobus—that old blind fart last week?*"

"*The one we had to hold you down from?*" asked Haskell.

"*Yeah, him. He challenged me to understand the first note of Beethoven's 'Kreutzer' Sonata, an A-major chord, in my head. At first I thought he was full of shit, but then I thought, What the hell? What better have I got to do in this place? What's the difference if I spend five minutes taking him up on it? But then, the more I started thinking about it, analyzing it, the more I understood. And it just kept going, you know? It took my mind with it. If I had to explain everything I was thinking while you were watching, it would take more time than I've got left.*"

"*You know,*" said Haskell, carefully choosing his words, "*I noticed you been angry for a long, long time, and then when the blind man come, you get angrier than ever. Then you start with your phantom practicing a few days ago and every day you get calmer and calmer. Now you almost sound grateful that the man have a hand putting you in this place.*"

"*I cursed him every day for that, don't you worry,*" said BTower. "*But you know what, Haskell? I've learned something about music—life, maybe—that I never would've if I hadn't ended up here. So maybe I lucked out in a way. What's better, to live a long time, make a lot of money, be famous, and not understand anything, or learn something worth knowing even if it means getting your neck stretched at an inconvenient time?*

"But what did you mean when you said 'partly,' when you asked if I was going to practice my left hand? That was kind of curious."

Haskell replied, looking BTower steadily in the eye, *"Only, young man, that I wanted to learn how to do it before it's too late."* Then his face loosened into a smile. *"After all, I'm over sixty. Who knows how much longer I got."*

Returning Haskell's gaze, BTower took a moment before replying, then said, *"You know, I've never taught before because I've never thought about stuff before and I never wanted to waste time when I had my own life. So what the hell, you wanna be my first student?"*

"As you say, what the hell?"

"So first thing to know is," said BTower, *"what each hand is responsible for. The right hand is responsible for the sound, see, and what the left hand does is play the note in tune—what's called intonation—and create vibrato. That's all."*

"Seems simple enough."

"You think so? What does 'playing in tune' actually mean?"

"Can't you just tell, just using your ear? Like that Supreme Court dude who knew obscenity when he saw it. You really need a definition?"

"Well, let me tell you what it really means, 'to play in tune,' and then you can tell me if it's important.

"A note on a violin's like any sound; it's a set of frequencies—a certain number of vibrations per second. The quality of the sound, see, depends on what's making it—a violin, an alarm clock . . . a lovely lady screamin' for more," he said with a smile, which Haskell returned. *"You following me so far?"*

Haskell nodded. *"So far."*

"The A that an orchestra tunes to is 440 vibrations per second, more or less, and

it's the same note as the A-string of the violin, which has its own quality. The decision to call 440 vibrations per second A is a totally man-made definition.

"*Now a good thing, see, about the first chord to Beethoven's 'Kreutzer' Sonata is that it's an A-major chord, using the A an octave below the open string, and also the A an octave above, with the notes E and C-sharp in the middle, filling out the chord.*"

"*You're way ahead of me, boss. What's an octave?*"

"*I'll tell you what, Haskell. Let me give you the lecture, and you pick up what you can. Otherwise, when they come get me, I'll still be on Lesson One.*"

"*Go ahead, then.*"

BTower defined an octave, and explained what it meant to play it in tune with the instrument, and went on to do the same with the other notes of the chord. He talked about fifths and thirds as well and how to practice them. BTower demonstrated microscopic adjustments, insisting they would totally change the intonation, even though to Haskell it appeared that his finger stood stock-still.

Most of what he said went right over Haskell's head, but Haskell was more interested in BTower's recent transformation.

"*So are we done playing that chord in tune?*" *asked Haskell.*

"*Not quite,*" *said BTower.* "*Like I said, in this sonata the opening chord is A Major—all the music in the minor mode comes later in the movement—so you have to consider how much English you want to put on that C-sharp.*"

"*So that's it, then?*" *asked Haskell.*

"*Only one other thing before playing this chord with both hands, and that's vibrato.*"

"*I've heard of that,*" *said Haskell.* "*You give your hand a shake, right?*"

BTower laughed and explained the intricacies of the mechanics and aesthetics of vibrato, demonstrating some of the exercises he had been practicing to get his hand moving again.

"*If vibrato's so tricky, why bother with it, then?*" *asked Haskell, whose efforts at imitating BTower's vibrato were a fiasco.*

"*By itself, vibrato doesn't do anything for or against the music, see? It's like a car idling in neutral; it can purr all it want, but it ain't about to go nowhere. To make it musical, I got to make decisions about the music first. I can make vibrato faster or slower, narrower or wider. I can use my finger, my wrist, my elbow, my arm to change the color. Vibrato that's all the same is no better than no vibrato.*"

"*Where'd you learn all this stuff?*" asked Haskell.

"*Some of it I came up with myself. But a lot of it—most of it—came from the older guys. Jacobus . . . Allard.*"

Haskell looked intently at BTower and noticed the skin on his face had a gloss of sweat.

"*You really didn't kill him, did you?*" he asked, though it was more of a statement.

"*It doesn't really matter now, does it?*" replied BTower. "*I can live with it. And I can die with it.*"

"*Well, I got to go now,*" said Haskell. "*Got to do my rounds before they start bangin' on the doors, and I already learned more than I can remember anyway. Thanks for the lesson, son.*"

As he was leaving BTower's cell, he asked, "*You got anything you want to say to anybody? Family? Any kind of a message? I'll let 'em know.*"

BTower thought for a moment. "*You can tell my mama I was still practicing.*"

"*She'd appreciate that, I'm sure.*"

"*You can tell her, if she wants to think I had God-given talent, see, that's her right, I guess.*"

TWENTY-FOUR

Jacobus choked down an allergy pill, then knocked on the door with his left hand. In his right he held a bouquet of flowers. That touch had been Nathaniel's idea, and Jacobus had balked at it so grievously that it almost nixed the plan the two had formulated after Novak's call. At first Jacobus thought Nathaniel was only joking and dismissed it out of hand, but Nathaniel was uncharacteristically insistent.

"Even though Ziggy isn't alive," he argued, "BTower is. Maybe we don't have what you could call a *trail* of information, but we do have a messy pile of it, and how would you feel if we give up now and BTower dies, and then find out we could have prevented it? At least we should try to understand the reasons for Ziggy's death, and I don't see how holding a bunch of flowers is gonna kill you if it'll do the trick."

Nathaniel had hauled him bodily into the car, bouquet and all, and prodded Jacobus all the way back to the city.

Jacobus almost hoped she'd be out, but then he heard the lock bolt being released and the door open.

"Mabel!" he said. He held out the flowers and affected a smile. "Surprise!"

"How sweet!" said Mabel. Her hand grabbed his, and Jacobus allowed himself to be led back to the familiar couch, where Mabel deposited him while she put the flowers in a vase, cooing all the way.

"Now, where were we?" she said. She regained Jacobus's hand and close to his ear crooned a quiet rendition of "Getting to Know You." Mimi the Siamese cat promptly joined in with a wail that did not sound too dissimilar.

Jacobus cleared his throat and made his best effort to sound sincere and unrehearsed expressing his awe at how much Mabel recalled of Bonderman Building's history. It was just so enlightening talking to her, he said. She had known so many famous people over the years! "Tell me some of the famous people, especially musicians, you've known," he asked. "After all, living next to René Allard . . ."

After a half hour of saying *wow, hmm,* and *ooh,* Jacobus still hadn't learned anything new. At one point he interjected, "You must have seen some pretty interesting shenanigans, I'll wager."

Mabel then launched into another half hour of the parties she attended with the privileged class. "And then that last night, the farewell party. That was going to be something special!"

It had been almost two years and Jacobus hadn't thought much about the soirée that never happened.

"Were you invited, Mabel?"

"Oh, yeah! Of course I was invited! You see, I'm in Apartment 4C—"

"Was there a big crowd?"

"Nah! Only a few people that he and Hennie really thought good of. You should've seen the food and wine they ordered! I was getting ready to go over, just before René was found dead in the hallway, when I looked out into the corridor and saw that pianist, Virgil Lavender."

"You mean BTower."

"No, he was later."

"Who was Lavender with?"

"He was all by himself. He never did make it to the party, which was of course canceled on account of René being murdered."

"How do you know he never made it there?"

"Hennie told me. She couldn't figure out why. After all, next to Hennie there was no one closer to René."

"Did you tell this to the police?"

"No."

"Why not?"

"They didn't ask. Those police are creepy."

Jacobus now had yet another world to overturn, and there was so little time. Could BTower have arrived on the scene after Lavender had killed Allard? And why in the world would Lavender do such a thing? It made no sense.

"So many mysteries," he said.

Mabel said, oh, yeah, there was a lot of that, but expressed the notion that they had done enough talking and it was time to move on to the next stage. Jacobus felt Mabel's hand on his knee. Cringing, he promptly removed it.

"What's wrong?" she asked.

"Nothing! Nothing at all! But maybe first you can tell me something mysterious. That always gets the ole engine runnin', Mabel. You know, me being a violinist, ever see any strange people bringing violins here, for example? Ever? Tell me a mystery, Mabel."

Mabel perked up. "That's what turns you on? Mysteries?" She thought for a moment. "Ooh, I have just the story for you. But first, I'll get us a drink. Don't run away!" She returned shortly, handing Jacobus a glass. "Sangria," she said, as if it were a long-lost aphrodisiac. She clinked her glass against his. "*Cin cin!*"

Jacobus took one sip of the sickly sweet fruit and wine concoction and almost vomited.

Mabel curled a lock of Jacobus's unkempt hair around her index finger, which he forced himself to tolerate, and she began a once-upon-a-time tale of how in the 1950s and '60s a dark European man in a trench coat—"just like Bogey's"—would come about once every six months late at night with lots of violin cases and leave empty-handed a couple of hours later. Mabel always knew it was him because he walked with a limp. She would look out from the crack in the door after he passed.

"Mmm. That's just the kind of story I like," said Jacobus. "But tell me, Mabel, where did this mystery man go with the violin cases?"

"Why, René's, of course! Next door in 4B. You see, I'm in 4C and—"

"Yes, yes," said Jacobus, and then reminded himself yet again to be patient. "Yes, you're in 4C. And this mysterious man with the limp and the trench coat, he always left empty-handed?"

"Uh-huh. Always."

"But here's something I don't understand, Mabel. If he had lots of cases, how could he carry them all? Maybe four cases, max, but that's not very many."

"Well, that's an easy one. Sometimes he made more than one trip up and down the elevator. Sometimes Ziggy would help carry them."

"Ah. And what was this man with limp's name?"

"How do I know? I never ever talked to him. Besides, he didn't speak English."

Jacobus marveled at Mabel's logic but didn't push her.

"And how long did you say this went on, Mabel?"

"This is really turning you on?"

"Can't you tell? I can barely even think about drinking the sangria."

"Well, the man kept coming through the sixties, but I remember Ziggy stopped helping him in 1965."

"This is so fascinating! And how can you be so sure about the year, Mabel?"

"That was the year of René's heart attack, when everyone thought he was going to die. You can't forget a date like that!"

"No, but it was strange about Ziggy."

"Ooh, you want to hear something strange about Ziggy? You'll like this story, I'll bet." Mabel related how, after Allard's hospitalization and subsequent recovery, Ziggy would come to 4B to assist Hennie more frequently than before with various requests, like moving a piece of furniture or carrying a heavy carton. Not many people were aware of it, but Hennie almost left René after his heart attack. Jacobus was surprised to hear this and inquired if Mabel knew why. She wasn't sure but thought it might have had to do with him divesting himself of his famous violin without consulting Hennie first. After all, Mabel explained, Hennie had been his business associate as much as his lover over the years. In any event, Ziggy was happy to do favors for her. He was smitten with her, but so was everyone.

"One afternoon, in the summer of 1965—that was the year of the heat wave—I was in Hennie's apartment. We were just having an aperitif—a Campari, or was it Cinzano?—and chatting, but it was so hot Hennie decided to take a shower. I stayed out on the balcony with my drink. Then the doorbell rang. It was Ziggy, who was delivering some groceries that Hennie had ordered but forgot about. Hennie was wearing only her bathrobe when she answered the door, and it was open almost all the way down to the sash and her hair was all wet. She didn't care she was half naked. It was hot and she was French. Well, Ziggy couldn't take his eyes off of Hennie's cleavage, which was at his eye level. Ziggy's head started sweating. Hennie knew why and it made her smile. She was so sexy at that time. She's still sexy now even though she's sixty. But Ziggy mistook her smile. He thought she was trying to seduce him by having him bring the groceries and with her all exposed and René gone. So he drops the bags and just grabs her and pulls her robe open and starts kissing her breasts as the grapefruits go rolling all over the floor. He didn't realize I was on the balcony. At first Hennie was so surprised, but then she burst out laughing, saying, 'Oh, Krinkelmeier, the shiny little head,' and then, I couldn't help it, I started laughing too. Ziggy immediately realized he had made a fool of himself and ran out. And that was the last time Ziggy ever went to 4B."

Jacobus thought, uncharitably, that Ziggy had literally been in over his head. Poor guy, he only wanted a life and made the mistake of trying too hard.

"How did you like that one?" Mabel said, whispering in Jacobus's ear. "How'd *you* like a shiny little head?" She put her bony hand between his legs and squeezed.

Jacobus jumped up and pretended to wheeze. "Cat! Can't breathe!" he choked. "Can't breathe! Need air. Damn! Wish I could stay." And, miraculously overcoming his arthritis, ran out.

TWENTY-FIVE

Jacobus sat in the waiting room of the law office of Phoebe Swallow, trying to ignore the insipid Muzak. "Waiting" room was the appropriate term—Swallow kept him sitting there for a half hour. No matter, Jacobus thought. At least it'll allow me to work on the mental jigsaw puzzle.

He could not dismiss the conclusion that René Allard and Hennie had engaged in a smuggling racket dealing in good, but not great, violins with the specific intention of flying under the radar. According to Novak, the instruments were made by reputable contemporary Italian luthiers. They would of course be in mint condition and sound fine, and there would be no question of authenticity. In a nutshell, they were eminently marketable and quickly disposed of. The result would be a steady stream of income, more so, Jacobus reasoned, if it was quietly made known to the buyer that the instrument had been in the possession of the inimitable René Allard. Quite enough extra stash, on top of Allard's performance fees, to massage his ultra-extravagant lifestyle. Ziggy had been a middleman—maybe just one of a cadre of middlemen—and pocketed enough of a cut to have kept his mouth shut, year after year. Perhaps there were others as well,

Jacobus thought. Others he already knew. Maybe Fuente, maybe the guy Zipolito, may he rest in peace. Jacobus determined to check that out also, if there was time, but that could all wait. It was important only if it somehow connected with Allard's murder.

He was increasingly confident the pictures Ziggy had hidden from Malachi were instrument photos, a common accompaniment to certificates, and that Oehlschlager's name on Novak's certificates served as a cover to keep Allard's and Ziggy's names out of the picture. Jacobus wondered yet again what, if anything, he had said to Ziggy in Salt Lake City that had triggered a tragic chain of events, or whether the attempt on his own life was somehow related to the end of Ziggy's.

And Rose Grimes? At some point she became involved. Until Jacobus had pieced together the tidbits he had unearthed from Novak and Mabel, he could not have assumed this, but now it appeared that she either was aware of the smuggling or somehow took advantage of that knowledge and stole the Garimberti from either Allard or Ziggy. Maybe Grimes even tried blackmail, threatening to reveal them. In any event, when Ziggy and perhaps Allard found out what Rose knew, they planted the music in her purse to trump up a reason to get her fired, because they of course couldn't go to the authorities. Formally accusing Grimes of stealing or extortion would risk their own exposure, potentially putting a quick and painful damper on their activities. Did the smuggling, if it actually took place, have anything to do with Allard's murder?

And now there was the Lavender factor! Was he somehow involved in all this? Was his presence in the fourth-floor corridor just before Allard's murder purely a coincidence? Pianists have

amazingly strong hands. Even the diminutive Alicia de Larrocha
had a handshake like steel. Could Lavender have twisted Allard's
neck into a string of taffy and vanished before BTower arrived on
the scene?

How this all led to the murder of Allard and BTower's in-
volvement or noninvolvement, Ziggy's suicide, and the attempt
on his own life was still murky. At least Jacobus now had a trail
that was sufficiently strong to coerce Phoebe Swallow, Hennie's
attorney, to agree to a meeting at her office. There might be a
statute of limitations on some crimes, Jacobus warned Swallow,
but the IRS would not take kindly to twenty years of tax evasion.

"*Allo,* Jake," said Hennie, placing her hand in his. "It has been a
long time, no?"

Her voice, as always, was bell-like and seductive. Jacobus let
go of her hand, as soft and alluring as the Parisian perfume she
wore, that clung to his just long enough to be suggestive. Jacobus
had no way of knowing whether Hennie's physical beauty had
declined, but her voice was still that of a twenty-year-old. If Swallow, at that precise moment, hadn't intervened in a poorly considered attempt to protect her client who needed no protection,
he might have dropped his case there and then. Idiot lawyer, he
thought, you just blew it.

"My client will make a statement," said Swallow, "and you will
then understand how you have completely misconstrued what you
claim as evidence of fraud." They sat down around a conference
table, Jacobus on one side, the two women on the other. "After
that it will of course be your option what to do. If you make the
unwise choice to pursue your harassment of my client, it will

then of course be our option to file slander charges against you. Is that clear?"

"I just have one question."

"Oh?"

"Do you have any mouthwash?"

"Why?"

"Because what comes out of your mouth is offensive."

He heard Hennie stifle a chuckle.

"It's okay, Phoebe," Hennie said. "Let me tell you the whole story, Jake."

"No legal gobbledygook?"

"No, Jake," she said, a smile in her voice, "no gobbledygook. Then I hope you will understand. It's not so evil as you think."

Hennie explained that the violinists in René's heyday were glamorous matinee idols, and not just figuratively. They actually starred in movies to complement their concertizing.

"But, you see, instead of sneaker manufacturers paying them millions and millions of dollars to wear their shoes, like Michael Jordan, instrument makers would clamor to have their instruments played by people like René, or Heifetz, or Fritz Kreisler. It would be a great shot in the arm for their reputations and for their careers. But the dilemma arose for us when the luthiers wanted to actually give their violins to René for free. Yes, of course they would lose a little money for the moment—after all, a violin takes only three or four weeks to make—but in the long run it was a profitable marketing tool for them. You know, 'If it's good enough for René Allard, it's good enough for anybody.' But René, who was such an idealist, he didn't want anyone to think he was playing favorites or was being bribed, so he insisted, absolutely insisted, on paying the luthiers the cost of making the violin, plus he would throw in a little gift to the courier to make the long trip worthwhile.

"So, you see, Jake," Hennie professed fervently, "René had only the best intentions for his actions. It was all totally innocent. One hundred percent."

"Well, that's the buying part," said Jacobus, thinking about the mysterious foreigner with the limp, "but what about the selling?"

"The ground rules," interrupted Swallow, "are that we are not entertaining questions."

"Don't worry," said Jacobus, "you're not entertaining in any way."

"It's all right, Phoebe," said Hennie. "I have no problem to answer Mr. Jacobus's question.

"You can imagine, Jake, the cost of buying all those instruments, and René, he had no intention of performing with them. They were good, but they were not Stradivari or Guarneri, and the cost all adds up just the same. And where would we keep them? In our closets? After all, New York apartments are not so spacious. And then there would have been the insurance on all those violins. And, René, you knew how busy René was on the concert tour. How could he have time to dispose of violins? Just selling one could take months. So he would ask his friends—"

"Like Ziggy," Jacobus said. Why not Dedubian? he asked himself.

"Yes, like Ziggy, who knew lots of people, to find buyers. And of course, René did not want to impose upon their friendship, so it was only natural that he would give his friends a small monetary gift for their trouble. So you see, Jake, there is nothing so nefarious here as you thought. Do you see?"

"How many violins, Hennie? Total."

"Ms. Henrique does not—"

"I would like to say about two hundred, maybe a few more, Jake," said Hennie. "That may sound like a lot, I know that. But remember it was over many, many years. I never knew who the buyers were or else I would of course tell you."

"Was one of the fences Rose Grimes?"

"We object," said Swallow, "to the use of the term 'fence' to represent my client's acquaintances."

"Was one of the acquaintances Rose Grimes?" asked Jacobus.

"You mean the cleaning girl?" Hennie laughed. "Now you're being silly, Jake. What could someone in her station do for us?"

"What is it she stole from René?"

"Oo-la-la! So you know about that! It was his most precious possession, Jake. It was his music to 'Danse Macabre,' signed by Saint-Saëns himself when René performed it for him as a boy. You're a musician. Only musicians can know how much those things mean."

"Was another of the acquaintances Virgil Lavender?" he asked.

"Jake, I am astonished at you!"

"I'm flattered, but what about Lavender? No way René could've paid him what he would have otherwise gotten in soloist fees."

"Perhaps, Jake."

"Just count the hours, Hennie. The recitals, the rehearsals, the travel, the students he accompanied at lessons. Did René pay by the hour, or what?"

"It was 'or what.' He gave Virgil a salary—a retainer, you might call it."

"And who actually paid him, Hennie, you or René?"

"What do you mean?"

"You were the business end of Allard Enterprises. Weren't you? Did René ever see the inside of a checkbook?"

"So I made the checks. Yes, it is true that Virgil maybe did not become wealthy by us. But we paid him fairly. He never complained and he loved René."

"Did Lavender go to the soirée the night René died?"

"Of course! Wait, no, he never did arrive. I can't remember. The party had just begun, people were still coming, and then . . . And then everyone had to leave. But that has nothing to do with the violins, and believe me, Virgil had nothing to do with the violins."

"Did the sale of the ex Hawkins have anything to do with the violins?" he asked.

"The ex Hawkins? That is a totally different story," said Hennie. Her voice, to Jacobus's trained ear, subtly but suddenly lost its luster. "I'm not going to talk about that."

"Mr. Jacobus," said Phoebe Swallow, "my client knows neither to whom the violin was sold, nor why, and I have another meeting. However, before you leave, Ms. Henrique has a gift for you in consideration of your long friendship."

Swallow pushed something from her side of the table over to Jacobus. He felt it. It was some sort of thick document, over a foot long, almost equally wide, enclosed in a plastic sheath.

"What's this, Hennie? A 1960 *Playboy* with you on the cover?"

Hennie didn't respond.

"Something even more valuable than that, Mr. Jacobus," said Swallow. "We understand Beethoven is one of your favorite composers, Mr. Jacobus, and Ms. Henrique thought you'd appreciate this more than anyone. It's a first edition of the Beethoven Violin Concerto, signed by René, signed previously by the great nineteenth-century virtuoso Joseph Joachim, signed by the violinist Franz Clement on December 23, 1806, the date he premiered the concerto, and signed by Beethoven himself."

Jacobus allowed his hands to linger on the music. It would probably be the closest he would ever come to immortality. If he was mercenary, he could sell it for tens of thousands of dollars. Jacobus departed, leaving the treasure on the table, wondering whether Hennie was capable of murder and thinking that she was wearing more perfume than she used to.

TWENTY-SIX

An hour later Jacobus was seated at the bar at Boynton's Steaks and Chops, nursing a Johnny Walker Black, double, to settle his nerves. He had chosen the location for several reasons. First, it was close to the Columbus Circle station, which he would next be visiting. Second, it was not the kind of watering hole musicians would frequent. Dingy, smoky, and generally uninviting, it was the appropriate place for him to deliver an unwanted message. He knew a fight was in the offing and he didn't want it to spill over into the public domain. He would have preferred a better solution, but time had just about run out.

After leaving Swallow's office, he had called Nathaniel and asked him to call Sheila Rathman at InHouseArtists, then call him back. In the meantime, Jacobus himself called Martin

Lilburn, the music critic who, at the urging of his readers, had been reinstated at the *New York Times,* having previously resigned from his long-held position, part of the fallout from the Piccolino Strad fiasco. Then Nathaniel had called him back.

"I impersonated a concert series presenter," he explained.

"Shameful," said Jacobus.

"Yeah, I suppose. But I got what you want."

Jacobus heard the door to the bar squeak open, felt an onrush of hot, smelly air from the city pavement, and heard steps moving toward him faster than someone merely just craving a brewskie. He took a last swig of his scotch.

"Here you are, Jacobus," said Virgil Lavender.

"Hello, Virgil. Drink?"

"I'll pass. What's all this cloak-and-dagger stuff? What's with this dive? I'm freaked enough having to get ready for this recital without having to take time off from practicing."

"Why didn't you tell anyone you were in the hallway moments before Allard was murdered?"

Jacobus waited for a response. And waited. Would it be the answer he sought? He heard the ceiling fan spinning, easy listening FM on the radio, tables being set in the restaurant, the bus pulling away from the curb. But not a sound from Lavender. Would he just turn around and walk out?

"I had nothing to do with it," Lavender said.

"You better tell me about it."

"I went to the party. At least, I tried to go to the party. Jacobus, try to imagine what it felt like. It was like waking up from a thirty-year dream. I had played with the greatest violinist of the century and he was leaving the next day. But I was staying. For what? It was like purgatory. I knew I had to say good-bye, so I forced myself to go to the party. My legs could hardly move. I got to the door of his apartment. I didn't know he hadn't arrived yet. I thought he was there. I thought once I got through the door everything would be okay. It would be another René and Hennie show, all laughs, all bubbly. But I couldn't. I couldn't knock. I just stood there like an idiot. And then I left. I guess you could call me a coward. But you can't call me a murderer. I wouldn't have harmed a hair on René's head. I loved that man."

"No resentment? No grudge?"

"Grudge? For what?"

"I understand your career's on the skids. That your concert calendar is almost totally open for the foreseeable future. That you're paying the expenses for your Carnegie recital out of your own pocket. That, as a result of all your years with Allard, your own playing is considered to have no individuality. No personality."

"Where did you hear that?"

"They call you Mr. Osfa—'one size fits all'—behind your back. Though I'm told you've heard that yourself."

"Jealousy, that's all."

"Or the review that said when the two of you played together, Allard was the sun and you were moon, your light merely a reflection of his. Or the one that said you fit Allard like a glove, but since he died you're a glove without a hand. I'm sure you've read those reviews. No grudge?"

"After thirty years, who reads reviews? I'm telling you. No grudge."

"How about an alibi? Do you have one of those?"

"For your information, I don't. I left the Bonderman. Alone. I went home. Alone. And I cried. Alone. And I think you've played detective more than enough. BTower killed René. It's been proved and that's the end of it. Good-bye, Jacobus. I wish you well."

Jacobus heard the footsteps recede and the door open, felt the hot, smelly air rush in, and heard the door close with finality. He felt even worse than he had expected.

"Give me another double."

TWENTY-SEVEN

"Hold, Mortal, lest thou will surely perish!" said the voice.

"You can knock it off, Drumstick Man," said Jacobus. "I've heard the spiel, and I'm in a hurry."

"Ah! 'Tis Gloucester from the terranean sphere. 'O brave new world, that has such people in 't!'"

"I come on a quest," Jacobus improvised. "A noble quest, for which I need my Sancho Panza."

"Sancho *who*?"

"Never mind. I need your help."

After Jacobus got the kiss-off from Lavender he called Nathaniel again, who was on his way to meet with the VA administrator in person because that was the only way they'd provide the information he needed about the catatonic in Grimes's apartment.

"Who're you going to impersonate this time?" Jacobus asked Nathaniel. "Freud?"

"I don't believe he was African American," said Nathaniel, "and I haven't worked on the accent for a while. I was thinking more of an adjuster investigating outstanding health insurance claims."

Jacobus hung up laughing. He envied Nathaniel's affable indefatigability and wished he had been blessed with the quality of patience.

Through a thickening haze of blended scotch, Jacobus had come up with a scheme of his own that now brought him back to Drumstick Man. Though he recognized it had little likelihood of success, he reasoned that if he could get Ziggy's photos of the violins—the ones *with* the pinholes—he could use that as evidence to contradict Hennie's explanation of innocent under-the-counter buying and selling, because having the photos demonstrated intent to profit. He shuddered to think that charming Hennie might have had something to do with Ziggy's disappearance or with the attempt on his own life. With Ziggy dead and with access to his apartment sealed off, Jacobus had decided that a look from below would be his last hope to get the photos, if they were there. Almost literally, it was a shot in the dark.

As Drumstick Man tapped happily with his sticks, Jacobus explained where the Bonderman Building was located in the "terranean world." Aboveground, where it was hot, sunny, and bustling, the building was only a few blocks away, but Drumstick Man no longer had a concept of a grid. The shadowy, serpentine tracks of abandoned New York were his only guide. Here, in the chill, damp, dim underground, Jacobus could only suggest it was about a ten-minute radius by foot from where they were and that recently there had been major construction to reinforce the basement with steel girders, tons of cement. Maybe the noise of the construction—

Jacobus felt his hand grasped by Drumstick Man's. It was like a steel vise. "I know this place of which you speak. Let us tarry not," he said. " 'Screw your courage to the sticking-place, and we'll not fail. Into the breach we go!' "

Using Drumstick Man's ceaseless tattoo as a guide, Jacobus was soon enveloped by the catacombs of New York City. He limped along as they traversed abandoned track beds, station platforms, and creaking catwalks, escorted always by the conspiratorial skittering of rats. They climbed flights of crumbling cement stairs whose railings had rusted off.

"Keep your hand to the wall lest ye plummet!"

The sound in the three-dimensional labyrinth had an eerie dreamlike quality. Jacobus could not pinpoint the location of the distant rumble of trains, an occasional teasing honk from the world above, the incessant dripping. It was almost like being underwater. There was also the rancid pungency of rotting garbage, and always of mold and decay.

"Step high here, man."

"Third rail?" asked Jacobus.

"Dead cat."

At one point the sound of what could have been distant voices barely infringed on his consciousness. Was it a human sound? Whispering? Or just tepid air being sucked out of the tunnel by the movement of a distant train? He stopped to listen more carefully.

"You hear it too?" asked Drumstick Man.

"What is it?" asked Jacobus.

"The Denizens of the Darkness. The Gatherers. No other. We best be moving apace."

They rounded a bend.

"Off with the shoes now, mate," said Drumstick Man.

"You must be kidding," said Jacobus.

"To ford the River Styx, mate. Don't want shit in no shoes, do we now?"

They waded shin deep in their bare feet through the mucky effluence of the underworld rivulet. Regaining the far shore of the accidental canal, Jacobus was retying his shoelaces when his guide proclaimed, "How now? A rat?" and he recoiled in response to an ungodly screech followed by a plop in the mucky water.

" 'Dead for a ducat, dead!' " announced Drumstick Man triumphantly. "No need for alarm. Just need to wipe off me little spear."

They arrived at a massive steel door embedded in a seemingly endless wall.

"Eureka!" Drumstick Man exclaimed.

"Pray thee, how the hell can you be so sure? Perchance we're at the Garden of the Square of Madison."

The door had no handle and opened out. Jacobus, feeling along its surface for a fingerhold, was baffled how they would open it.

"Fear not, doubter. Trust in the magic stick."

Jacobus heard Drumstick Man probe with his stick. He had assumed it was a wooden stick, but now he clearly heard the rasp of metal on metal as Drumstick Man sought the door's Achilles' heel. Finally finding the spot, he used the stick as a lever.

"Put your shoulder to it, man!" he said to Jacobus. They both pushed against the stick with all their weight. Within moments the door surrendered, its heavy weight scraping along the rough cement floor, giving way just enough to snake through.

There was no question they were in a basement. Jacobus recalled the general layout of Basement Two from his visit there almost two years earlier, and began to reconnoiter by feel. Girders springing from every direction, like a monstrous monkey bar apparatus, blocked his way.

"It's a damn Eiffel Tower in here," he said. For a moment he was uncertain they were in the right place but then realized that the steel maze was the extensive infrastructure that had been constructed to support the new elevator above.

"I know not this edifice of which you speak, but verily 'tis a pain in the ass."

When Jacobus was a little kid, he went to a birthday party where they had a game in which each kid, blindfolded, had to guess the object put in his hands. It could be anything from a green pepper to one of those foot-long stuffed alligators they used to sell. Since his blindness, he had played this guessing game over and over. It was part of his life, and now he was playing it once again. Nearest the door through which they had entered he fumbled his way past the extinct incinerator, then the old furnace, then the abandoned elevator entrance, the obsolete massive washing machines and dryers, the utility room—where he literally kicked the bucket—and the dressing room, where he again tripped over a wooden crate and, reaching out to right himself, tore the skin off his fingertip on the end of a wire screen mesh around head height—all the while ducking under and climbing over the gargantuan metal lattice.

Ah! Finally! The apartment! Jacobus turned the knob. Locked.

"Put your shoulder to it, man!" Jacobus said to Drumstick Man, and began leaning into the door.

"No need, kind sir," said Drumstick Man. "Never has mere lock met my match."

Within moments, the door clicked open.

Entering the apartment, Jacobus felt for the desk, opened drawers, searched for photos with pinholes. Photos of smuggled violins. Suddenly there was a clank and a bang from inside the apartment. He straightened up.

"Just a bit of foraging, fair prince," said Drumstick Man. " 'Man does not live by bread alone.' Sometimes he must also have canned goods."

"That's not Shakespeare," said Jacobus. "That's Deuteronomy."

"Well," mused Drumstick Man. "Almost as good."

"You smell something? Other than your own hide?" asked Jacobus. There was the remnant of something in the air, neither the general fetid underground must, nor the moldy odor of an abandoned apartment, nor the smell of dust-encrusted oil on the obsolete incinerator and furnace.

"We reside not in Denmark, but perchance 'tis rotten?"

"Forget it," said Jacobus, and returned to his search. He uncovered no photos, though he did find a small locked metal box. He shook it. It could be photos. Maybe not, but it was the best he could do. Together they left, the blind man and the crazy man, each bearing his treasure.

Jacobus paced all over Nathaniel's apartment, waiting for his return. If the box contained the violin photos it would convince

him there was something fishy going on. He could take them to
Dedubian, who could trace the owners, and then he'd be able to
ID more of the middlemen who were part of Allard and Hennie's
grand scheme. No doubt, if there were others like Gottfried and
Rose Grimes—and at this point it was clear to him that Rose was
involved; violins don't just show up on your doorstep, especially
the kind that Gottfried was fencing—a compelling motive for
murder would emerge. His attempts to open the metal box had
proved futile. He had tried prying it open, picking the lock,
throwing it against the wall several times, all ineffectual.

Jacobus heard the key in the door. Before he could open his
mouth, Nathaniel said, "Jake, have I got news for you!"

"Yeah?" he said hurriedly. Jacobus was not anticipating that
anything from Nathaniel would be of equal import to the contents of his box. "What've you got?"

"Well, first of all I got all those hand and arm measurements
you wanted from Malachi. He also did measurements on Allard's
right arm as well as his left, chest, and everything else. I think you
finally got to him." Nathaniel had written it all down and he
slapped his pad onto the table for Jacobus to hear. Then, to reward
himself, he went to the fridge, got out last night's chow mein, and
put it in a pan on the stove. He said over his shoulder to Jacobus,
"Malachi said it sounded like you were thinking of ordering a new
shirt."

"I'd like to take a little of the starch out of Malachi's, and before you go ahead and stuff yourself, measure me," said Jacobus.

Nathaniel nosed around in the drawer next to his sink for the
measuring tape he knew he had put there once upon a time, and
actually found it. Jacobus got down on his knees, approximating

Allard's death position as he had done in his room at the Waltz Rite Inn in Salt Lake City, and Nathaniel extended Jacobus's left arm the distance Malachi had reported, then did the same for the distances between the fingers, altering the angle of his arm as determined according to the specifications, gradually working his way all the way down to Jacobus's feet. Jacobus still wasn't sure what to make of the bewilderingly complex arrangement of his limbs and joints, except to note that they were aching. The only thing that felt familiar was the orientation of his left hand.

"First position?" Jacobus muttered as he rose stiffly to his feet, dusting off his pants. "Why don't you sweep your floor sometime?" he said to Nathaniel. "Any other good tidings you want to share?"

Nathaniel had patched together bits of information from the VA hospital and the hospital where BTower had been born that by themselves were seemingly innocuous data, but put together were potentially explosive.

"It wasn't that difficult, really," he said. "It seems that Shelby Freeman Junior—aka BTower—was born in March of '66, five months after Shelby Senior returned from Vietnam. Junior's was a normal, no-complications full-term delivery. Shelby Senior was listed on the birth certificate as the father. Problem is, not only was the five months not long enough for Rose to become pregnant and have a child by Senior, according to medical records at the VA, Senior, as a result of his war injuries, was totally incapable of inseminating anyone by any means whatsoever, even with Rose's alleged assistance.

"What this means," said Nathaniel, "is that Shelby Freeman Senior no way can be the father of Shelby Freeman Junior."

"What this means," bellowed Jacobus, "is she lied again!" He was not so much surprised as he was simply frustrated and discouraged. Who BTower's father was at this point was anyone's guess. And he had no idea whether it had anything to do with anything.

Nathaniel asked Jacobus what information he had gathered.

"Shit, I don't even know," he said.

In a nutshell he related to Nathaniel his underground excursion with Drumstick Man. Then he showed him the metal box. Nathaniel got out a hammer and a screwdriver. The small lock was no match for his bulky strength. With one whack it was off.

"So what do we got?" asked Jacobus. "Baseball cards, love letters, or violin photos with pinholes?"

"Oh, dear," Nathaniel said. "Oh, my Lord!"

"Well, are we going to share?" asked Jacobus. "Are they photos or what?"

"Yeah, Jake, they're photos," Nathaniel said. "And with thumbtack holes. But not of violins. They're photos of Rose. Old ones."

"Rose?"

"In these here she's taking her clothes off. And in these . . . Jake, in these she's being assaulted. By René Allard. There's no doubt."

Jacobus was stunned. Allard! Ziggy! What could Ziggy have been doing with these photos? And tacked up on his wall! Assuming it was Ziggy who shot them with his trusty Leica, was he in cahoots with Allard to photograph his victim? Were they that perverted? And maybe there had been more than one victim! How long had this gone on? A thought jolted Jacobus. The date! Could Allard be the father of BTower?

Jacobus asked Nathaniel. He checked the dates on the backs of the photos, just as Malachi had done with the unpinned ones. Ziggy had been true to form. These were from 1964, too early, they determined, for the attack to have caused the pregnancy that led to BTower's birth. There could have been later attacks, certainly, but there were no later photos.

"That doesn't mean there weren't any," Nathaniel cautioned. "Just that they weren't in the box."

Jacobus asked Nathaniel what was in the background of the pictures. Maybe they could figure out where they had been taken.

"Well, it's a weird angle. There's only the upper parts of their bodies, almost a bird's-eye view, but not quite. And there's blurriness."

"Out of focus?"

"Yes and no. There's a pattern. Kind of like they were taken through something gridlike. Maybe a window with little panes."

Jacobus felt the bile rise in his gut. He knew he would have to ask, though it made him sick to do so.

"Nathaniel, you've got to describe the pictures. I need to know."

Nathaniel took a deep breath and, in sequence, described the photos, slapping them angrily on the table, one at a time, like cards of a losing hand.

In the earliest dated pictures Rose was alone.

"She's taking off or putting on her street clothes or work outfits in these," Nathaniel said. "The work outfits are all the same, plain white industrial-style dresses, but the street clothes seem to vary depending on the season."

"Which suggests they were taken over an extended period of time," Jacobus speculated.

"Yeah, I suppose. Some she's got a coat and hat hanging up. Others just a sweater, but whoever took the photos was more interested in what she wasn't wearing than what she was."

"Is there any chance she's posing?"

"Nah," said Nathaniel. "She's oblivious.

"Here are the nasty ones with Allard. It looks like they were shot all in one sequence. First, here's Allard grabbing the top of Rose's dress and pulling it apart. Second, Rose is struggling. There's anger. And fear. Third, Allard's ripped Rose's clothes off. He's squeezing her breasts. He's pushing her against a wall. He's pressing himself against her. He's taller than Rose. His head is angled down, forcing his lips against hers. Rose is trying to turn her head away. Allard is pushing his body against hers. She's pinned against the wall. She's trying to push him off. Her eyes are closed.

"That's it," said Nathaniel. "It's too much."

Jacobus was staggered. Who was this person, René Allard, whom the world had revered? Whom he thought he knew? Could he be this monster? What did this all mean? Did Rose murder Allard out of revenge? Could she have been capable? Could Ziggy's complicity in this outrage have been the reason for his suicide?

Jacobus and Nathaniel sat in silence, trying to fathom the meaning of it all. Finally, Nathaniel called Malachi and told him what they had. Malachi listened quietly, simply making some grunts of recognition from time to time.

"I'll call Brown," he said when Nathaniel finished. "One

thing I want to make clear: I'm not on your side yet regarding
BTower. You might even have just put the last nail in his coffin."

"Meaning?"

"Being the son of Grimes. If a crime of this magnitude was
committed and the victim was even tenuously connected to the
deaths of its perpetrator and his accomplice . . . Well, you can
finish the sentence. But let's just say I'm willing to keep the conversation going."

"Damn," said Nathaniel as Malachi hung up. He ran to the
stove, where the chow mein had burned in the pan, and in a rare
display of anger hurled it into the sink. "Not that I could eat it
anyway at this point," he said. He put the photos back in the box,
then he and Jacobus took yet another drive to Harlem.

TWENTY-EIGHT

Traffic was heavy and the cars were honking. The Yankees must
have beaten the Red Sox again. But with Nathaniel inching
through the gridlock, Jacobus had time to try to piece things together. There had been so many lies. So many secrets. The number of questions was escalating with dizzying frequency, the
number of answers was still hovering around zero, and the number of days left in BTower's life was down to one. Did Rose and
BTower conspire to murder Allard, who, as far as Jacobus was
concerned, deserved no less? Or did Rose do it herself? Or did
BTower, to avenge his mother? Who was BTower's father? Was
Shelby Freeman Sr. truly incommunicado with the outside world,

or was he faking? Was the man in the wheelchair in fact Shelby Freeman Sr.? And where oh where did Sigmund Gottfried fit into all this? Ziggy the humble courier, he with the Leica. And what did any of this have to do with Hennie and smuggled and stolen violins?

Yet again they stumbled up the dark stairs. Nathaniel knocked on Rose Grimes's door. "Mrs. Grimes," said Nathaniel, "we need to talk to you."

There was no answer. Maybe she was asleep. It was late. Even so, it was a hot night outside and Jacobus heard the fan on in the apartment. Nathaniel knocked again. "Please open the door."

Still silence. Nathaniel said to Jacobus, "Wild-goose chase. Let's go."

Jacobus put his face to the door and said quietly so as not to rouse any hostile neighbors, "Rose, I know you're in there. I smell the food. I smell the chicken soup. It may be the one thing we have in common, but I would recommend dill instead of parsley. Open up."

"Go away," she said. "I'll call the police."

"You do that," Jacobus said. "And you can explain how you stole a violin from René Allard. You stole it because you were going to sell it to help pay for your invalid husband's care, didn't you? Hey, I can understand that. But it didn't end up working out that way, did it? Rose, we know what Allard did to you, and it wasn't just getting you fired from your job. We know the real reason you killed him."

Jacobus heard Rose start to cry softly.

" 'Fear ye not the reproach of men,' " he heard her say, " 'neither be ye afraid of their revilings.' "

"The second irony, Rose, is that after Shelby Junior began playing the violin, you just couldn't bear to sell it. Isn't that right, Rose? You had to choose between your husband's life and your son's future. But then there was the argument with your son and you destroyed the violin, but you never filed an insurance claim on it because you had stolen it, and collecting the money would expose what you had done. And the third and last terrible irony is that when you killed Allard, BTower took the blame for the murder. He took the blame to protect you, even though with your zealous religious fervor you still couldn't forgive him for having renounced God. You refused to go to your son's aid. Isn't that the way it happened, Rose? Isn't that the truth you've been hiding from us?"

"You know nothing," she said in a voice hardly above a whisper. "Nothing. Now please leave."

Jacobus heard Rose's staggering, shuffling retreat from the other side of the door and had a hasty, whispered conference with Nathaniel.

"Knock down the door," Jacobus whispered to Nathaniel. "And haul her down to Malachi."

"Jake, if we did that, even if she was guilty, breaking into the apartment of an old lady with an invalid husband would give her the sympathy vote and could just as soon land us in jail."

"But there's no time to wait anymore, dammit. The execution is tomorrow morning, and with Grimes in custody there might be a chance it'd be temporarily stayed."

"You're forgetting, a confession from Rose won't necessarily help BTower. If anything, like Malachi said, it could incriminate him even further."

"Ah, fuck it. You're right."

Nathaniel spoke to Grimes through the door. "We'll go now, but we'll have to come back. I'm sorry, but we will be back with the police. Soon."

Nathaniel opted that they go back to his apartment, but Jacobus was afraid Grimes would flee, even if it meant leaving her invalid husband behind. He proposed standing vigil outside her building. Nathaniel told him he was crazy—the chances of him being mugged that late at night far exceeded the chances of her taking off. They compromised. There was an all-night diner on the corner from which Nathaniel would be able to keep an eye on the building. From there, they would call Malachi on Nathaniel's cell phone.

They crossed the darkened street, the traffic light turning from green to red and back again. The only traffic was the occasional cab searching for fares, like fireflies flittering through the night. Flanked on one side by Cinnamon Buns, a boarded-up nightclub sporting a graffitied poster advertising an all-black, all-girl revue, and on the other side by the humble yellow brick First Church of African Liberation, the outline of the '50s vintage diner was obscured in darkness. Only the dim light from within and the faulty red neon sign that said DI ER allowed it to emerge from hiding.

"Menu, gentlemen?" asked the slow-speaking waiter, after they seated themselves in a corner booth from which Nathaniel had a direct line of sight to the apartment building. They were the only customers.

"We got a special. Beans and franks. Four ninety-nine."

"Any other specials?" asked Jacobus.

"Yeah. Beans or franks."

"I'll have the beans and franks," said Jacobus.

"Make that two," said Nathaniel.

"Good choice, gentlemen. Drink?"

"Coffee."

"Comin' right up."

Jacobus borrowed Nathaniel's phone and dialed Malachi's number. He answered on the first ring.

"You always at your desk, Malachi?" asked Jacobus.

"Occasionally I do take a bathroom break. Is that why you called?"

Jacobus filled him in on what had transpired. Malachi was furious that the two of them were taking the law into their own hands, and warned that if they continued to interfere, any chances they might have to save BTower would go down the toilet. Jacobus argued that if it hadn't been for them, nothing would have been done in the first place.

"You think so, Jacobus?" said Malachi. "Well, it happens that I've just had an enlightening conversation with the Davis County, Utah, police."

Malachi then regurgitated a seminar on the geological history of the Great Salt Lake that he'd just heard from Detective Baylor Minnion of the DCPD.

"Skip the overture," said Jacobus. "You're curing my insomnia."

Minnion had explained that something was weird about Gottfried's alleged suicide.

"Alleged?" asked Jacobus.

"That's what I said," said Malachi. "Turns out he might've been offed. Listen to what Minnion told me.

"First of all, the Great Salt Lake fluctuates greatly. No one knows exactly why, but in any event it's not very deep. Lately it's been especially shallow, so someone would have to walk about a quarter mile from shore before the water would be up to his armpits. But the main thing, which just about everyone knows from the picture in their elementary school social studies book, is that the Great Salt Lake is so salty that you'd have to chain yourself to a lead weight in order to sink, and it wouldn't be very practical to carry a lead weight a quarter mile. If Gottfried killed himself, in Minnion's opinion he couldn't have done it near the Avalon. That meant that either he parked the car there and walked a long way from it to go kill himself—unlikely. Or he killed himself somewhere else and then someone else moved the car—possible. Or someone forced him to write the note, then abducted or killed him—probable. Minnion assured me that at this point he was investigating all possibilities. I guess they're not total rubes out there.

"Go home, Jacobus. Nathaniel's right. Rose Grimes isn't going anywhere. In any event, there's no evidence to arrest her for anything." Malachi told them he would follow up and even thanked them for their efforts.

The waiter, who had courteously waited until Jacobus hung up, brought their meals. The beans were spicy and the franks crisp, and the meal came with fresh corn bread. Jacobus, who had had no appetite for days, ate with unanticipated relish. He sensed they were near a resolution, though with the new mystery

surrounding Gottfried's death, he had no idea what that would
be. The two of them threw around countless theories and sce-
narios as they ate.

"Maybe someone had been stalking Gottfried at the concert,"
Nathaniel said and suggested they call Yumi. "She went to the
Markner concert. Maybe she saw something."

Jacobus was reluctant. He would have to tell her what had happened to Gottfried, and thinking about her unsavory encounter
with Kortovsky in her quartet, he felt she already had enough on
her plate to deal with. Nathaniel suggested Jacobus might want to
ask her how that was going anyway, to find out how she was doing,
so Jacobus ended up agreeing to the call. They calculated she was
at the Sunriver Music Festival in Oregon, where the time was
three hours earlier, and after making a few inquiries were connected to the home of Yumi's hosts.

Yumi said she was delighted to hear from them. For Jacobus
to actually be calling her was an unaccustomed honor.

Jacobus began by asking how the concerts were going and
gradually got to the issue of the harassment she had experienced.
Yumi reported that she had had no further incidents and would
take Jacobus's advice if anything happened.

"And you can just tell that creep, Kortovsky," Jacobus said,
"to keep his hands off you or I'll cut his balls off."

Yumi laughed. "I'll be sure to do that, Jake. I'm sure that will
do the trick."

Jacobus then had to broach the bad news about Gottfried.
Yumi was saddened, but as he had been only a peripheral personality in her life, his death didn't have a deep emotional im-
pact on her. She asked if there was anything she could do.

Jacobus asked if she had seen Gottfried at the concert of the Markner Quartet, and if so, was there anyone with him? He described Gottfried but needn't have, as Yumi remembered what he looked like.

"I don't think he was there," she said. "As you know, the hall at the Garr Ranch only holds about a hundred fifty people. I'm pretty certain I would have seen him."

"But Ziggy's suicide note mentioned how hearing the G-Minor Quintet was a beautiful way to end his life."

"The G-Minor Quintet?" Yumi sounded perplexed. "There must be some mistake. They didn't play the G-Minor Quintet. Simon Baker never showed up."

"What do you mean, 'never showed up'?" asked Jacobus.

"His flight was delayed at O'Hare," said Yumi. "Thunderstorms. He couldn't make the concert, so they didn't do the Mozart quintet. Instead they did his 'Dissonance' Quartet. They said afterward they hadn't even rehearsed it for over a year, but it was incredible. I thought that's what you were talking about the last time we spoke."

"I don't believe it!" Jacobus bellowed into the phone.

"Why wouldn't I tell you the truth, Jake? His flight was delayed. He couldn't help it."

"Never mind, Yumi. Of course I believe you. It's just that every time I learn something new, it adds ten more questions. But everything's fine. Gotta go. Bye."

Jacobus slammed down the phone. He had heard about people pulling out their hair in frustration, but this was the first time he ever understood it was more than a figure of speech.

"Ziggy never went to the concert, dammit!" he said to

Nathaniel. "The suicide note had to have been written in advance. What the hell was going on with that goddamn little mole?"

How many billion neurons does the human brain have? Jacobus asked himself. Somewhere in my brain there's one damn neural pathway that can connect the information that's stored up there and arrange it in a rational pattern. Shit.

Jacobus snarfed down his last mouthful of beans and wiped his mouth with his sleeve. Suddenly he froze.

"Jesus Christ," he said, putting his hands to his head, as if to prevent it from falling off.

"Jake," Nathaniel asked, fear in his voice, "you been poisoned again?"

"Yeah, but not with cyanide. You can take your big mitts off me. I'm okay." Everything was clicking dizzyingly inside his head. "What day is today?" he asked. With this one small piece of this ghastly mosaic, the world was rearranging itself into a totally new picture.

"Tuesday. Why?"

Jacobus said there was no time to explain. He had to get back to Nathaniel's apartment to retrieve the metal box and get to Columbus Circle as fast as possible. In his agonized heart, he apologized to Rose Grimes.

TWENTY-NINE

Even before Nathaniel's Rabbit came to a skidding stop after
rounding the curve at the southwest corner of Central Park,
Jacobus had opened the door and had a leg out, metal box under
his arm.

"C'mon, Jake, let me go with you," Nathaniel pleaded.

"Just amscray and get your heinie over to Malachi," said Jacobus, slamming the door.

Even this late at night, Jacobus had to push his way through
the human congestion as he charged down the escalator into the
Columbus Circle station. He shouldered his way through
the turnstile, hobbling as fast as Grandpappy Amos in a three-
legged race in the opposite direction from humanity along a
path now familiar to him but to few others.

"Drumstick Man!" he called out into the dark. "Hey! Drumstick Man!" he repeated. "Yoo-hoo!" He heard his voice echo
back, but no other sound. He called again, but the result was un-
changed.

"Damn," he said. He pondered his alternatives, quickly deciding there weren't any. He couldn't wait. Maybe he was already
too late, so he began to retrace his underground expedition to
the Bonderman Building alone, hoping he wouldn't get irretrievably lost or attacked either by the Gatherers—whoever they
might be—or more likely by the rats.

The going was faltering and no more agreeable than the first time, but he was ambivalently reassured of his bearings when, directly in front of him, he smelled the river of ordure he had forded earlier in the day. With minutes dwindling, he forced upon himself the excruciating patience to take off his shoes and socks. As he did, he perceived what sounded like human footsteps, *sans* tapping, somewhere behind him, though with the cavernous resonance of the stone and brick surrounding him it could have come from anywhere, even from within his own imagination.

He concentrated on recollecting Drumstick Man's route, swallowing his fear of the steep stairway with no railing and its slimy, unevenly worn treads. With his left hand on the cold, clammy bedrock of Manhattan Island as his guide, he slowly and resolutely willed his way up those steps, and as he did, he heard from behind the sloshing of someone crossing the canal. Jacobus hurried his pace, his hip aching from exertion and dampness, steeling himself against the prospect of plummeting off those steps in the hope of finding a safe haven in the Bonderman basement. Hands against the side of the ancient subway wall, he felt his way through the tunnel. Finally he arrived at the massive steel door, still slightly ajar from his earlier visit with Drumstick Man. At least now he didn't have to open it with his own strength, which would have been a wasted effort. He sidled his way in, hoping that whoever was following him had lost his trail.

He groped his way through the steel maze to Gottfried's apartment, ignoring the pain of repeatedly whacking his head and body against the unyielding infrastructure. Gottfried's door was still unlocked. He prayed, to the extent he ever did, that he was in time to return the metal box to the desk where he had found it. First, though, he groped for the link chain that he recalled dangled from the ceiling light. He wasn't interested in turning on the light, of course, but only to ascertain whether the lightbulb was warm, which would indicate it had been recently used. He was hoping it was still cold. He found the chain and, holding the box under one arm, reached for the bulb with his free hand.

"Aaah!" yelled Jacobus, his fingers seared from the heat of the bulb, at which moment René Allard began to play violin, tuning up on the first eerie chords of "Danse Macabre."

Jacobus, in shock, dropped the box as his knees almost gave way.

"Good evening, Mr. Jacobus," said a polite voice. "As I told you so recently—oh, though it seems so long ago—my father always said to me—"

" 'Better an hour early than a minute late.' And I'm a minute late. Is that so, Ziggy?" said Jacobus. "Back from the dead, are you?"

"Just so." Gottfried chuckled. "I'm sorry to have startled you with the recording, but I know how much you've always enjoyed Maestro's playing. I wanted to make you a nice surprise. I myself can listen to him endlessly. I know that playing a record is each time always the same, except maybe for the scratches as it gets older—just like people, wouldn't you say?—but with Maestro, somehow every time it seems like a new performance.

"But that's neither here nor there. I have been expecting you, Mr. Jacobus. In fact, in a way I have been looking forward to this visit. There is no longer the exhilaration of solitude for me here in this place which I used to enjoy, which I yearned for. I knew if anyone could find me it would be you, with your great analytical capacity. And it is precisely because of you, Mr. Jacobus, that I am back here in my lonely apartment instead of in the glorious Utah sunshine. But when you inquired after Rose Grimes in Salt Lake City, I knew it was just a matter of time, even though it hadn't yet occurred to you."

"You said she was Negro."

"Yes, but since you hadn't mentioned that, if I didn't remember her, how could I know her race? As you now understand, I had no choice but to disappear."

"With the assistance of your dear sister, no doubt," said Jacobus. "Nice of her to pick you up hitchhiking from Antelope Island, wasn't it?"

"Schatzi and I have always helped one another. But now she is there, I am here, and you have come to visit. And just for your information, sir, in case you were still wondering, the light in the apartment is on, as you so painfully determined. I can see you very clearly. I'm glad to see you are looking so well. I trust you have made a complete recovery from your accident in Utah. But, just out of curiosity, how was it that you concluded I was here and not dead or somewhere else perhaps?"

"Tuesday. Beans and franks. That's what was in Malachi's report. That's what I smelled when I was here earlier today. I just couldn't place it at the time. And, I'm sorry to say, it's Tuesday."

"So clever, Mr. Jacobus. I am more impressed with you than ever. I myself have never been clever. I am just a simple elevator boy, a victim of routine. Ah, I see that you have returned my little box. Doubtless you had the contents examined. I'm sorry you did that. Life would have been so much simpler if you hadn't. And for you, longer.

"But why should we be so gloomy now? After all we are old friends, are we not? May I make you some tea, Mr. Jacobus?"

"Sounds great," said Jacobus. He didn't know the clinical nomenclature for Gottfried's condition, nor did he really care. All he knew was that Mr. Elevator Boy was crazy as a loon. Two subterranean madmen in one day, but this one was a menace.

Should I try to escape? he asked himself. Or should I play the talking game and hope Nathaniel or Malachi will show up?

He was momentarily spared the decision as Gottfried, brewing the tea, spoke.

"Let me describe to you a little bit about the history of my room here, Mr. Jacobus, because it is important you understand the world from which I thought I had escaped. I think you will find it very interesting since you can't see it yourself. When the Bonderman was constructed in 1904, this entire level was dedicated to producing heat for all twelve stories. All the little rooms on this floor were only afterthoughts, like my humble apartment. Even though the ceiling was very low to begin with, they filled it with ducts and pipes of all sorts to carry the heat and the water and the electricity and the sewage, though at first I believe the building must have been heated by coal, because as I'm sure you have discovered, there is such an unpleasant grimy black coating covering all these things and also the impressively large furnace near the door that goes out to the underground. And of course there is the incinerator next to the furnace, where they used to burn all kinds of garbage. Thankfully, scientists now understand that type of burning is very bad for our health and we don't do it anymore. These things are no longer used since they closed this floor, but I want you to remember what I am saying. One time long ago this place was clean, but now everything looks black, and with so few lightbulbs there is very little to cheer up my world. I don't complain, though, because here I was comfortable enough."

Jacobus heard the teakettle begin to whistle. It stopped immediately as Gottfried removed it from the hot plate. Should I try to run for it? Jacobus asked himself again. Not a good idea. I can barely walk as it is, and I'd get clobbered finding my way through the maze of pipes and ducts. But Gottfried knows his way around like the back of his hand, and Gottfried also has a kettle of boiling water.

"Other than my little apartment, there was a room on the opposite wall that housed the washing machines and dryers, to clean the linens and towels that were provided to the residents and guests. I should remind you that the Bonderman Building's residences were half hotel, half apartments, but linen service was provided to all, for a fee of course to the residents, but the towels were very nice and soft. Before these modern washing machines there were much less automatic ones, and of course in the earliest days I imagine most of the laundry was done by hand. Can you imagine all that work, Mr. Jacobus? It is too bad none of these machines are being used anymore because of the new elevator construction, but that is progress, I suppose. Here is your tea, Mr. Jacobus. I hope it is not too hot for your taste."

"I'm sure the tea will be as delightful as your company."

"There was another room, next to the laundry room, for the maids and other service people to change from their street clothes into their uniforms in the morning and back again at the end of their shift. It was not much of a room, more just a space with walls, a bench, a few hooks for hanging clothes, and a shower. So little by little I got to know the other employees who used these 'facilities,' as the room was called. Not all employees did, though, only the ones who had jobs that made them perspire. Mostly the maids and sometimes a mechanic or other repair person. That is how I got to know Rose Grimes, by the way," Gottfried concluded.

At that moment the recording of "Danse Macabre," which had faded into insignificance, tapered to its close. The apartment was left with only the sound of the rhythmic scratching of the worn stylus on the brittle, still-spinning 78.

"Ah!" said Gottfried. "There's something I'd like to play for you, Mr. Jacobus. I think you'll enjoy this."

Jacobus heard Gottfried stand and take a few steps to his left, then the cardboard sound of an old album sliding out from among its neighbors.

Well, aren't we having the quaint little tea party, he said to himself.

He heard the needle drop and the music begin. He immediately recognized the famous fourth movement variations from Franz Schubert's "Trout" Quintet, a jaunty little tune that Schubert had adapted from his song of the same name, about an angler gaily going about his task of hooking the reluctant trout, which is finally enticed out of its safe haven in the clear, running brook by the angler's craftiness, sealing its fate.

"This music always cheers me up!" said Gottfried. "Schubert! With Schubert I always feel so young and carefree!

"Now, Mr. Jacobus, tell me why you are here," said Gottfried, his tone changing. "Why did you steal my box?"

"I don't know why you say I stole it, Ziggy," said Jacobus. "If I stole it, why would I have brought it back? I just needed some evidence, and I'm glad to say you've provided it for me."

"Evidence?" asked Gottfried. "What evidence?"

"To prove that Rose Grimes stole the Garimberti and then killed René in revenge for raping her. It wasn't your fault, Ziggy. That's what I've come to tell you."

"That's very interesting, Mr. Jacobus," said Gottfried. "Please go on."

Jacobus, sipping his tea, reiterated what he earlier said to Rose Grimes through her apartment door. He had been convinced of the story then and hoped he would sound that way now. As Jacobus talked, he listened for other potentially helpful sounds, but he heard nothing except his own voice.

"That is a remarkable story," said Gottfried when Jacobus had concluded. "Poor Rose. She has had a troubled life. But neither of us believes that fairy tale. Do we, Mr. Jacobus?"

Suddenly, Jacobus found himself on the ground, reeling from a concussive blow to his forehead. Through pain and dizziness he felt blood seep between his nose and eye.

"I should also have mentioned, Mr. Jacobus," said Gottfried, "I have a gun, my father's beautiful Pistolen 08, what you call a Luger here. My father fought with it during the war. It is of course mainly for shooting, and for shooting it is wonderful accurate, but as you have just experienced, it is effective in more than one way. You seem to be bleeding, Mr. Jacobus. The gun must be heavier than I thought. Here, take this." Jacobus felt a handkerchief being pressed into his hand. "This should stop it," Gottfried said, as he hauled Jacobus by the collar back into his chair as if he were a rag doll. The final pieces now fit into the puzzle. Jacobus fully comprehended the scene in which Allard was killed and realized that trying to escape now was futile.

"As you can see," Gottfried said, "fairy tales don't interest me. Anytime I hear a fairy tale it upsets me, and I don't know what I might do if I hear another. Now, Mr. Jacobus, please tell me a real story."

"When did you start smuggling violins, Ziggy?" asked Jacobus. "Or did that come with the elevator job?"

Gottfried laughed. "So is that what you wish to know?"

"For starters."

"So. I had only begun my elevator boy job a few months before. Other than a pleasant nod or a polite hello, Maestro Allard barely acknowledged my existence. And why should he? Someone so famous! Nevertheless, I always responded as politely as I was addressed, even more politely, in the way I had been trained by my mother. Then, one night when there were no other passengers, out of the blue, Allard said, 'Ziggy, I have this violin. Of course, it's not anything special,' he said. 'Just a modern Italian violin that's been sitting around my apartment.' Allard stopped talking, and I asked myself, am I supposed to say something?

" 'I like you,' said Allard. 'You're polite and you're discreet.'

" 'Thank you, sir,' I said.

" 'This violin,' Allard continued, 'since I don't need it, and since you know so many people from going up and down in the elevator all day, every day . . . well, I thought to myself, maybe Ziggy would know somebody who would like a nice new violin.'

"I found this a very strange statement coming from René Allard. I assure you, Mr. Jacobus, at that time I didn't know one person in the world who could afford such a fine instrument, except of course the people in my elevator who already had one!

" 'Ah!' said Allard. 'These violins, they are good but they are not, how shall we say, in the same league as a Stradivarius, a Guarneri, nor even a Gagliano. But they are good, nevertheless, for the advanced student, maybe even the young professional.'

"Allard was so famous, so dashing, already the most sought-after violinist in the world. And not only that. He was always doing such nice things for people. For charities. For countries. He was an ambassador of goodwill. But as you know, in very reduced health. Probably from all that smoking and all that fast living. When he talked to you he often had to stop between sentences, even words, to catch his breath. What is the name of that disease, Mr. Jacobus?"

"Emphysema."

"Ja, just so! Emphysema! I believe you have a bit of that too. I myself had no such bad habits, but on the other hand I was a young nobody. So here we were, two people in the same elevator, yet a world apart. At least here in this one place Maestro treated me like an equal. I responded as I thought Allard would want.

" 'Maestro Allard, sir,' I said. 'I will keep my eyes open, but if I find someone who would like the instrument, how much should I say it costs?'

" 'I think five hundred dollars would be a fair price,' he said. 'What do you think?'

"Why was he asking me this question, Mr. Jacobus? He must have known I knew nothing about violins.

" 'That seems like a reasonable price, Mr. Allard,' I said.

" 'That settles it,' he said, as I opened the elevator door. 'And if you should be so fortunate as to find someone who buys the instrument, I will give you twenty-five dollars for your trouble.'

"That was half a week's salary for me, Mr. Jacobus! You can imagine I would look very hard for a buyer.

"I was very proud of myself for finding a Juilliard student who had outgrown his inadequate German violin. I had discovered him by keeping my ears open in the elevator—the teachers, they come and go all the time to the dealers—but it wasn't easy for me. To begin with I didn't have much free time, and searching for a buyer almost eliminated entirely my time to eat and sleep. So I was quite pleased that it took me only five days to sell the violin for Allard, who in turn was equally pleased. I received the twenty-five dollars with sober dignity on the outside, Mr. Jacobus, but inwardly you can imagine how giddy I was. I wish you could have seen my face, but of course you can't.

"At first I wanted to spend all my new fortune at a great restaurant like Delmonico's, but then I heeded my dead father's admonition to save my money and spend it wisely. Since the money was a gift from heaven, I decided to put it away until I either needed it or, God willing, I had so much that it didn't matter. So I put the money in my little metal box that you were so kind enough to return, Mr. Jacobus, along with the other money I was saving. Am I boring you, Mr. Jacobus?"

"Go on. Please," said Jacobus. "You're fascinating me."

Gottfried was silent. It was like the silence before a thunderstorm, made all the more ominous by Schubert's music dancing merrily along in the background. Jacobus decided to refrain from further sarcasm.

"A few months later I was working my shift," Gottfried finally said. "Again it was late at night.

"'Up, please. Floor twelve, Ziggy,' said Allard. This was very strange because there was nothing on the twelfth floor that would be open so late. Dedubian's shop would have closed hours before, and Allard lived on the fourth floor.

"'I'd like to talk to you,' he said, 'and since it's late at night I trust no one will be discommoded.'

"I pressed the lever forward, and so up we went.

"'Slowly, Ziggy, slowly,' said Allard. 'We have much to talk about.'

"I said nothing, though already my mind was racing.

"'It seems,' Allard said, 'that I am able to procure additional violins. Violins of similar quality to the one for which you recently found a buyer. I was very proud of you for that, Ziggy. I'm sure the young man at Juilliard is very pleased, and it is no longer wasted just sitting around unplayed, taking up space. It is being put to good use, maybe creating a future Allard, eh? And you have been rewarded—I hope you will agree, reasonably rewarded—for your efforts.'

"At that moment, I remember the buzzer went off in the elevator. A passenger in the lobby was waiting, but I kept going upward.

"'There is a man, an Italian man,' Allard continued, 'who can bring me as many new Italian violins as I may wish. From Bologna, from Cremona, Brescia, Venice, Naples, and so on. These are all first-rate instruments. No 'schlock,' as the Jews say. So I was thinking, Ziggy, perhaps you have more friends who would be interested in a purchase.'

"My father, Mr. Jacobus, had taught me to always be on the lookout for new opportunities, to think sharp. Now I saw the previous favor I did for Mr. Allard in a new light. It had been a test, I realized. You see, I had done the right thing—worked hard, kept my mouth shut, asked no questions. All the things my father had taught.

"I was good at doing sums in my head. The violin I had helped sell for five hundred dollars. I had been given twenty-five. That left four hundred seventy-five. Assuming that Maestro made some money—and why would he really do it if not for money?—so then I think he probably paid only about two hundred fifty to three hundred dollars for the violin. Three hundred fifty, tops. But now Maestro has just told me there was this 'Italian man.' So this go-between man must have his portion too, leaving the poor maker probably only somewhere between one hundred to two hundred dollars. I didn't know where all this was leading, but it helped me see things clearly.

"As I brought the elevator to a stop at the twelfth floor, I had a sudden thought somewhere in the back of my brain. I couldn't yet put my finger on it but I knew it was big. I had never had such excitement from only a thought, and such a vague one at that. Then the idea vanished as suddenly as it had arrived, passing like a puff of air, but I knew it would return.

" 'I think I might be able to find some more friends,' I said to Maestro. 'I will certainly do my best. Perhaps it may ease me in my retirement someday.'

"Allard laughed at my little joke, perhaps a little too hard. 'Thank you, Ziggy,' he said. 'You are to be congratulated.'

" 'I try my best, Mr. Allard. My father always told me, "No

matter what you do, you must do your best. In such a way you will
never disappoint yourself." '

" 'That's good to hear, Ziggy,' Allard said to me. 'We will work
out the details soon. You may now take us back down to the
fourth floor.' Then, I remember, Allard began to cough his terrible cough, and he was still a relatively young man. 'I might not
make it to retirement, myself,' he said, doubled over by that terrible body-racking cough. I could hardly understand his words.

" 'Shall I get you some water, sir?' I asked him.

" 'Doesn't help,' Allard wheezed. He was barely audible. 'It
will end, sooner or later. We can go. Please go.'

" 'Yes, sir. I hope you feel better.' "

"And that sudden thought you had," Jacobus interrupted,
"the one that went *poof*, was to somehow sell a really valuable old
violin actually owned by Allard. No middlemen, no five percent
here, ten percent there. A violin that to begin with is worth a
hundred times more than the stuff you were peddling. And with
all the chatter going on in your elevator over the years, you'd
have to be deaf not to hear a lot about how the market value of
such an instrument would be that much greater if it had been
owned by someone famous, especially if the famous violinist had
just died. So when Allard was in the hospital, seemingly on his
deathbed, you were there by his side, the loyal servant. Except
you weren't there to console Allard. Just like Lavender thought,
you were there for another reason. But Lavender didn't know it
was to blackmail Allard to get the ex Hawkins del Gesù using the
photos you took of him raping Rose Grimes."

"Rose!" said Gottfried. "Oh, Rose! Of all the housekeepers,
she was the one I liked the most. Always a smile for everyone.

She dressed so neatly and always wore a hat and gloves to work and always on time. She took pride in her work, Mr. Jacobus! That is a very important way to judge character! If she arrived during one of my shifts and there were not too many people around early in the morning, even though she was Negro I would give Rose a ride in the elevator so she wouldn't have to walk up all the stairs. I must say that I am kind to people of all races, and here I am more like my mother than my father. No one can help it if they were not born white, so what good does it do to remind people of that by being mean?

"Rose and I became good friends. I knew always when her shift was, so that I could say hello and good-bye. We gave each other small Christmas presents, and I gave her a little present for her husband too. It was so sad that her husband was wounded in the war. War is such a terrible thing.

"Mr. Jacobus, on your way here, did you perhaps notice the changing room?"

"Our secret voyeur heaven, you mean? Wouldn't miss it for the world."

"I don't understand this word 'voyeur,' Mr. Jacobus."

"I'll be happy to explain, Ziggy," said Jacobus, "because I literally fell upon it when I tripped on the stool my last visit to your little world here. Us blind folk are so clumsy, aren't we? I reached out to get my balance, and that's where I found that small screen that lets out the steam from the shower. There it was, high up on the wall, the one separating the changing space from the furnace area, on the side away from the elevators and the washing machines. I cut my finger on it when I grabbed on to it. Knowing your height, I would say that it was on that stool and through that screen that you took your pictures. That explains the weird angle and the blur in spots that Nathaniel couldn't figure."

"Just so, Mr. Jacobus! Just so!" said Gottfried. "But this was not so easy because I had to stand on my tiptoes, as you Americans say, and lean against the wall, and even so I could only see down about halfway, because as you know I am not very tall.

"I did this because I liked to watch Rose change her clothes, especially at the end of her shift when she took off all her clothes for her shower. She was very careful to hang them up or fold them neatly so that she never looked liked she had been working. She was very pretty. Her underclothes were white and it made her dark skin, the color of Bavarian chocolate cake—I see you think that is funny—look especially lovely. As I said, I could not see all the way down, so even when she was totally with no clothes I could only see her top half. I couldn't see her remove her stockings because she would sit down for that, but I could imagine it. I liked watching her remove her undergarments and then lift her arms to hang them up and then pin her hair up so I could see her large bosom. I also liked to watch her dry herself off when she was wet. Sometimes she would rub herself with an ointment.

"I know when I say things like this you say to yourself, 'What a deranged, sick, lonely man.' I know that's what most people would think, but I say that I was harming no one, and who wouldn't want to see Rose, or another beautiful woman, without her clothes on? I believe all men think the way I think. I am just being honest. Look at all the people today who buy the magazines and go to the movies to see people doing terrible, obscene things to each other. Well, I don't want to go on and on now, but I took my pictures and looked at them on my wall. It was harmless."

"And how long did your innocent fun go on, Ziggy?" asked Jacobus, holding his teacup. He hadn't really drunk any, thinking he might have to throw it at Gottfried at some point if all else failed. Somehow he would have to escape and notify Malachi if BTower's life were to be saved. Tomorrow was the last tomorrow for him, and tomorrow was almost today.

"I watched Rose change her clothes whenever I could," said Gottfried. "Of course, most of the time I was busy with the elevator, but over the years I watched her dozens of times, at least. You would have envied me, Mr. Jacobus."

"I'm sure I would have, Ziggy. But then one day things changed, didn't they?"

"One day everything changed, Mr. Jacobus. It was a spring day because she was wearing my favorite of her dresses, with a big pattern of cherries and bananas with a white background, and it had those big shoulders that women once believed fashionable. It was the end of Rose's shift and she had removed her uniform and had taken her shower, and she was putting her dress back on. As she was buttoning the dress—it had big red buttons going from top to bottom—there was a knock at the dressing room door. I could not see who it was since I was around the corner against the side wall with my Leica.

" 'Who is it?' Rose asked. I could tell by her voice she was immediately nervous.

" 'It is me, Allard. Something was left in the apartment. Perhaps it is yours.'

" 'I'll be out in a moment, Mr. Allard.'

"Rose continued to button her dress, faster. But before she could finish, Allard opened the door. I strained to see what I could. Rose's brassiere was still showing.

" 'Mr. Allard, what are you doing?' There was fear in Rose's voice that made me angry at Allard.

"Allard didn't say a word but grabbed the top of Rose's dress and pulled it apart. And then . . . but now I don't need to describe the details, do I, Mr. Jacobus? You have seen the photos.

"Finally, when Allard was finished with her, he said, 'I must have made a mistake. It must belong to someone else.' After he said this he just left.

"Rose stood there for a moment. Then she sat down on the wooden bench and cried. I couldn't see her but I could hear, and it was an interesting thing that it wasn't like usual crying, which everyone knows. It was almost not human. It disturbed me greatly and made me feel too sad.

"I had to get back to work so I was ready to get down off the box when Rose stood up. She turned on the shower and walked into it without even taking her clothes off. I wanted to say to her, 'How will you get home with wet clothes?' She was not thinking straight but it was too late, she was already wet. Now it was time for me to go to work, so to this day I do not know how she got home.

"When I was back in the elevator I was thinking there was something I had learned from what Allard did to Rose, but I wasn't sure what. Of course I wasn't going to say anything about what happened. Ah, you are thinking again, I am a terrible person for doing nothing, but think again. Who was I going to tell?

And *what* was I going to tell? I don't like to speak unkindly of the dead, but if I told Mr. Zipolito, our boss, he would shout at me, 'Keep your rotten German mouth shut! It's none of your business! Mr. Allard is a famous man and has paid his rent on time for years! Those Negro women are all the same and get what they deserve . . .' Am I not right, Mr. Jacobus? Isn't this what people in this country say? Or if I confronted Allard himself? Then what? He would have a quiet chat with my boss and Rose would be fired and I would be fired. And I knew that this is what Rose thought also. She and I had much in common, being at the bottom of the ladder. She would say nothing and she *did* say nothing. No, no! I know when to keep my mouth shut, Mr. Jacobus. That is what my father taught me."

"You're such a thoughtful guy, Ziggy," said Jacobus. "And when Rose was eventually fired for stealing Allard's music, you felt so bad that you gave her the Garimberti, one of the violins that you were fencing, just so she could make ends meet."

"Yes, you are correct again, Mr. Jacobus," said Gottfried. "You are uncanny!"

"Now it's *you* who's telling a fairy tale, Ziggy," said Jacobus. "Because Rose didn't steal the music. That's not what happened at all, is it?"

Gottfried was silent while Schubert's music cheerily ambled on. Jacobus recalled the last verse of the "Trout," because it was in that verse that the poet finally makes his metaphor, cautioning pretty young girls to be wary of the crafty angler, lest they become hooked against their will.

"Cat got your tongue, as we say in America, Ziggy?" Jacobus said. He dabbed his brow with Gottfried's handkerchief. The bleeding seemed to have stopped. He tossed the handkerchief onto the floor.

"I'll tell you what really happened. You stopped taking pictures of Rose after the rape because for your purposes—your 'big idea'—her usefulness was over. And you're absolutely right, she didn't say a thing to anybody, except to Jesus maybe. But funny how Rose continued to work at the Bonderman for over a year even after she was raped by Allard. The answer is, she had to. She had a husband overseas in a war, and she couldn't afford to lose her job. So why do you suppose it is that she waits for a whole year, and then one day out of the blue she decides to steal, of all things, Allard's music? Was it for revenge? Profit?"

Gottfried remained silent. The recording had come to an end, and now the only sounds were the damp groans and sinister knockings of the underworld around them, but none of a knight in shining armor galloping to Jacobus's rescue.

"No answer? Then let me tell you why," continued Jacobus. "But first I have to go back in time a bit, to when your sacred elevator was defiled by Allard and Hennie. You didn't like it, did you, when they screwed in your sanctum sanctorum and made you watch. It was pretty disgusting behavior, wasn't it?"

"Yes, it was disgusting. This was their private business, but I was the one who had to clean it up."

"But even so, that Hennie, she was something, eh? Young and wriggly. Sexy. Alluring. Watching her do what she did with Allard—you couldn't stop thinking about her here in your dungeon, could you? The way she looked at you in the elevator. Maybe there was a spark there, eh? Maybe that's what got you started peeping at Rose, taking pictures. If the Frenchies could be so kinky, why couldn't the Germans join the fun? Right, Ziggy?"

"I know little about women, Mr. Jacobus," said Gottfried. "The only one I have ever understood is Seglinde."

"Yes, sisterly love, Ziggy. So pure. But still, you continued to do little favors for Hennie over the years—kept the flame alive—and then when Allard and Hennie became alienated—we'll get to that in a minute—you thought, Oh, boy, this is my big chance with the lady. Then one hot summer day, lo and behold, Hennie asks you to bring groceries to her apartment, and there she is, standing half naked in front of you with that cunning little smile on her pouting lips and the curl of her wet hair clinging to her cheek. What else could she mean, you thought, other than that she wanted you?

"This was your big moment, Ziggy, the climax of all your dungeon dreams. You took her in your arms, embraced her, and what did she do? She disappointed you, didn't she, Ziggy?"

"She laughed," said Gottfried. "And the other one—"

"Ah, the omnipresent Mabel Bidwell! She was there, and she laughed too. What is interesting about this, Ziggy, is the timing of this little tryst gone awry. One day before Rose was fired. One day! Coincidence? I think not. What I think happened is that you were so humiliated, enraged even—and who could blame you?—that when you saw the sumptuous Rose down there in the basement—a woman you could trust, a woman of your station—your frustrations and your urges won out over your reason. Remember, Rose had no idea you had ever seen her dressing or showering, no idea that she had been one of your secret fantasies. No idea you had seen her bosom. She still thought you were her friend."

"Yes, I was her friend."

"So when she saw you there, when she was changing her clothes at the end of a long, sweaty day at the office, she never suspected you'd do the same thing to her that your mentor did. But, hey, why not? After all, you emulated him in so many other ways. You followed him in the smuggling business. You followed him in your adoration of the irresistible Hennie. You couldn't actually play the violin, but you collected all his recordings and pretended. Raping Rose Grimes was just one more way to be René Allard himself, wasn't it?"

"I loved Maestro Allard. Who understood the ways of the world better than Maestro? Not me, Mr. Jacobus. I lived my life in my elevator and here in my room. It was all I knew. Who else was there to learn from? What better example? All the world loved him. All the magazines and all the newspapers with his picture, all the parties—there were always women, and they were always smiling at him. He made them all smile, and I thought when Rose saw how I felt, she would smile at me too. Why shouldn't I follow his example?"

"Why not indeed, Krinkelmeier? Oh, I'm sorry, I bet you don't care to be called that."

"Names don't offend me, Mr. Jacobus."

"I'm glad, Krinkelmeier, because I'm sure Hennie and Allard just called you that in jest. Why would that offend anyone?

"But, to answer your question, you realized after you raped Rose that you weren't as immune to tattling as your idol—or should I say former idol. That if Rose went to the cops and accused you of what you did to her, you could conceivably lose not only your job but also your liberty. Maybe mean Mr. Zipolito would not want to keep a rapist on staff. This, after all, was the civil rights era. What better way to show off the new American justice than to convict the son-of-a-Nazi rapist of a hardworking black woman whose husband was a disabled Vietnam War hero?

"So you were shaking in your boots, weren't you, Krinkelmeier? You went back to 4B and got your hands on Allard's 'Danse Macabre' music. You then planted it among Rose's belongings, reported her to Zipolito, and voilà! as the French say so well, Rose is history."

It was clear to Jacobus that Gottfried had been caught off guard by how much he knew, but whether it would help prolong his own life was up in the air. It could even shorten it.

Gottfried broke the silence. "I have one more record for you, Mr. Jacobus. It's very special, one of the few in existence of Maestro Allard playing chamber music."

Again there was a pause as Gottfried went to retrieve the recording, which from the established pattern Jacobus gauged was in a stack located between the old Victrola and Gottfried's seat on his bed, all within a few feet of each other. Jacobus was losing the battle of endurance over the stalemate with this madman. In fact, he didn't think it would be a stalemate much longer. The story was coming to an end, and then what? He would have to do something soon. He would have to act, even if it killed him.

THIRTY

The music began. It was the last completed work of Jacobus's only hero, Beethoven, the final movement of his string quartet, Opus 135. Beethoven had been totally deaf for years when he wrote this masterpiece shortly before his death. He was also violently sick and socially reviled, yet the music had the freshness and vitality of one who had overcome all obstacles.

This movement in particular had its own unique message. Above the score Beethoven had written, *"Der Schwer gefasste Enschluss."* "The difficult decision." The music begins slowly and ominously with a questioning three-note motive based upon words Beethoven wrote, *"Muss es sein?"* "Must it be?" Then, from out of nowhere comes the affirmative Allegro, the main motive here twice inverting the original question. *"Es muss sein! Es muss sein!"* "It must be! It must be!"

No one knew for certain what Beethoven intended with these words. Scholars and music historians have postulated everything from death's inevitability to having to pay an unwanted laundry bill. Whatever Beethoven's reason, Jacobus asked himself, what was Gottfried's reason for playing it?

"And so," Gottfried asked, retuning to the subject, "how do you know Rose did not steal the music, Mr. Jacobus? Or the violin?"

"I asked myself, Ziggy, if Rose were to risk her job by stealing something, why would she steal sheet music? Sheet music has no value to her, even music owned by the great René Allard. She knows nothing about music except for listening to her gospel on the radio. Hennie was right when she told me that only someone who knew music could appreciate the value of something like that.

"So the next question I asked was, if Rose didn't steal it, and someone else planted it on her, for whom would that music have value? The answer was you. No one on earth prized that music as much as you—'Danse Macabre' owned by René Allard and signed by Saint-Saëns himself. And who other than Rose had easy access to Allard's apartment? The fact that you were the one who reported the theft to Zipolito made it that much easier for me to understand the whole picture.

"As far as the Garimberti was concerned, yeah, I thought Rose stole it. She had no plausible explanation for how she got it. But then again, she chose not to profit from it when she could easily have."

"That is surprising," said Gottfried. "It was a good violin. It should have been no problem to sell."

"Exactly. But she chose not to sell. She gave it to BTower when he was a kid and then broke it when he wouldn't join her in praising the Lord."

"BTower? How did she know BTower?" asked Gottfried.

"It's a small world, isn't it, Ziggy? BTower just happens to be Rose Grimes's son, a prodigal son maybe, but definitely her flesh and blood. And when he went astray and she broke the fiddle, she could have made an insurance claim but didn't. So, unlikely as it may seem, Rose Grimes was indeed telling the truth.

"And here's a simple, simple truth that took me too long to figure—Rose is not capable of stealing. To her, one sin is as bad as another, and stealing would send her to hell just as quickly as murder or rape, wouldn't it, Ziggy? You were the one who left the violin on her doorstep, aren't you? Out of guilt for what you had done. No note, no acknowledgment, no way to trace it. Until I found Novak."

"You see? That was my weakness," said Gottfried. "I was too soft with poor Rose. She had lost her job, and then her husband came back with his injury. But it is so ironic. If I hadn't given her the violin, which I bought with my own money, neither you nor I would be here now having our conversation. You would never have come to Salt Lake City to ask me if I knew Rose, and I would never have had to eradicate you. I failed at that once, I admit, and so had to make myself disappear and return here for the time being. It is a very difficult situation for me, I tell you, being a very wealthy man and having to hide here.

"But who could have guessed? Who can read the future, Mr. Jacobus? I accept my fate, but it is so sad that my momentary lapse with the Garimberti will be responsible for your demise. But, these minor indiscretions of mine aside, we are still a long way from your accusation of murder. Are we not?"

"We're getting there," replied Jacobus, hoping to talk until something—preferably something good—happened.

"Back when Allard had his heart attack, the one that almost killed him, you thought, My God, everything is fitting into place. This is my opportunity of a lifetime. I can trade these photos of Maestro raping Rose for his ex Hawkins del Gesù, and the day after he dies, which everyone thought would be any moment, I'll get three times the million dollars it's worth."

"Yes!" said Gottfried. "Yes! Mr. Jacobus, you understand me totally! Maestro Allard was not so easily persuaded, though. I showed him the photos there in his hospital bed and suggested how much his reputation would suffer were they to be seen. At first he couldn't believe someone had seen him with Rose. He was sure no one knew. I must commend him, though. For a Frenchman he tried very hard to be brave and sturdy, especially in his weakened condition. For that I must give him credit.

" 'You can't blackmail me . . .' he said. His voice was like a whisper and he had to work so hard for each word. 'I'm going to die anyway. What do I care what happens to my reputation when I'm dead?' He thought he had me there. He smiled the smile of a skull. I confess I had to think.

" 'True,' I said to him. 'But what if you *don't* die? Then what?' And so, Mr. Jacobus, Maestro really had little choice, because if he survived and the pictures were known, his life would have been hell, which for him, without the adoration and the fast living, would have been worse than death. So he gave me the violin. When he told Hennie it was gone—of course he didn't say to whom—she was furious. She was planning on that for their retirement in Paris. That made me doubly happy."

"And you kept the photos anyway," said Jacobus. "For insurance against him saying something in the unlikely event he survived his heart attack. Which, amazingly, he did. And that was your problem, wasn't it, Ziggy? His will to thwart you was so great that he lived on and on and on. He understood you and your greed. Of course, he cut off your lunch money. No more wheeling and dealing violins for you. No more quick trips to Laszlo Novak, eh, Mr. Oehlschlager? And Allard knew you'd be too stubborn to sell the ex Hawkins until the day he died because that's when you'd really cash in, but he figured the longer his life, the shorter yours would be to enjoy the fruits of your hard-earned extortion. And that's why you had to kill him on that particular night, isn't it? Because you knew the day after that final Carnegie recital he was going to leave for France forever, and this was your last chance."

"No murder weapon was ever found, Mr. Jacobus. And there is no proof. There were no witnesses, except to see BTower with blood on his hands. All that you say is mere fantasy."

"But I do know the murder weapon, and I have proof," said Jacobus. "You can tell me what happened in the elevator that night, Krinkelmeier, or I can tell you. It doesn't matter to me."

"Very well, Mr. Jacobus. We will see what you think you know."

Gottfried paused. Beethoven's Allegro was electric and Allard's playing commanding. What are they telling me? Jacobus asked himself. What's the message? "It must be! It must be!" What must be?

"I answered the buzzer to go to the lobby," Gottfried resumed. "It was midnight. When the elevator door slid open, the two of them were standing there. 'Good evening, Ziggy,' Maestro Allard said to me, and he stepped in with his violin case in his hand. He turned his back to me, as he always did. BTower stayed in the lobby.

" 'Good evening, Maestro,' I said to the back of Allard's head. 'Congratulations on your great triumph tonight.'

" 'What are you to me?' he said. 'You are nobody and your

words mean nothing. Good-bye, Ziggy. You will die your proud little German death here in your precious little castle, and I will live forever. I will outlive you and you will never see a pfennig from *my* violin.' I let him talk this way if it made him feel better. I didn't care. That is all that happened. I will admit this."

"That's all that happened," said Jacobus, "until the elevator arrived at the fourth floor, Allard's floor. You see, I went up to the fourth floor a couple days ago to see Hennie. Your building superintendent, Fuente, took me up there. Fuente's not the art- ist you are when it comes to operating the Stradivarius of eleva- tors, and so I got my finger stuck in the grate when he slid the safety door only partially open. That's when it occurred to me. When you opened the door for Allard, you intentionally opened the safety grate only partially. As Allard began to step forward, you quickly looked up and down the corridor as if routinely to see if anyone needed a ride, but really to make one hundred per- cent sure no one was there, which wasn't likely anyway, since it was midnight on Halloween and all the revelers were still out and about. Seeing no one, you stepped back into the elevator, behind Allard, as was customary. As Allard began to exit the elevator, you lunged at him from behind and with your gloved hands rammed his head through one of the diamonds of space in the safety door lattice, lacerating his scalp. He wasn't dead yet. Only injured, dazed, and trapped. Next you slammed the safety door closed again, in doing so reconfiguring the diamonds so that the one around Allard's neck closed like a vise, choking him, rendering him incapable of calling out. Then you thrust for- ward the lever to ascend, jolting the elevator up toward the fifth floor. As it shot toward the top of the door opening, Allard's exposed neck was crushed instantly with the force of a reverse guillotine as he hit the top of the elevator doorway. His neck broke and his windpipe collapsed. That done, you immediately put the brake on the elevator and lowered it back to the fourth floor. You yanked Allard's almost disconnected head back through the grate, holding on to his collar as you opened the elevator door. You then shoved Allard, still gripping his violin case, out into the corridor. How long would that all take? Not long, I bet."

"That would have taken less than a minute, Mr. Jacobus, if it had happened that way. And for the sake of argument, what would I have done then? Perhaps if I were a clever person I might then have gone back in the elevator and ascended at normal speed to the top floor. You can imagine I probably would have been panting from exertion if not exhilaration, but otherwise I might have been quite calm. I might then have removed my white gloves, taken a cloth and a spray bottle of all-purpose cleaner from my tool kit, and wiped the grate and the floor. I might have put the cloth into a plastic bag, returned it to my kit with the cleaner, and put my gloves back on."

"And then, Krinkelmeier, you might have returned to your routine, and until Fuente needed you to take him to the fourth floor after the emergency call came in, you just went about your job. When you went back down to your apartment, you were so terribly upset, but you still had time to toss the plastic bag into the incinerator, which was then still burning like hell. That's why the missing bits of scalp and hair were never found.

"And you were lucky yet again, weren't you? You hadn't expected to see BTower in the lobby, and you certainly didn't plan on him being spotted next to the body, the result of which deflected any possible suspicion from you. This was a real windfall, but you decided to wait until BTower's conviction before putting the ex Hawkins on the market, first to make sure BTower would take the fall, and second to maximize your profit. So the day after the conviction, when you were safe, you yourself permanently disabled your prized elevator in order to provide a cover to leave your cherished old dream job. At the same time your darling sister, Seglinde, under the name of Oehlschlager, made a call to Boris Dedubian to begin the transaction to sell the ex Hawkins. And here's a funny thought! It's also almost to the very day that dear Mr. Oehlschlager met his timely demise from symptoms suspiciously similar to long-term cyanide ingestion. Quite a set of coincidences, don't you think?"

Jacobus heard Ziggy's applause. "Well done, Mr. Jacobus. Well done," he said. "But as we know, the only witness to the murder was dear Mrs. Bidwell, who saw with her own eyes BTower with blood on his hands. I feel terrible about the young man, a fine violinist and I liked him so, I truly did, but in the end all wars have their casualties."

"Except that there *is* a witness, Krinkelmeier," said Jacobus. "René Allard himself."

Ziggy laughed for a long time, but Jacobus heard a hint of alarm in it.

"Oh, Mr. Jacobus! How you retain your sense of humor even at such an anxious time! I suppose Maestro spoke to you from the grave."

"Exactly."

"Please explain your joke to me. They say we Germans have no sense of humor. Maybe they are right."

"Allard's strange pose when he was found," said Jacobus. "They said he couldn't have survived more than a minute after his neck was broken. Only his instinctive motor skills might still have functioned, like the proverbial headless chicken. But with a musician, especially one like Allard from the 'old school,' instinct and trained muscle memory are essentially one and the same. Just imagine, repeating the same physical gestures an infinite number of times from the age of three or four! Hour after hour, year after year, until you can do it in your sleep. It becomes almost as automatic as breathing.

"When a dead person is thrown to the ground, he doesn't end up resting on his elbow. He ends up flat on his face, if he still has one. Allard, in his last moment, raised his left arm, even if his own brain didn't truly compute what it was doing. And the alignment of his fingers. Malachi thought it was rigor mortis. I first thought maybe, just maybe, it could've been Allard giving the finger to his killer. But that wouldn't be Allard's style, would it?"

"I suppose not, but where are we going with all this, Mr. Jacobus? As you know, I am not a musician."

"Neither is Malachi." At that moment, gathering inspiration as the last three triumphant chords of Beethoven's final work rang out, Jacobus decided what he would do. "But I am. And after I got all the measurements from Malachi of Allard's arm and finger position, I knew that it was you who killed him."

"Now this is interesting, Mr. Jacobus. Very interesting. Please continue."

Jacobus hurled his tea in the general direction of Gottfried's voice. He knew the tea was no longer hot, but Gottfried didn't. It was just a decoy.

Jacobus had no intention of trying to escape. He had concluded he was a dead man long before. Instead, he sprang for the Victrola, tackling it with all his waning strength. As it toppled under his weight he heard and felt the ancient acoustic horn shatter into pieces.

If he was going to die, Jacobus told himself, it wouldn't be by groveling in front of an insane extortionist, rapist, killer. He would not allow music to soothe *that* savage breast. He would not.

Just as he ripped the tone arm off its mooring, Gottfried's foot slammed into his ribs, rendering him immobile and unable to breathe. A second vicious kick caught him in the mouth. He heard the click of Gottfried's Luger next to his temple. He had done what he had to do and was exhilarated even through his pain. At least his hip didn't hurt anymore, he said to himself. He waited calmly for his fate. He was victorious.

"I don't understand you, Mr. Jacobus," said Gottfried. "I don't know why you did that. As you can imagine, it doesn't help your situation."

Jacobus still could not talk.

"But before you meet your untimely end, I am curious to learn how it is you think you know how I killed Maestro."

Jacobus lay inert for several minutes. Slowly his ability to breathe returned. He tried to stand but was able to get only as far as his elbows and knees. Funny, he thought, my position isn't all that different from how they found Allard. Concussed, Jacobus slowly probed his swollen mouth with his tongue, seeking broken teeth. His speech was slurred.

"Remember, Krinkelmeier, how famous Allard was for his improvisations on people's names?"

"Remember! Who could forget? It was like a miracle how he could do that so easy. And please, Mr. Jacobus, I am getting tired of you calling me that name."

"I suppose you don't go for Oehlschlager either, Ziggy. How about Sigmund? Yes, I think Sigmund will do just fine. Now suppose Allard's pose was indeed to hold a violin, Sigmund. With the measurements Malachi took, Allard's left hand would have been in first position on an imaginary D-string." Jacobus, still on his knees, demonstrated through his pain. "Allard's soon to be cold and dead first and third fingers would have been playing the notes E-flat and G."

"And I'm sure they were very beautiful," said Gottfried. "But do we know anyone whose initials are E–G? I am sure I do not."

"Not E-*natural*," said Jacobus, "E-*flat*! In Europe, the note E-*flat* is called S. S–G, Sigmund! Sigmund Gottfried. So you see, Sigmund, Allard's final deathbed instinct was to identify you as his murderer. And just to be sure you wouldn't steal another violin from him, he instinctively cradled his violin case underneath his body with his right hand to protect it. Violinists do not like to part with their dearest possession. It's amazing what a trained musician can do instinctively. Don't you think?"

"Well, I must say that is quite an accomplishment you have made, Mr. Jacobus," said Gottfried. "Bravo, bravo, bravo. It is almost as miraculous as Maestro's playing itself. I knew so well that if he had left for France the next day I might have had to wait, who knows, another ten or twenty years before I could make the money that should have been mine decades ago. And by then I would have been too old to enjoy it. It was unfortunate that Maestro didn't die in the hospital when it was meant to be. So it was a case of either

his time would run out or my time would run out. You see, in a
way I really had no choice.

"But now, Mr. Jacobus, your time has run out, and you have a
problem that I don't. There are only you and me here, and soon
it will be only me."

Jacobus again heard the soft click of the Luger being readied.

"In our conversation here you have understood so much that
I feel I have been preaching to the choir. But unfortunately for
you, you are only a choir of one. I am sorry to say, Mr. Jacobus,"
said Gottfried, "*Es muss sein!*"

THIRTY-ONE

The blast of a gunshot rang out. Perplexed, Jacobus found
that he was not dead, or even wounded. The gun, it occurred to
him, had been fired from farther away than Gottfried. Then
Jacobus heard the last voice in the world he expected to hear.
"Mister, this choir's got another singer!" The clear voice of Rose
Grimes resounded through the gloom. "And I shall raise my
voice unto the Lord."

"Hallelujah!" called Jacobus. Had she shot Gottfried?

"And you better believe this singer's packin' heat!" she said. A
second, closer round went off that sounded like a cannon in the
confinement of the basement. "So, Ziggy, you gonna put down
your gun now, or else you're next."

Still alive, Jacobus cursed to himself. But probably as shocked
as he was.

"Rose," Jacobus shouted through his swollen lips. "Go! Now! He's after both of us."

"Don't listen to him, Rose. I'm so glad you're here," Gottfried said. "It has been such a long time. Here is the man you want. This Jacobus. The man who led your son to the gas chamber. You can put your gun down. We have him!"

In a way, Jacobus admired Gottfried's resourcefulness even as he cursed him again.

"What are you talking about? You're the man I want," she said.

"How can you say that, dear Rose? I gave you the Garimberti. I gave your son the chance to play the violin, and I'm very happy—no, I am honored—that I was able to be a small part of his success. There is no need to thank me for the Garimberti. Yes, that was me who gave it to you. As a gift. Now you know. You can ask Mr. Jacobus here if I am telling you the truth. Hearing BTower play was all the thanks I needed.

"But then this man here, he had to testify against BTower at the trial. He said terrible things about your son, Rose. I did the best I could. I said only nice things about your son, Rose. I said I couldn't believe he would do something like kill any man, let alone René Allard. But they wouldn't believe me and it made me cry, because you see I'm not an expert witness like Mr. Jacobus. They convicted your son because of this villain, Mr. Jacobus.

"But now we have him, don't we, Rose? 'And ye shall know the truth,' Rose, 'and the truth shall make you free.' So now you can put your gun down and we can take care of this evil man."

Jacobus had been on his hands and knees all this time. He now felt Gottfried's grip on his arm and waited for another beating, but Gottfried only helped him, almost gently, back into his seat.

"Did you also cry when you got me fired?" Rose rebuked, but there was growing indecision and panic in her voice. "I've been listening. I just heard everything you did. You know what you did to me. And you set up my son when you murdered Allard just like when you put Mr. Allard's music in my purse, knowing that all the suspicion would be on my only son. You blackmailed and murdered René Allard and used my son's life to save your own skin. You used both of us and now you're using me again to get away with another crime."

"Rose," said Gottfried, gently, "there is one thing I know about you because we are so much alike, you and I. You are a religious woman. We both know our Bible, don't we, Rose? Unlike this atheist here. This wild man who just tonight accused you of killing Allard. We both know the sixth commandment. Don't forget the sixth commandment, Rose. Don't forget 'Thou shall not murder.' You would not be able to shoot me, Rose, even if I were the terrible monster you think I am. So put down your gun now. That's what the Lord would want. Of this, there is no doubt."

There was a long, terrible moment of silence. Then Jacobus heard the gun clatter on the floor.

"I'm sorry, Mr. Jacobus," Rose said. "I just can't."

"I know, Rose. It's all right," he said. "You did the right thing."

"So we are all in agreement," said Gottfried. "Now I must ask you both to please proceed to the incinerator. You have done me a favor, Rose, saving me the trouble of looking for you. But you needn't doubt yourself, I would have found you. Now I will open the door for both of you to enter, but please do not try to go anywhere else or I will shoot you. It is unfortunate for you that it no longer is being used because now your deaths will be that much slower. I am afraid no one will hear you. Please get in now."

"You're making a big mistake, Ziggy," said Jacobus. "You have your money. There's no reason to kill again. Hatred isn't profitable, you know."

"Hatred?" asked Ziggy. "What hatred? You are wrong yet again, Mr. Jacobus. I didn't hate Allard and I don't hate you or your race either. Allard was a wonderful man, a wonderful violinist. Famous people usually don't live up to their reputations, but if anything, Allard was even greater. I loved Maestro Allard."

"Even though Allard hated you? Even though he and Hennie called you Krinkelmeier and laughed at you? Humiliated you? You know why he gave you that recording? He was mocking you! And you know why he played 'Danse Macabre,' don't you? It was so he wouldn't forget what people like your father did. What you're doing now. It was his way of making sure he wouldn't forget."

"Ah, Mr. Jacobus. And was René Allard such an angel? Both you and I, and Rose, know what he really was. In the end, Mr. Jacobus, he was just like you and me.

"And now it is time for us to disappear," Gottfried continued. "You, permanently, I'm sorry to say. Me, for a little while. For me, it is not so difficult. I have always been invisible. Yes, people see me and even talk to me, but I am like wallpaper. I am there and I am not there. So when I reappear soon as someone else with dear Seglinde, no one will know the difference and no one will care. Good-bye, Mr. Jacobus. Good-bye, Rose."

Jacobus heard the creaking cast-iron door of the incinerator being opened. Suddenly there was a shove at his back, and he toppled into the sooty filth, with Rose tumbling on top of him. They were entwined with each other half sitting, half lying, like laundry in a washer, but the space was so cramped that it was impossible for them to disentangle.

"Gottfried," Jacobus said, his face pressed against the toxic brick-lined incinerator wall. He lay painfully twisted on a metal grate from under which arose the odor of dank ash from countless tons of burned garbage. "There's one more thing you need to know."

"Mr. Jacobus, you are beginning to bore me," said Gottfried.

"If you kill us, Gottfried, BTower will die as well. Tomorrow."

"This is unfortunately so."

Jacobus heard the heavy door begin to close.

"But there's one thing you don't realize, Gottfried."

Gottfried did not respond.

"Tell him, Rose," said Jacobus.

"I can't."

"Tell him. This is your last chance! Tell him why you couldn't kill him!"

"What is it, Rose?" asked Gottfried. "It won't change anything."

"You're his father," said Rose.

"Whose father?" Gottfried asked.

"You are the father of BTower. If you kill us, your son will die too," said Rose.

Jacobus sensed Gottfried's hesitation in the ensuing silence, but he could do nothing except wait.

"I am proud of my son." Gottfried finally said. "He was a

good boy, and I am sorry to find him only to lose him so quickly. Good-bye."

Jacobus heard Gottfried clamp the door handle shut with unmistakable finality.

He yelled out, "The onus is on you, Gottfried! The onus is on you! He's your own flesh and blood! Do you hear me?"

From the other side, as if from a distance, he heard an unnaturally calm voice. "Mr. Jacobus, you simply underestimate the inexhaustible capacity of greed."

And then, nothing. Jacobus and Rose waited in silence. Waited for what? He had told Nathaniel where he was going but not how to get there. They were in a crypt within a crypt, and Jacobus had no hope.

The tension of Rose and Jacobus's involuntary embrace began to relax, but what little air there was inside the incinerator was noxious. The rancid redolence of age-old creosote made them gag and wheeze. Rose began to pray in a fervent whisper, "'For the Lord loveth judgment, and forsaketh not his saints; they are preserved for ever: but the seed of the wicked shall be cut off.'"

Jacobus tried to listen for signs of Gottfried through Rose's prayer, but he would not interrupt her now.

"'Evil men understand not judgment: but they that seek the Lord understand all things.'"

Through the thick iron walls of the incinerator he heard Gottfried close the door to his apartment, probably taking his little metal box with him. No need for him ever to return now, Jacobus thought. If Gottfried had any second thoughts about killing them, now would be the last opportunity to change his mind. Jacobus called out one final time, "Gottfried!" but as his footsteps approached, passed, and then receded from their prison, Jacobus realized that Gottfried would be having no doubts.

Jacobus listened as Gottfried pushed open the massive steel door that led to the underground passageway and freedom, and heard it being closed. Then there was no more sound but for Rose's hushed, zealous praying.

" 'The righteous cry, and the Lord heareth, and delivereth them out of all their troubles.' "

Nothing more happened. Jacobus asked Rose how she was doing. She told him she'd probably be more claustrophobic if it wasn't black as Hades. Jacobus chuckled and replied that that hadn't been an issue for him for a long time. Then he asked how she had managed to find him at Gottfried's apartment.

She laughed. It was the first time he had heard her laugh. It was rich and honest. She had overheard his furtive conversation with Nathaniel outside her apartment and kept an eye on them at the diner while they thought they were keeping an eye on her.

"Then when you exploded out of that diner like you were trying to escape the clutches of the devil himself, I said uh-huh. So I kissed Shelby on his forehead and told him that something big was up, I wasn't sure what, but that I had to go. I told him, 'If I don't make it back I will see you again soon in heaven, where you'll be whole again.'

"I followed you in a cab and then on foot into the subway station. You think it's hard following a blind man down a railroad track when you're shining a flashlight on his back?"

Jacobus laughed too and asked, hadn't she been concerned for her own safety down there in the tunnels?

"I'd already abandoned my son twice, Mr. Jacobus. I wasn't going to do it again. Besides, ain't no one going to molest an old Negro lady walkin' down the tracks, especially one carrying a gun."

They laughed again.

As breathing became more difficult, so did thinking. Before he lost consciousness, Jacobus told Rose that he was proud of her.

"You did the right thing, Rose, not to shoot Gottfried. I gotta tell you, I've never known a more moral person than you, not that there are that many. But still.

"And you know what? I talked to BTower last week, and I'm sure he still loves you," Jacobus said. Even though he had no idea if this was true, he wanted to say it because the lack of oxygen was quickly depriving him of his ability to speak.

"Now I'm gonna tell you something I never told anyone, even Nathaniel. Y'know, it was my parents, my mother and my father, sent me to New York. Sent me here to study violin when I was a kid. They stayed in Germany. They died in Auschwitz. In the incinerators. I lived and they died. Every time I played the violin . . ." His voice trailed off.

" 'Blessed be the God of all comfort," whispered Rose in short gasps, " 'who comforteth us in all our tribulation, that we may be able to comfort them which are in any trouble, by the comfort wherewith we ourselves are comforted of God.' "

Then Jacobus started to tell her something he rarely admitted even to himself, something that had happened to him when he was a participant in a violin competition as a youth—what one of the judges had done to him—when he realized Rose was no longer conscious. He kissed her forehead and then leaned back against the cold iron wall. In his mind's ear he began to listen to the most beautiful performance of the Mozart G-Minor String Quintet he ever heard, and he thanked Gottfried for ending his life's struggle.

CODA

THIRTY-TWO

DAY 7: WEDNESDAY

"Is he sleeping?" asked Gundacker.

"Nah," said Haskell. "He just contemplatin'."

It was early morning, well before dawn, and it was quiet. BTower lay on his back with both hands behind his head, eyes closed, a trace of a smile on his lips.

"He just be practicing that first chord of Beethoven in his head," Haskell added by way of explanation. "He's ready to play the whole thing now."

"But he's been doing that for hours," said Gundacker.

Haskell ignored the comment, following his own train of thought.

"That young man play in all the concert halls of the world, connecting with folks. And what's the difference between a violin and concert hall anyway, Gruber? One's a small box, one's a big box, but they both vibrate when the music's going, now don't they? That means the audience is vibrating too, so when I say connecting, I mean connecting.

"But now his concert hall is in his head, and you know, I think he's connecting with *more people than ever. I think he's connecting with his mama, with that old blind Ja-cobus, with Beethoven, and with George Augustus Polgreen Bridgetower himself. Just from that one A-Major chord. And you know what else, Gruber, I think they can hear him. That's just my personal opinion, of course. Mr. BTower looks to me like he's ready to die a happy man."*

Haskell turned off the monitor. He and Gundacker, both dressed in their uniforms, which Haskell had insisted they clean and press for the occasion, met BTower's lawyer, Cy Rosenthal, outside the surveillance office. In a way it was a comical sight as the three men silently, contemplatively made their way through the quiet corridor to BTower's cell, with the brawny Haskell and Gundacker flanking the diminutive lawyer in the middle.

"Go ahead, Gruber," said Haskell. "It's time."

Gundacker moved forward to insert the key to BTower's cell door, giving Haskell the opportunity to wipe away a silent tear. The heavy door opened smoothly on well-oiled hinges.

"Ah, my posse," said BTower, smiling. Rosenthal smiled back. "Cy, I just want to tell you, I know you did your best. I'm ready."

"I have some news for you, BTower," said Rosenthal. "Good news. You're a free man."

BTower looked at them a moment before his eyes lost their focus. Haskell caught him before he hit the ground.

THIRTY-THREE

It had been billed the "recital of the century." The energized audience had arrived at Carnegie Recital Hall hoping for—expecting—fireworks. Now it was almost intermission. The performance had been one long fizzle, and even the fizzle was sputtering.

BTower and Lavender had begun the program with the Handel Sonata in D Major, a wonderful piece of music imbued with operatic lyricism contrasting with joyful ebullience that was nevertheless not too technically challenging. As this was the first time the pair was performing together and only a month after BTower had been freed, the thinking was that this piece would be ideal to get them off to a good start, settling any jitters before embarking upon more demanding fare.

BTower had decided to play this recital "straight"—no light shows, no jazzy contortions, no special effects—intent on claiming the mantle of a serious musician that Allard had left behind and that Jacobus had challenged him to grasp.

Lavender's solo recital two weeks before in the same hall had been a qualified success. Martin Lilburn of the *Times* had described it as "workmanlike, in the most positive sense," but no one was knocking down doors to engage Lavender for future engagements.

Their Handel strategy, though sound in concept, backfired. BTower and Lavender tried so hard to be calm and collected that the music went nowhere. The interpretation was tentative, dry, and lifeless. Each of them waited for the other to do something to get the music off the ground, but neither took it upon himself to carry the flag. BTower, the younger of the two, deferred to Lavender, the veteran accompanist of René Allard, for leadership. Lavender, considering himself the subordinate, waited for BTower. The audience fidgeted as they sleepwalked from one movement to the next.

BTower had vowed to perform within a week of his release from prison, but upon his return to practicing with a real instrument, he realized just how much he had lost in his two-year incarceration. What had been natural now had to be relearned, but worse, the youthful swagger he had acquired during his soaring career was in abeyance.

The second piece on the program, the Brahms Sonata in A Major, began where the Handel left off. Brahms uses the unique term "Allegro amabile" for the first-movement tempo indication: an Allegro that's lovable, pleasant, kind. In the hands of the BTower/Lavender duo, unfortunately, it became more of an Allegro funebre. By the time they neared the end of the last movement, Allegretto grazioso, rather than spinning out the golden-hued radiance that Brahms intended, they fumbled over notes amid phrases that were vacuous and meandering, ending in almost apologetic relief.

"That's enough!" Jacobus muttered more to himself than to Yumi, as the disgruntled audience headed for the lobby, and some for the exit. This was more painful than his broken teeth (now reassembled with temporary crowns) and cracked ribs. He kicked himself for having come up with the idea of putting the two musicians together. More than merely for the blatant poetic justice of it, he had thought a joint recital would resurrect both of their careers in one fell swoop, so he brought them together and coaxed them into the enterprise. But rather than killing two birds with one stone, he now thought, he was just killing two birds. So much for trying to be a do-gooder.

"What will you do?" asked Yumi. She had squeezed his arm in dismay every time the duo, particularly BTower, had blundered. Jacobus was sure he was now black and blue.

"You mean before or after I throw up?" he said. He rose from his seat on the aisle, where he always sat so as not to trip on people's feet, and, feeling for the seats one by one in front of him, made his way backstage.

It had been a difficult, bittersweet month for Jacobus. The day after his rescue, Pit Bull Brown had hastily organized a press conference on the steps of City Hall, claiming victory over the forces of darkness. Tireless police work and a race against time, she reported, had uncovered the identity of the true killer of René Allard. At her urgent behest, the governor's eleventh-hour decree had spared the life of BTower. "Justice never sleeps, and mercy never falters" were the words with which she ended the session, a line calculated to vault her to the DA's office.

A week later, by which time Jacobus had sufficiently recovered, he met with Detective Al Malachi at the Carnegie Deli. Malachi reluctantly admitted to Jacobus over a chopped-liver sandwich that he never would have, nor could have, figured out that Allard's death pose was in reality a violin position, let alone an indictment of the murderer.

"All that money my parents paid for my violin lessons," said Malachi, "and what good did it do me?"

"I gotta confess, Malachi, it wasn't really my idea either," said Jacobus. "It was BTower's."

"BTower? What are you talking about?"

"When Rosenthal told me he had observed BTower doing mental practicing, holding an imaginary violin, it got me to thinking about Allard's arm. In the end, it was BTower who freed himself."

"Yeah, well, maybe you can get him to figure out how you freed yourself from that damn incinerator. We just don't know how the hell you did it. There was no handle on the inside of the door, no way for you to open it. But there you were, you and her, lying there next to each other like a pair of corpses, outside the incinerator. We thought you were a goner, but Nathaniel wouldn't let the EMTs stop. They finally got your pulse going."

Jacobus took a sip of his chicken soup, but he wasn't hungry.

Malachi filled him in on the details. The police had responded to a 911 call from "a crazy guy that spoke in verse, telling him where and how to find 'sightless Gloucester and the dusky damsel.'" The dispatcher had asked his name, but all he said was, "I'm but a walking shadow, a poor player, that struts and frets his hour upon the stage, and then is heard no more," and then hung up.

Sigmund Gottfried's apartment had been ransacked, stripped bare like a picnic basket devoured by a swarm of famished ants. Somebody, though, had left the recording of "Danse Macabre" and the little metal box neatly arranged by Jacobus's side.

Following a trail of blood that began just outside the Bonderman basement and continued through the underground maze, the police had found the shriveled body of Sigmund Gottfried, eviscerated by some kind of spear or lance. Naked with several of his teeth ripped out—for the gold, Malachi surmised before being unable to look any longer—Gottfried had bled to death slowly, apparently crawling the last fifty yards before he died at the sewer, where blood and excrement merged.

"Any idea who might have saved you or killed Gottfried? Or why?" asked Malachi.

"Haven't a clue," said Jacobus.

The rest was all follow-up stuff, Malachi explained. Laszlo Novak, in thick eyeglasses, had confirmed Gottfried's identity from photos shown him by the police. Gottfried was indeed "the little guy" who had visited him for violin certificates. Though many years had passed, Gottfried's appearance had changed remarkably little.

Camille Henrique, Hennie, endured protracted meetings with the IRS, Phoebe Swallow diligently by her side, charmingly but unsuccessfully trying to explain why the profit from the sale of over two hundred violins over a twenty-year period should be tax free.

Seglinde Oehlschlager was placed under arrest by Salt Lake City police as a coconspirator in the blackmailing and murder of René Allard, the illegal sale of the ex Hawkins del Gesù violin, and the attempted murder of Daniel Jacobus. The police were, for the moment, offering her a plea bargain if she identified the accomplice who served Jacobus the cyanide-laced cognac at Un Peu de Paris. Boris Dedubian confirmed that it was indeed Seglinde who was the anonymous seller of the ex Hawkins. The Salt Lake police also initiated an investigation into the possible slow poisoning murder of her late husband, Orin Oehlschlager. An exhumation was already under way. Seglinde's bank account was frozen and Cy Rosenthal was in the process of having the money from the sale of the ex Hawkins transferred to Sigmund Gottfried's closest living relative, his son, BTower, who intended to use it for the care of his stepfather, Shelby Freeman Sr., and to start the Rose Grimes School of Music for disadvantaged children of color.

Jacobus arrived at the door to the backstage area.

"May I help you, sir?" rang the strident voice of the usher. Jacobus ignored it.

"Sir! *Sir! Sir!!*"

"I'm going backstage."

"The artists have given explicit instructions. They don't want to see anyone."

"I don't care whether they want to see me or not. Let me in. You want me to start screaming that you're abusing a blind man?"

"Just wait here a moment, then. I'll find out if they'll make an exception. But may I say, sir, that you are an embarrassment to all those with your special need."

"May I say, madam, that your comment explains why you are backstage and not onstage."

Jacobus heard the indignant footsteps recede. He waited impatiently.

"What do you say, Jacobus, of being the dean?" BTower had asked him two weeks ago over a cup of coffee at Solid Grounds. "I need someone in that position, see, who's got the respect of everyone in the profession in order to get good teachers to come to Harlem. It won't be an easy sell."

Jacobus had laughed his coughing laugh and dismissed BTower's offer out of hand, telling BTower gruffly that the new music school would be an administrative shambles after a month if he were the dean. What BTower could not see were the tears forming behind his dark glasses. He had been wrong about BTower and wrong about Rose. He had been wrong about Allard and wrong about Lavender and wrong about Ziggy. He wondered if there was anything he had been right about, yet here was a hand being held out with an olive branch he did not deserve.

Jacobus did agree that if BTower wanted to send him any of

the students he deemed worthy, "even the little runts still in first position," he would teach them at his home in the Berkshires, tuition free. And, thinking of Yumi, he told BTower he had a former student whom he should hire to be on the faculty. But, Jacobus warned BTower, he would never teach a student to do the watusi while they were playing, like BTower did on the stage. BTower had laughed.

"You've got a deal," said BTower, and they shook hands. "And I already have a student signed up. He's kind of a 'special student,' and he's still in first position, but he ain't no runt. Name of Haskell. Bailey Haskell."

It was at that point that Jacobus made the suggestion, springing from somewhere deep inside that he hadn't even consciously thought about it, that BTower and Lavender perform together. It had seemed like a match made in heaven.

The usher returned.

"The artists will meet with you now."

Jacobus heard the two soloists talking in the greenroom. He banged on the door and barged in.

"What the hell is going on out there?" he raged.

"I don't know, Jake," said BTower. "I just can't get juiced."

"Juiced! You can't get juiced! I paid forty bucks for a damn ticket to hear you jokers play. You're professional musicians. You *owe* me—you *owe* the public—a good performance. It's your *job* to be juiced.

"And you, Virgil! Why don't you give him something to go on, Mr. Osfa? You play like a limp dick."

"What can I do, Jake? Ever since René died—"

"Bullshit! Did it ever occur to you, even for a moment, in all those thirty years with Allard that maybe, just maybe, he was feeding off of *you*? Off of your musicality? That in fact it was a true collaboration? That the only difference between the two of you was his savoir faire, not musicianship? That if not for you he wouldn't have been the success he was?"

He returned to BTower. "So what's the problem? You're playing like you're in a trance. Where's the energy? Where's the passion?"

"I know. I know. But, see, when I was practicing there in prison, in my head, it sounded so perfect. It was pure sound. I went over every detail to get it just right. No moving around, the way you like it, no show. I was so sure I got it. Just pure sound. But now, it just isn't working."

"Hey, in case anyone hasn't told you, you're not a Buddhist monk. Music's a living thing, but it's the performer who has to get its pulse going. So forget the mantra. Go out there and be BTower. I gotta go take a leak." He left, slamming the door behind him.

A few minutes later, Jacobus returned to his seat. He was supposed to have had a date, not Yumi, sitting next to him. Earlier that evening, as the elevator ascended to the fourth floor, Fuente commented on how natty Jacobus looked. Clean shaven for once, and wearing his dark glasses, his steel wool shock of thinning gray hair vaguely brushed, dressed in a new pair of blue corduroy pants and wearing his cleanest flannel shirt, Jacobus was on his way to Apartment 4C. He had made what for him was an unprecedented gesture—a dinner reservation at the trendy and expensive Columbus Avenue restaurant Nouvelle Dijon, and concert tickets, as a thank-you to Mabel Bidwell for her enthusiastic assistance.

The elevator rose in more fits and starts than ever.

"Don't worry. Today's the last day," said Fuente, reading Jacobus's thoughts. "Then they're shutting this baby down forever. I still can't believe about Ziggy. He was such a nice guy. To think, all those years . . ."

" 'All those years' is right," Jacobus said. "All those years in an elevator and in an underground hole. Alone. It wasn't a life. It was an imitation of a life. Imitating Allard, he and his sister imitating their parents. Y'know what separates a great musician from a second-rate, Lon? A real life from a fake life? A true maestro interprets. A fly-by-night imitates. An Allard from a BTower. But now BTower has a chance to be an Allard on the violin. He's already the better man."

They arrived at the fourth floor and Fuente slid the door open. Jacobus almost recoiled at the sound—the serpentlike smooth metallic sound of the weapon used to murder René Allard—and the elevator seemed to groan.

"There are ghosts of a lot of musicians in this building, Mr. Jacobus."

"And of one guy who was a ghost, dead *and* alive."

Jacobus knocked on the door of 4C.

"Ready?" he asked when the door opened.

"I can't go, Jake," Mabel said. "It's Mimi."

"Mimi?"

"She's choking on a fur ball. I can't get it out. I have to wait for the petbulance to come and drive her to the ER at the vet."

"Can't you just pour some sangria down its throat? That should dissolve anything."

"I don't appreciate that comment, Jake," Mabel said. "Maybe another time."

She closed the door.

BTower and Lavender walked onto the stage. The applause was sparse and tepid. BTower tuned to the piano's A, preparing to begin the Beethoven "Kreutzer" Sonata. There was a long silence before he started. Finally, as Yumi's fingers dug into his arm yet again, Jacobus heard BTower's first note. The moment of truth.

The sound was pure as a bell and perfectly in tune. It was absolutely correct. But it wasn't music. It came from nowhere and went nowhere. There was no musical connection between the first and second notes, nor between the second and third, nor thereafter. Jacobus's heart sank. When should one die? he asked himself. Should one try to live as long as possible with the chance of dying miserably, or should one choose the moment of greatest joy to bring life to a close? BTower had been ready to die a happy man a month ago, but now he's shattered, an empty shell.

The music stopped, even before Lavender had played his first note. There was unsettling murmuring in the audience, even a few boos. Jacobus put his hand on Yumi's, preparing to tell her it was time to leave.

But before he could rise, he heard the first note again. BTower had started over. Technically the note was identical to the way he had played it the first time, but musically it was entirely different. It had direction, conviction, purpose. It was music.

He completed the first phrase, and now it was Lavender's

turn. He grabbed on to what BTower had given him, only changing the color of the sound because whereas the violin's music was in A Major, the piano's tonality suggested a darker minor. Together, they wended their way through the opening Adagio sostenuto with increasing confidence, and dove into the Presto in full throttle. By the time they finished the first movement, they had regained the trust of the audience, which was providing them with the inimitable cosmic energy that distinguishes a live performance from a recording.

The second and third movements rose to greater heights. The performance was technically superior and musically uninhibited, gaining momentum as the music progressed. Even before the final triumphant chords sounded, the audience was on its feet en masse, screaming *bravo*! It was a moment that would go down as one of the greats in the annals of the violin. BTower and Lavender were recalled to the stage four times, five times, six times.

Finally, the crowd quieted as BTower began to speak.

"We would like to dedicate our encore to Daniel Jacobus, and to the memory of my mother, Rose Grimes." He paused. "And to the memory of René Allard."

The crowd was silent.

From out of nowhere emerged the most distant sound, a silvery sustained D-natural from the violin that was simultaneously plucked twelve times, once per second. The stroke of midnight.

"Danse Macabre!" Yumi said.

"Allard's ghost," said Jacobus.

When it was time to play the diminished fifths, the indication that the devil was tuning up for the diabolic waltz, BTower had a surprise for the audience. Rather than play them loud, as

Saint-Saëns had indicated in the music, BTower continued to play almost inaudibly, and slowly. Lavender took his cue and followed suit. They played the entire piece that way. The effect was chillingly intimate, as if it were embedded in the subconscious of every member of the audience. Allard had never penetrated that deeply, and if Allard hadn't, no one had.

The final phrases faded into insubstantiality. Jacobus wasn't even sure they had been played, though he thought he heard them. When the music finished, no one applauded. No one moved. Finally, the audience quietly filed out, the ghost of René Allard at last laid to rest.

ACKNOWLEDGMENTS

I am deeply indebted to the usual suspects for guiding me through *Danse Macabre*: Josh Getzler, my buoyantly supportive agent at Russell and Volkening; Michael Homler, my uncannily perceptive editor at St. Martin's Press; Geraldine Van Dusen, my production editor, and a violinist to boot; and my copy editor, Cynthia Merman, whose spicily insightful comments keep me on my toes. Thanks also to Anne Gardner, my former publicist at St. Martin's, for holding my hand through the learning process of marketing my first novel, *Devil's Trill,* and for energetically promoting the book as if it were her own; and to my new publicist, Bridget Hartzler. It has been a wonderful collaboration with all of them.

With *Devil's Trill* it could be argued that the main character was the Piccolino Stradivarius violin. One could make the same case for the elevator in *Danse Macabre*. I couldn't have learned about the workings of antique elevators without the information and photos enthusiastically provided me by Stephen Showers, the corporate archivist of the Otis Elevator Company. And though

278 Acknowledgments

the elevator in *Danse Macabre* is a figment of my own imagination, it is based upon the actual early Otis models, those wonders of turn-of-the-twentieth-century technology.

I also need to mention Jennifer Toth's disquieting 1993 book, *The Mole People: Life in the Tunnels Beneath New York City*. Years ago, there was in fact a gentleman we nicknamed "Drumstick Man" who played "the drums" using the asphalt of Fifty-seventh Street and a pair of sticks as his instruments of choice. I simply transferred his performance venue to Ms. Toth's realm *under* Manhattan, where he could assist Jacobus in finding the subterranean lair of Sigmund Gottfried.

A thank-you is in order to Beethoven for his Opus 135 String Quartet and his "Kreutzer" Sonata. Perhaps someday we'll learn definitively what disagreement caused Beethoven's dedication of this monumental masterpiece to be switched from George Augustus Polgreen Bridgetower, who had played it with Beethoven, to Rodolphe Kreutzer, a violinist whom Beethoven never met and who didn't even like the sonata. For now, though, that's another mystery to be explored.

Thank you to Mozart, Schubert, Mendelssohn, Brahms, Wolf, Shostakovich, and all the other composers whose music is part of the story of *Danse Macabre* and who have inspired listeners over the years and the centuries.

Finally, thanks to Camille Saint-Saëns for his evocative tone poem *"Danse Macabre."* In his deft hands, the "devil's interval" never sounded more diabolical.